EVERYTHING TURNS AWAY

ALSO BY MICHELLE BERRY

EVERYTHING TURNS AWAY

Michelle Berry

This is a work of fiction. All characters, organizations, places and events portrayed are either products of the author's imagination or are used fictitiously.

Published by Buckrider Books
an imprint of Wolsak and Wynn Publishers
280 James Street North
Hamilton, ON L8R2L3
www.wolsakandwynn.ca

Editor for Buckrider Books: Paul Vermeersch | Editor: Jen Sookfong Lee | Copy editor: Ashley Hisson
Cover design: Ingrid Paulson
Interior design: Jennifer Rawlinson
Cover image: iStockPhoto/urbancow
Author photograph: Fred Thornhill
Typeset in Adobe Caslon and Interstate
Printed by Brant Service Press Ltd., Brantford, Canada

Printed on certified 100% post-consumer Rolland Enviro Paper.

10 9 8 7 6 5 4 3 2 1

The publisher gratefully acknowledges the support of the Ontario Arts Council, the Canada Council for the Arts and the Government of Canada.

Library and Archives Canada Cataloguing in Publication

Title: Everything turns away / by Michelle Berry.
Names: Berry, Michelle, 1968- author.
Identifiers: Canadiana 20210255935 | ISBN 9781989496398 (softcover)
Classification: LCC PS8553.E7723 E94 2021 | DDC C813/.54—dc23

For Stu, Abby and Zoe
And especially for my parents, Margaret and Edward Berry

– With all my love –

In Breughel's *Icarus*, for instance: how everything turns away
Quite leisurely from the disaster.

– W. H. Auden, "Musée des Beaux Arts"

SEPTEMBER 11, 2001, 4:32 A.M.

When the babysitter wakes she is in a strange kitchen. It is dark. Her neck is stiff and she is bent awkwardly over a table, leaning forward on a hard chair. Her arms are asleep from resting her head on them. The babysitter shakes herself out and groans. Something is wrong with her head. Something hurts. Everything hurts. Where is she? It is pitch-black out. She can hear nothing. No sound. Has she lost her hearing? She looks around frantically, trying to figure out where she is. She isn't at her boyfriend's, at Derek's. She isn't at her house. Or any of her friends' houses. Or even back with the baby waiting for the drunk parents to come home from that dinner party. The time on the microwave is lit up. It says 4:32.

Then the babysitter hears a noise. She leans back down on the table, puts her head in her hands the same way she'd been resting before and closes her eyes. Hiding. She doesn't want to be here. She doesn't want to be seen. A sliding glass door behind her opens. Someone comes into the kitchen in the dark and disappears into another room. The babysitter can hear the squeak of running shoes on tile. She doesn't open her eyes. She hears footsteps moving around a room off the kitchen.

She can hear. It just occurs to her that her hearing has come back. She stifles a sob. The babysitter wants to go home. She'll never do drugs again. Never, never, never. She'll straighten up her life. Honestly. Please, she thinks. Please don't let anything happen to me.

A strangled cry. A groan. The sound of something ripping. Muffled noises. A struggle? The babysitter stiffens. She suddenly remembers a man and a woman in this kitchen talking to her. Where the hell is she? What is going on?

There are more sounds coming from the room. Quiet sounds. Thumping. Ripping. Like cloth. Or tape. Something ripping. Wet sounds. The babysitter has never heard sounds like this. She doesn't even know how to explain them to herself. How will she tell people later? If she survives. She can't figure out what they could be. Slurping noises. Strangled crying. Oh God, she thinks. Oh help. What if she just got up quickly and rushed out the back door into the night? Maybe she could do that? But her legs are as stiff as her neck. She is not sure they will work. It will be like one of those lame horror movies her friends love to watch where the girl always trips. She always trips when running away from the murderer.

The babysitter hears the footsteps coming into the kitchen. A sigh. Light, airy, feminine. A whimper. She hears breathing. Heavy, as if running. The person stops. She can feel someone looking at her. She can feel the eyes as if they are burning holes into her shoulders. There is nothing like this. Nothing she has ever experienced in her sixteen years has prepared her for this. It's so hard not to begin shaking. Or screaming. The babysitter somehow knows that if she moves, if she shows any indication of being awake, something awful will happen to her. There is a smell in the air suddenly. A rusting metallic smell. Also the smell of shit. Breath and breathing all around her. Panting. The person stands there breathing. Catching breath. The babysitter stops breathing. And then the person leaves. Out the sliding glass door. Shutting it silently behind them.

Gone.

The babysitter stays there, in the same position. Not daring to move. Then she gulps air again. Panic breaths. In out, in out. She tries not to gag on the smell that is becoming more and more prominent. It is overtaking the kitchen. It's a fishy, rusting smell.

The babysitter raises her head slightly. The clock on the microwave says 5:10. She lowers her head. She hears noises coming from upstairs in the house. Someone walking down the hall. A door shutting. A toilet flushing. Water running. Then the footsteps walking back down the hall. Another door shuts. A bed creaks.

Where am I? The babysitter screams inside her head. Where the fuck am I?

She remembers her math textbook. A fox. A man with rotten teeth. She remembers her boyfriend, Derek, touching her stomach with his soft lips, bending to lick her belly button as she stood outside on the back steps with him and smoked the joint he gave her and drank the Diet Coke, while the baby slept inside. She remembers the mother, whose kid she was babysitting, yelling at her through the door, and Derek disappearing down the side of the house and running away, the mother telling her to walk home right now, alone. She remembers the length of Bloor Street and rushing across the bridge towards somewhere far from home. She aches for Derek. Where is he? Where was he when she was supposed to meet him at the bottom of the street? If he had been there nothing bad would have happened to her. She wouldn't have been in this strange house, hearing strange noises, smelling horrible smells. She would be home in her own bed, with her cat.

Blood, the babysitter, thinks. Suddenly her mind goes red. Blood. That's the smell of blood. Her period. She has smelled this smell once a month for several years now.

She stands up, tests her legs. They work. Her brain pounds, makes thick, slow connections. Blood. The heavy breathing. Was it a man? She isn't sure. There was the sound of someone. The bulk of a person. It's always a man, isn't it? The heat of a man? She assumes a man now but she isn't sure. There was a female sound to the noises, a sigh, a whimper. Running shoes squeaking on the floor. The smell. Shit. Blood. Oh God, she thinks. Before, in the kitchen, were a man and a woman. She remembers that. One is upstairs. Where is the other? Who was that person?

The babysitter turns towards the sliding back door. She turns just a bit, terrified that she will see a face looking back at her from the darkness. Her heart beats wildly. She sees only her reflection. And a black streak smeared on the white handle of the door. She reaches out and touches this streak and pulls her hand back. Smells it. Metal. Blood.

"No," she whispers. The floor is streaked with it.

Later she will regret this, but the babysitter can't help herself from walking towards the room off the kitchen. It sounds to her as if she is walking in tap shoes. Loud, clicking noises. But really she is quiet as a mouse. Towards the back room. There is no door on it. It is becoming dawn and she can see more now. The sun is coming up. She can hear more. Smell more.

She comes straight into the room in her tap-tap-tap, so-god-damn-loud shoes and looks, eyes open, at the sofa bed. On the bed is something. What? Something. The smell is fierce in here. The babysitter moves closer. She sees puddles forming on the floor, puddles of that thick black stuff soaking into the rug. She wonders, later, if she heard drips. Plopping. Thick.

"No."

She moves closer still. Why can't her legs move away, turn away, why can't she get out of there quickly? Something is compelling her to see what she needs to see. Something is telling her that if she doesn't see this she will never know what happened in this room and she will wonder for the rest of her life.

There is a body. Wet and oozing. Blood. Everywhere there is blood. And duct tape holding the legs, the arms. His face . . . it's a man. The babysitter turns and runs back into the kitchen. She stops. She turns wildly around.

They will think it was her.

She opens the sliding glass door, using the material from her shirt to grasp the handle, to wipe off that black smear she touched earlier, and disappears into the world. She takes off out into the early morning. Down the back porch and across the grass and down the side of the house and out into the street. She runs faster than she's ever run before. Sprinting. It's a race, she thinks. I'll be the fastest to get away. Around every corner she hears the murderer. Around every corner she hears the breathing. But no one is out. She passes no one. Even on the Danforth there is little traffic and the babysitter manages to cross the street quickly and rush south, down towards the water. She needs to get away, as far away as she can.

The babysitter cries. And she runs.

BEFORE

1.

Sophie thinks, much later, that a lot of it began with the butter dish.

A Wedgewood butter dish. Blue and round, with a solid silver lid and beautiful creamy Greek goddesses on the sides.

The butter dish is what sets her off. Paul's grandmother's butter dish.

Sophie carries the butter in from the table and thumps it down on the counter beside Paul. His hands are in the sink, up to the elbows in soapy water.

"Jesus, Sophie, you almost broke my grandmother's butter dish."

"What do I care about butter? Or dishes?" she says and walks back into the dining room. He said *his* butter dish. As if it isn't *hers*.

Back into the kitchen again, this time with the salt and pepper in the crystal shakers given to him by his mother. Sophie plops these down heavily on the island in the middle of the kitchen.

"Salt and pepper." She wants to shout, but she'll wake the baby. "I suppose they are yours too? Who cares?"

Another sip of wine. Paul is drinking the leftover wine in all the glasses from the dinner party. Helen had white, dry wine; Sophie had a rich red; Allan had beer. Allan stuck with beer all night. Paul doesn't want to sip Allan's beer. He drinks out of Helen's glass and wonders if this is what it would be like to kiss her. He tastes her lipstick on the edge of the glass.

Sophie brings in the tablecloth. His, his, hers, she thinks.

"Shake it outside."

"What do you know?" she hisses. "Shake it outside." But she goes to the back door and opens it to the chilly night air and shakes the cloth out into the rose bushes off the porch. The light goes on with the motion detector. She watches the crumbs scatter.

Paul has turned the radio on while he washes dishes. The dishwasher is chugging along beside him. He whistles to Mozart. He drinks out of Helen's glass.

Sophie comes back inside and kicks the cat out of the way. She stops and listens to the noise around her. The radio. The dishwasher, Paul's whistling. The swish of water on plates, the cutlery clinking.

"It was a good dinner," Paul says.

"The chicken was too dry."

"Sophie," Paul says. "Lighten up."

Sophie pours herself some of the leftover white wine in a new glass. Paul has washed hers. She notices that Paul is drinking out of Helen's glass. "Figures," she says.

"What?" Paul continues to whistle.

Allan had been drinking beer all night. He didn't even switch to wine for dinner. Sophie was appalled. Beer didn't work with her dinner. Wine did. It made her angry suddenly, as she sat down across from him, to watch him suck on his beer. That's another thing. He didn't pour it in a glass. The glass she offered. Instead he drank from the bottle and Helen laughed and her lipstick stained the rim of her crystal wineglass. And Paul laughed all night. With all of them. Open-mouthed laughing. They are in their thirties. All of them. It's 2001. Grow up, she thinks. We need to all grow up.

The baby gurgles. She can hear her upstairs through the monitor on the kitchen counter. Gurgling. Rolling over in her sleep. Allan and Helen's baby probably never gurgles in the night. Helen is probably never kept awake by the little sounds that come out of the monitor all night long. In fact, Sophie thinks, Helen probably doesn't even have a monitor, doesn't believe in them. Their damn kid probably sleeps perfectly.

Why is she so angry? Sophie doesn't know.

Paul wonders why Sophie is so angry. His hands are warm and wrinkled in the soapy water. Sophie forgot to run the dishwasher before the dinner party and so the dishwasher is cleaning both the lunch and breakfast dishes. Paul is cleaning the dinner dishes. And Sophie used so many dishes. It seems to Paul as if he's washed sixteen plates for four people.

"Should I check on her?" Sophie asks. "She's gurgling."

"She has a cold. Nothing to worry about."

Paul is always saying no. No, don't check on the baby. No, don't worry about anything. Colds. Flu. SIDS. Nothing to worry about. Don't worry about airplane travel, or public toilet seats, or leaving the oven on. Nothing will happen, thinks Paul. Everything will happen, thinks Sophie.

The house will catch fire from the faulty wiring in the oven; the public toilet seats will give you a rash you can't get rid of. It will spread to your internal organs and then slowly kill you. And airplane travel. My God, Sophie thinks. Airplane travel.

Paul wonders if Sophie will dry the dishes or if she will just stand there, looking at the baby monitor and sipping her wine. A scowl on her face.

Sophie thinks, Why am I always so upset? It's not like she wants to be this way. She used to be happy. Didn't she? As a child. Even as a teenager. Always laughing. And now, Helen's lips are on Paul's wineglass (or the other way around) and Sophie hates Allan for drinking out of his beer bottle.

That's another thing. It was his beer. He brought his own beer. As if their beer wasn't good enough.

"Was it?" Sophie asks out loud. "Was it not good enough?"

"What?"

"Our beer?"

"We don't have any beer," Paul says. "Allan drank it all."

"Oh."

So he moved on from his six-pack to their beer. He wasn't as picky as Sophie thought. But he was a drunk. Good thing he walked home. Staggered home. And Helen staggered along beside him. Although Helen doesn't even look drunk when she is. High heels. Rosy cheeks. And she managed the sidewalk down the front of their house with no problem.

The baby sobs. One quick sob. Then nothing. Paul and Sophie stop and stare at the monitor. They look at each other.

"Dream," Paul says.

"Fucking airplane travel," Sophie says.

Paul looks at her quizzically. But he says nothing. Better, he knows, to say nothing, pretend he isn't listening. Five years of marriage has taught him this. If only this. There are plenty of other mistakes he is always making and knows he is making. It's just that he forgets sometimes, forgets to do the things she has asked him to do.

Sophie begins to dry the dishes. She thinks about Allan and his macho ways, the way he says, "How ya doing?" with a little wink when he comes in the door. She thinks about the way he kisses her on both cheeks when he leaves. Hard kisses. Hard hands that grab her shoulders.

But he smells nice. She'll give him that. It's a smell that comes off of him. A warm, clean smell. Even his strong cologne doesn't mask it.

Paul licks around the rim of Helen's wineglass. He hopes she has a cold. He could use a sick day. Call in to work and lie on the couch watching TV. But with Sophie and the baby at home he would probably end up fixing something or cleaning something or moving something instead.

Helen, Sophie thinks. Sophie has known Helen for years, before they were both married, before they both had kids. They've become better friends now, since they had kids at the same time, but Sophie doesn't think she even knows her. Like what was Helen thinking when she looked at Paul and asked him to tell Allan how easy it was to get fixed. She said "fixed," just like he was a cat. Neutered. Paul was shocked. His vasectomy was a secret – only done because Sophie didn't want any more babies, only done because this pregnancy almost killed her, because the doctors said the next pregnancy would kill her.

"Fixed?" he said, looking at Sophie. "Who said I was fixed?"

And Helen laughed then and said, "Oops." She said, "Was that a secret?" She held her long painted fingernails up to her scarlet lips, her white teeth peeking through.

"Damn her," Sophie says.

That's another thing. She's been talking to herself a lot lately. Swearing to herself. She can't seem to help it. Days alone with the baby. She blurts things out all the time. In the grocery store, at the dentist even. Didn't he have to tell her to stop talking when he filled that cavity last Wednesday?

"Who?" Paul stops washing the dishes. He dries his hands on the towel and then turns to Sophie and says, "Who? Damn who?" Paul knows he should say nothing but he just can't help it.

"No one." Sophie puts the dishes away. She forgets to dry them and just places them in the shelves wet. Paul watches her.

"You're drunk," he says.

"Okay," Sophie says. She takes a deep breath. "You know that I hate when you say that."

"Yeah, I know," Paul says. "But you are."

"And you are too."

Paul looks at his wrinkled hands. "I am." He picks up Helen's wineglass and swallows the dregs. He wonders if her lipstick has come off on his lips. He wonders what he'd look like with red red lips. He wonders if his teeth would look whiter. Helen's certainly did. "I am not ashamed of being drunk."

"You should be," Sophie says. "And it's a drunk. Not drunk."

"So should you." Paul leaves the kitchen, moves into the dining room, looks at their dining-room table and remembers when they bought it, when they went into that horribly expensive store in Yorkville and handed over a credit card and bought it. Like it was nothing. Like they did that kind of thing every day. Spend five thousand dollars on a table. Not even the chairs. Just the table. That was before they were married. Before they had the baby. Paul imagined dinner parties on that table. Dinner parties like tonight's. When you would drink and eat and be merry. You would laugh and then clean up, all the while talking about how fun the night was. And then you would go to bed and lie together and continue talking and touching and kissing.

"Ha," Paul says to himself.

"You're doing it too." Sophie is right behind him. He didn't hear her come into the dining room. She's holding her wineglass. "You're talking to yourself too. I'm not the only crazy one in this house."

Paul looks at her. His wife. He hears the baby sigh on the monitor. He reaches out towards Sophie but she walks quickly past him and goes into the living room. She plops down on the couch and puts her feet up on the coffee table (another expensive purchase from before they were married). The coffee table has scratches on it from use, from time. Scratches on his heart, Paul thinks, and then snorts.

"Do you think Helen and Allan had a good time tonight?" Sophie calls to Paul in the dining room.

Paul steps back into the kitchen, grabs his wineglass, fills it and then walks into the living room and sits beside Sophie. He puts his feet on the coffee table next to hers. They both face the dead fireplace. Paul sips his wine.

"I don't know. Helen looked like she was having fun. Allan said something, though. About an argument they had earlier. There was some tension. Once Allan starts into a few beers he gets bossy. Have you noticed? Telling Helen how to eat her food, how to hold her fork. Like she isn't an adult."

"And she kept phoning the babysitter. Can't she go out for one night without checking on every crappy diaper?"

Paul laughs. "Is that what she was doing? Poop count?"

Sophie smiles slyly. "Their baby isn't perfect if she's pooping through the night."

"Yeah," Paul laughs. "Who shits in the night?" He touches his toe to Sophie's. A tender moment. She pulls back.

"Did you just notice that?" Sophie says. "About Allan being bossy. You just noticed it tonight?"

"No, I . . ." Paul thinks. Yes, he did just notice that. Usually Allan seems so easygoing.

"He's always like that. He makes me sick."

Paul looks at Sophie. Really looks at her. "You don't like Allan?"

Sophie shrugs.

"Why do we have them over for dinner so much if you don't like him?"

"I don't really like Helen either," Sophie says.

"Oh." Paul looks at the coffee table. He looks at Sophie's feet. "I like Helen. I think she's nice. She's smart." Why did he say that just now, he thinks.

Sophie hits him. Smacks his leg hard.

"Ouch. What was that for?"

"I'm going to check on Rebecca."

"Don't check on her. You'll wake her and then she'll be up all night."

Sophie rises. "I'm going. There's nothing you can do to stop me." She stumbles a bit, staggers. Almost spills her wine.

"I could hold you here." Paul reaches up and takes her hand.

"Let go."

"Don't check on Rebecca."

"I'm going to check on the baby."

"Helen isn't that great, actually. Now that I think about it."

"She's amazing," Sophie says. She sits back down again. She leans forward and puts her head in her hands. She rocks back and forth. "Things never happen the way you think they will."

Paul nods his head but Sophie doesn't see him. He is thinking about the chicken, about it being dry. Sophie was right. It was dry. Sophie is thinking about life, how it hasn't gone the way she hoped it would. Sophie wonders if she has postpartum depression.

"Do you think I have postpartum depression?" she asks.

"Maybe." The chicken was dry, Paul thinks. The rice was sticky. It wasn't supposed to be sticky. It was basmati, not Japanese.

"Rebecca is three months old. Can I still have it? Am I still post-partum?"

"I think postpartum means any time after you have kids."

"So when she is forty years old I could still have it?"

Paul laughs. And then shrugs. He thinks. "Maybe," he says. "Maybe not."

2.

Helen says, "I think Sophie is depressed. She doesn't look good to me."

"She looks good to me," Allan says. He burps loudly. All that beer. He didn't want all that beer, but he likes bugging Sophie. "She's a fine-looking woman."

"That's not what I meant. I mean that she doesn't look happy."

"Who's happy these days?" Allan holds up his hands, throws them into the cooling air. Helen looks up into the air at what Allan is indicating. There is nothing but more high-rises, an airplane way up high and no stars. Pollution. They are on Bloor Street, walking towards home.

"She is pretty," Helen says. "You are right there."

"I'm right here, honey." Allan laughs. "And I feel sick. That chicken was gross."

"The rice. My God, you'd think they'd know how to cook rice after all the goddamn dinner parties they have."

Helen is leaning into Allan as they stagger down the street. They left Sophie and Paul's house over an hour ago but they stopped at the Irish tavern on the Danforth and had another drink. It is getting late. The babysitter must be worried. At least Helen thinks she must be worried. Helen can't imagine that she may just be talking to her boyfriend on the back porch, whispering things like, "Do you want to touch me? Where? Where do you want to touch me? Oh God. Not there," and laughing. When Helen was sixteen years old she didn't have a boyfriend. In fact, she didn't have a babysitting job. Her mother didn't let her do anything. She stayed home every night and read books. No wonder she fucked the first boy who took her to the movies in university. Back seat of his car. Typical. Maybe if her mother had let her out more she wouldn't have lost her virginity in a silver Mustang with dog hair on the seat covers.

Allan is talking. Saying nothing but talking. Helen looks at him. She looks up at the condos around her, the office buildings, the closed storefronts. Some people walking, scattered out, on the street. Toronto at midnight. Lights on above, in the apartments, blue flickering lights, people up there watching TV. Everyone is always watching TV. Helen can't figure it out. TV doesn't interest her. That's one good thing about her mother. Helen likes books. Lots of books. Any books. She reads all the time. You wouldn't know it, she thinks, by looking at her. At least that's what everyone tells her.

"So then Paul said that Sophie won't let him touch her toes. She gets this freaky feeling when he touches her toes. That they'll fall off or something. That Paul will pull them off." Allan laughs. "That's kind of a turn-on, don't you think? Don't you think, Helen? Are you listening?"

Everything is a turn-on for Allan. Especially after drinking all night. He can't wait to get Helen home and undress her. He can't wait to take off her bra. He loves doing that these days, unclasping the back and letting her breasts pop out like two round eggs. Ever since she had the implants put in he can't help but think they are like eggs. Perfectly symmetrical now, perfectly round and formed and hard. Hard as rocks. As eggs. Allan has to pee. He's in agony.

"Why was Paul telling you about Sophie's toes?"

"I don't know. I was telling him about your breast implants."

"God, Allan. Do you have to tell everyone?"

"I wanted to know if he noticed."

Helen walks a little more quickly. Her heels catch in the sidewalk occasionally. She stumbles a bit. She must look a sight, faltering down the street in her long coat and high heels. Her breasts. When Helen couldn't breastfeed she got angry. What's the use of breasts when they aren't useful? she'd thought. So she decided to do something useful with them. Implants. What's wrong with that? If they aren't being used, she thought, why not make them useful in another way? Why should she be embarrassed by the fact? But she isn't sure now if she did the right thing. In fact, she knows she didn't do the right thing. She looks ridiculous now. She feels ridiculous. Everyone looks at her differently now. It makes her sad.

"Did he notice?"

"He said that he noticed something was different about you, but couldn't put a finger on it."

"What did you say?"

"I said he should put more than a finger on it, more like a hand. Squeeze." Allan reaches over and squeezes Helen's breast. She almost falls.

"Allan."

Allan laughs. Then he walks into an alley beside a building. Helen follows. Allan unzips and pisses beside the garbage dumpster. Helen watches the stream of liquid steam in the cool air. She steps aside so that none of it gets anywhere near her.

"That felt good," he says.

"Lucky you," Helen says.

They walk on down the street. Suddenly Allan stops. "Fuck," he says.

"What?"

"The car."

"What about the car? Our car?"

"We drove to the dinner, Helen. Our car is in front of their house."

Helen stops walking. "You are kidding me. You're kidding, right?"

"No. I picked you up at the house after the nanny went home and the babysitter came. And we drove over."

"You're right. God, you're right. Now what? We can't go back now and get it. They'll see us."

"So?"

"They'll see us sneak back after over an hour" – she looks at her watch – "and climb into our car. We told them we had to leave early to get back to the babysitter and now we're still out. We've been to a bar. Besides, you're drunk. You can't drive anyway."

"I can't just leave the car there. I need it for work first thing tomorrow morning. Oh shit, I can't believe I forgot the car. We'll get a ticket."

"You can and you will," Helen says. She pulls on Allan's sleeve. "Let's go home. You can get it in the morning."

"No." Allan takes his arm back. "I need the car now. I have to get the car."

"Come on." Helen begins to walk in the direction of home. "Men and cars," she growls. Allan turns and walks back towards Sophie and Paul's. "Jesus, Allan, come on home. You can't let me walk the rest of the way by myself. It's dark. And you have to walk the babysitter home. If you go, who is going to walk the babysitter home?"

"I want my car." Allan remembers his new cellphone is in the car. Also the new CD he bought on the way home from work yesterday.

He hasn't even listened to it yet. What if someone breaks into the car and steals his phone and his CD? He keeps walking away. Away from Helen, away from the direction home, back towards the dinner party.

Helen stops walking and turns and watches Allan as he disappears into the dark night. "Oh," she whispers. She looks around. There is suddenly no one around. Not a soul, she thinks. She'll probably get mugged. Raped. Helen tiptoes in her high heels down the street, towards Spadina and across, towards her house, towards her baby, her babysitter, her little goldfish named Pepper. She thought the night was fine. A good night. Even with the dry chicken and sticky rice. But now it's crappy. Plain crappy.

If she's quiet on her heels then she won't wake the muggers. The rapists will think she's wearing running shoes and can move fast ahead of them. That she can run into the night.

3.

You are tired of being alone. You are tired of being sad and lonely and depressed. Although she died only three months ago, it seems you've been alone far too long. Three months ago you lay by her side in her hospital bed and touched her hand and watched her breathe her last breath. Your wife.

There was a Labradoodle puppy for sale on the internet. All the rage. Half Lab, half poodle. Only $650.00. Male. Black. Free Delivery, you thought the ad said. He's all yours. Quiet personality. Only six weeks old. Completely trained. On paper. Newspaper. Kennelled, whatever that meant. His name was Gibson, after Mel. Gibson lived with his mom (Lab) and his dad (poodle) in the country. Out on a farm two hours north of Toronto. He liked to chase the chickens. There was a picture of him on the internet chasing the chickens.

Clicked on it. Why not? Bought yourself a puppy. Sent in your VISA number with the expiry date. It was a secure site so that was fine. Bought a puppy. Delivered to you. You wondered if he would come with the chickens? You wondered if you would step out on your front porch one morning, a fresh-squeezed glass of orange juice in your hand, and see a box with air holes waiting for you there? Would Gibson's nose poke out, wet and black? Would his tongue fit through the holes to lick your finger?

These were the kinds of things your wife used to take care of. Ordering things. Buying things. Shopping. Decisions that you avoided your whole life. Why make a decision when your wife could make it for you? Besides, your decisions were always wrong.

Like in this case when you realized there was no free delivery and you'd have to rent a car to drive two hours north of Toronto to pick up the dog.

You aren't sad, really. Just alone. And alone is sad. You guess you are sad. Your psychiatrist says you are sad. You miss her. Even with Gibson snuggled nearby, the aloneness makes you almost afraid to be in your house at night. You climb into sheets that are tightly tucked on the one side, untucked on the other. They are cold. There is no one there beside you. Gibson prefers the floor. You look at your bony arms and legs and the age spots on your hands. You think of your wife and how she will never age past the day she died. She will never grow very old. Just old enough.

You only have a few more years until retirement. Full time to spend alone. Or with Gibson.

You thought about adopting a girl? Or a boy? An orphan, so you won't feel so alone. You thought you could name him or her after your wife or your grandfather.

But you are too old to go down that road.

And your wife didn't want kids.

Aren't you. Too old?

A dog, for now, is enough.

4.

As Allan walks back towards Paul and Sophie's house he listens. He listens to the sounds of the night. Over the bridge, the Bloor Street Viaduct. He walks back towards the Danforth.

Allan hears the cars below, the traffic streaming even at this hour. He hears a dog bark somewhere in the ravine. And footsteps. Not just his. He hears his footsteps and then he hears more footsteps behind him.

Allan is a big man. Allan is a strong man. He lifts weights. No worries, mate, he says all the time, even though he has never been to Australia. No worries.

Footsteps.

Allan stops.

The footsteps stop.

But when Allan turns to see who is there, who is following him, there is no one there and he starts to think that maybe he did drink too much, maybe Helen is right and he shouldn't get the car, maybe he should just go home. After all, he is a father. He's been a father for three months. There should be some sort of test you have to take to be a father – will you drive drunk or get the car tomorrow? Check a box. Allan shakes his head and continues to walk towards Paul and Sophie's. Fuck it, he thinks. He'd fail the test.

Sophie and Paul. Paul and Sophie. Allan can't remember when he met them. He thinks Sophie did something with Helen before they were married. Maybe they exercised at the same place? Who cares.

Footsteps.

Not Allan's.

"Who's there?" Allan is off the bridge and has turned up the side street towards Sophie and Paul's and the footsteps are following him. But no one. Not a soul. No one's out tonight. It's windy.

When Allan stops the footsteps stop.

A ghost, he thinks. Then he laughs at himself and his laugh echoes. That's it, it's an echo. He begins to walk again and the footsteps walk. It's his footsteps, his echo.

"What a dork," Allan says.

He thinks of Helen and her new breasts and he wonders if she'll be in bed asleep when he gets home. He wonders if she'll be naked. Sometimes she is naked in bed after he's walked the babysitter home and he climbs in beside her and she pretends to be asleep and he makes love to her pretending she's asleep too.

Or dead.

Sometimes, he's ashamed to admit even to himself, but sometimes he likes to think she's dead and he's fucking her. He's not one of those necrophiliac guys, or whatever they are called, but the idea that Helen isn't alive anymore to bitch and boss and talk, well, sometimes that feels good. Just a nice hard, toned body, nice breasts, nice everything. Lying there. Still warm. That's what would gross him out. The coldness of a dead body. Helen is warm. And soft. But hard.

Here he is. At Sophie and Paul's house. With a hard-on. He definitely would fail the fatherhood test.

Their lights are still shining. The living room lights are on. The dining room. The curtains are open. Allan heads towards his car, sneaking there, bending a little to hide. He uses his key chain to beep the doors open. The light goes on in the car. The alarm shuts off with a chirp. Can they see him out here?

But then he stops. Before he gets in the car, Allan stops and looks back at Paul and Sophie's house. Those two. They act like everything is so great. They act as if they are perfect. The food was crap tonight, but generally the food is good. The wine is always the "right" wine. They drink their beer from glasses made especially for beer (different kinds of glasses even for different kinds of beer). That's why Allan drank from his bottles tonight. He brought crappy beer just to piss Sophie off. It worked. Sophie was getting all hot and bothered every time he opened another beer. And he piled the beer caps up beside him at the dining-room table, made a little tower next to the fancy china and crystal. Allan smiles to himself. He presses the button on his key chain again and his car chirps back to darkness, back to being fully alarmed. The doors lock, the lights go off. He walks towards Sophie and Paul's house, towards the lit up windows.

No one is around. The street is empty.

There is something about Sophie that intrigues him. Ever since she had the baby she's been compelling. It's like she's giving off a scent or something. Allan has been meeting Paul for squash once a week for the last six months, since before both babies were born, and lately he finds himself trying to smell Paul. As if Sophie's scent will be there on Paul. But he never smells anything. One day Paul caught him after their showers trying to sniff his T-shirt. It was lying on the bench. Allan said he was wiping his nose and Paul's expression was interesting. Allan wonders if Paul threw the shirt in the garbage. He's never seen it on Paul again.

The kid.

The babysitter.

The wife.

He's got it all now. The house, the mortgage, the car with the alarm and chirping keyless entry. He's got the huge TV in a glass cabinet, a top-line stereo with a six-CD player. The Peg Perego stroller. The ensuite bathroom. The wife with new breasts. The wife who wanted new ones. He didn't even have to ask her. She did it herself.

So why is he creeping up to Sophie and Paul's house to take a look inside?

Why not?

Allan has a tendency to wreck a good thing. That's what it said on his report card in grade five. He's never forgotten. His parents never let him forget. "Allan has a tendency to wreck a good thing." Self-destructive. It probably said he was self-destructive. That's the kind of language in report cards. Like the teachers are looking at a cheat sheet when they fill in that stuff, like they just jot things down according to what the books say. They never really look at the kids. Never really pay attention. Allan thinks he'll try and put his kid in a different kind of school when the kid grows up. Something with a little more personal attention. Smaller classes. Teachers who know your kids' names.

Footsteps. This time he's not walking.

He looks around. He is on the front lawn.

A man passes by, walking his dog. A big, black, curly haired dog. Like a poodle, but not a poodle. Allan breathes heavily.

"Hello," Allan says. "Nice night."

The man nods sadly, as if he has the weight of the world on his shoulders. His dog nods, Allan swears it does. The man walks by. They look like they are walking a great distance, going on a long journey.

5.

Inside the house, in the living room, Paul says to Sophie, "Did you know that Helen got her breasts done? Implants?"

Sophie puts her wine down beside her feet on the coffee table and looks straight at Paul. She opens her mouth to say something but nothing comes out. She can't think of anything to say. Her mind has seized up. She never thought she would be the kind of woman who had a friend who got breast implants. The whole thing knocks her out.

"Allan says they are hard," Paul says. "Squishy, but hard, if that makes sense."

That starts her mind whirring. This is it, Sophie thinks. This is what I am mad about. Maybe subconsciously she noticed Helen's breasts. Because she was mad before the butter dish. Maybe Helen's breasts set her off in the wrong direction tonight. Got her up on the wrong side of the dining-room table, so to speak. Sophie says, "I thought something was different. God. I thought she looked bigger. I thought she was wearing a push-up bra, or was padded or something."

"I didn't notice at first," Paul says. "But then Allan pointed it out."

"And then you couldn't stop noticing." Sophie grimaces. "Right? You couldn't stop looking? Why didn't she tell me? She should have told me or asked me before she did it. I would have talked her out of it."

Paul laughs quickly. Like his wife just made a joke. Good one, he wants to say.

"Figures she'd get her boobs done," Sophie says. "Jesus Christ, implants? Doesn't she ever watch the news or read the newspapers? Doesn't she know that they leak? Doesn't she know anything?"

Paul sits silently. He thinks about Helen's breasts. He wonders what they would feel like to touch. Would the nipples still be sensitive? Sophie's breasts are now so soft and flat, as if the baby has sucked everything out of them. And she has. Paul has seen her. Sucking for forty-five minutes sometimes, with such an intense expression on her face. Sophie's milk draining out of her. The baby getting bigger, Sophie's breasts getting smaller.

"Why are we friends with them?" Sophie asks the black window in front of her. "What do we have in common? Is there anything we share? Philosophies? Morals? Ethics?"

Paul shrugs. "We all drink," he says. "A lot. That's something we share."

6.

Jack Kerouac wrote *On the Road* in three weeks. On Benzedrine and coffee. Helen read this somewhere. It makes her walk faster towards home to think of Jack Kerouac hopped up on caffeine and pills. She imagines his shaking fingers and hands, his handsome smile all torn up inside, his aching belly. Because wouldn't your belly be aching from all that crap?

But he wrote something good, didn't he? Something different.

Helen isn't sure anymore. What is different? What is good? Good is subjective.

She walks forward, all wobbly. The alcohol – the wine, and then the gin and tonic later, and then the vodka and soda, and then the manhattan. What was she thinking? All of it is swimming in her stomach. It's so dark out.

She is almost home. Woozy.

Allan left her. He went the opposite direction, went back instead of forward.

Fuck him, Helen thinks.

There is a noise coming from an alley down the street. She hopes it is rats and not humans. She can hear shuffling and scurrying.

A car whips past, ignoring the traffic lights.

What time is it? Helen thinks.

The babysitter will be asleep on the couch. She's sure of it. And how will Helen walk her home? She guesses she can leave the baby asleep and walk the babysitter home. Why not? What's the worst that can happen? The baby wakes up and cries for fifteen minutes?

Or she can let the babysitter walk home alone. But then what if she gets raped or someone, some freaky Paul Bernardo, asks her for directions and then pulls her into the car and cuts her up in little pieces.

After torturing her.

How the hell was someone like that allowed to be born?

She comes close to the alley and quickly runs past it. A man is pulling something out of a dumpster.

A body? Oh God, Helen thinks. Was he pulling a body out of there? Was it too small for a body? A child's body? She wants to go back and look. But she wants to run too. Why would anyone be pulling anything out of a dumpster?

It astonishes Helen always, as she walks down Bloor Street on her way to work most days, or back from the gym, how many homeless people there are. Lying here and there. Easy to trip on. Easy to not see them. Because there are so many of them, she doesn't see them and that makes her feel awful.

Is Benzedrine a pill or a powder you sniff? And did he get hopped up on caffeine from coffee or Pepsi? If he lived today, Jack Kerouac, he'd have such choices. All those new drinks that have way more caffeine in them than Pepsi or Coke or coffee. The ones that make you jittery just holding them. Helen sees her students all crazy on them; their hands shake as they take notes.

Students. She has to teach tomorrow.

Big breasts, hard body, working husband. And she's a professor. When she married Allan, and all his movie buddies came to the wedding drunk, her mother was horrified. A professor marrying the film crew? They were drunk before they got there. It was kind of funny. One guy threw up at the back of the church. And they sang some sort of song, a song that you could only know if you were used to filming a lot in the wind and rain first thing in the morning before the sun came up. And most of them didn't know the words. And they slurred the song and then that guy threw up.

Helen knows she shouldn't start her sentences with *and*. Not even her thoughts. She should use proper grammar even in her mind. Because if she isn't doing it for herself, then who the hell is she doing it for?

Doing what?

God, she's drunker than she thought she was.

Stumble, stumble. That's what she thinks. Then she thinks of stubble. Then she thinks she needs to shave her legs. She can feel the stubble under her nylons.

The man in the alley is long gone behind her. The man with the dead body. She's moving forward.

And Allan is long gone. What the hell was he thinking? Helen stops. She doesn't even have money to pay the sitter. Or her keys. Allan has everything. She left her purse in the car. The babysitter will open the door for her. Surely.

What was her name again? Ashley? Mary-Kate? Some damn teen star's name. Lindsay, that's it. What is it with parents? Naming their kids Dakota and Britney and Paris. Although maybe those are stage names?

Her little baby has the perfect name. She couldn't have done any better. When you grow up with a name like Helen, an old lady name, then you make sure your baby has a perfect name. Katherine. What more could she have asked for? A blonde baby named Katherine. She can be Katie later. That's a fun name for a girl. And then Katherine when she is a lawyer or banker or doctor or professor. Or, god forbid, in the movie business.

Not that there is anything wrong with the movies, Helen thinks. After all, it pays. And she likes movies as much as the next person.

But Allan's hands are so rough from outside shots in the hail and the rain. His hours are so crazy. Sometimes he works and sometimes he doesn't. He's not a thinker. He's a doer.

Mind you, that's what she likes about him. His roughness.

Maybe he'll pass her going home. Maybe he'll drive past her and stop and pull over and say, "Hey, good looking, want a ride?"

Or maybe he'll get pulled over for drunk driving and end up in jail all night.

What an idiot.

TV. Katherine is only three months old and so she has no idea what Saturday morning cartoons are. Who Bugs Bunny or the Roadrunner are. That's kind of sad.

Helen doesn't like TV, but she did like the repeats of Saturday morning cartoons when she was young. And *The Love Boat*. And *Gilligan's Island*. And *Fantasy Island*. *Bewitched*.

"Hey."

Helen stops. There is a man standing in front of her. She freezes. Panics. What the hell do I do? she thinks.

"Got any money?"

Helen holds up her hands, showing no purse. She wants to pull out her pockets to show the man they are empty but she's afraid if she puts her hands in her pockets the man will think she's armed with pepper spray and he'll stab her.

But he's not carrying a knife.

And he's drunk. As drunk as she is. She's drunk and she's cold too. She's just realized how cold she is. She's always cold when she drinks. But fall is definitely coming. September evenings, like this, are crisp.

They stand there, wobbling slightly, checking each other out.

"Thas okay," the man says. "I only wanted a coffee."

He pushes past her and wobbles down the street. Helen smells him. The horrific smell of old urine and stale body odour. Of someone who never washes. Her stomach drops. She rushes up her street and towards her safe, safe house. With the babysitter and her baby snug inside. Everything warm and rosy and clean.

7.

Sophie and Paul are still on the couch. A candle burns on the side table. Their feet are touching. Just the side of Sophie's right foot against the side of Paul's left. No toes. They are both wearing socks. Paul's socks are worn; his toe shows through just a bit. The radio is off, the dishwasher chugs in the background. There is no sound from the baby monitor. The baby is asleep. So is everyone outside, in the world. Or so Paul assumes. He yawns.

Paul thinks about work tomorrow. He wonders if he'll be hungover. He sips Helen's wine. Or his wine now, as Helen's leftover wine is long gone. Her lipstick stains are gone too. Licked off.

Why would Sophie plan a dinner party for a Monday night? Now Paul has the whole week ahead of him. No chance to recover. Sophie said something about having the dinner on a weekday and the guests leaving early. Ever since the baby came Paul and Sophie have a hard time staying up all hours.

Especially on a Monday night.

Getting old, Paul thinks.

And responsible.

He hears something out the side window, in the gap between their house and their neighbours'.

Sophie looks towards the window too. The cat, lying on the floor, perks up.

"Raccoons?" Sophie says.

Paul grunts. Did he remember to put the top on the garbage can? Did he remember to tie it down with bungee cords? Toronto has more raccoons than people, Paul thinks. And then he says that and Sophie groans.

"You always say that," she says.

What does she care? Paul thinks. Sophie doesn't have to fight those rodents day and night. She didn't do anything when he tried to resod their lawn in the summer and the raccoons rolled it up every night. Every morning Paul would come downstairs and, sipping his coffee, he would look out the back patio door and see his lawn rolled up. Sophie said they could take it back to the store every fall and get new sod the next spring. If they moved they could take the grass with them.

Paul tried staking it down with clothes hangers. He tried spraying his hose on the raccoons in the morning, but they stayed there and watched him, crouched low on the fence, waiting for him to go to work so they could climb back down and roll up the lawn again and eat their grubs. He tried hitting them with his hockey stick. He tried spraying them with Endust. (It was the only spray can available in the house at that moment. Endust or hairspray and Endust seemed somehow more therapeutic for Paul's state of mind. End Raccoon.) The raccoons just hissed at him, yes hissed. And rolled up the grass. And now they are outside digging through his garbage.

"Oh man," Paul says. "I hate this."

"Just leave them. They might have rabies. You'll get bit."

Paul looks at Sophie.

"And then I'll have to take you to the hospital and you'll get all those shots in your stomach and we'll have to find the raccoon who bit you and cut his head off or something and carry the head in a bag to the doctor's office."

"You've been watching way too much TV," Paul says.

"It's true."

"Cut the head off?"

"They test the head."

"Who is they?"

"The doctors. I don't know, Paul. Just don't go out there and disturb them."

Paul thinks that Sophie wouldn't think twice about disturbing him when he is in the middle of a meal, like the raccoons. "I'm going to have to clean it up in the morning."

"Whatever."

"Whatever?"

"Whatever. I mean it's not like I don't do anything around here."

Paul thinks.

"I wipe the baby's ass every ten minutes, it seems. I do a lot." Sophie glares. "I made the dinner, didn't I?"

"I helped clean . . ." Paul stops. Why get into this with her? What's the point? He'll never win.

At work Paul has legions of people working under him. They would do anything he asks them to do. They would scratch his butt if he told them they had to. Whoever said a man's castle is his home really didn't know Sophie. Or any woman. Any married woman. Something happens to women when they get comfortable. They get angry. Did Sophie used to be so angry when they were dating? Paul doesn't remember anymore. He can't imagine dating again. He imagines it would be tiring.

Many of his colleagues are doing it, though. Dating again. Or rather, cheating. Leaving the wives at home with the babies and heading out with the younger, happier women.

"Sorry," Sophie says. "I didn't mean to be angry."

Paul's lawyerly instincts tell him to argue, tell him to say, "You're always angry these days." But his husbandly instincts take over and quickly tell him to shut up. He is saved by the raccoon outside. The trash cans crash over.

Paul stands.

Sophie holds her hand up to pull him back down. "Don't go. Just do it in the morning. Maybe they'll eat most of it anyway."

Paul stands quietly for a minute, relishing Sophie's hand on his arm. His stomach feels a bit sick. Dry chicken. Too much wine. The bay leaf he accidentally ate. She's right. If he goes outside and cleans up he'll feel even sicker. Seeing all the chicken bones. Smelling the wrappings the raw chicken came in from the butcher. It's amazing, come to think of it, why anyone eats chicken after they smell it and see it raw. Disgusting stuff. Beef doesn't have that rotten sulphur smell. Neither does pork.

"I think we should make love tonight," Paul says suddenly. Quite loudly. He didn't mean to be so loud. "It's just that we haven't made love in a long time."

"Are you afraid you'll forget how?" Sophie laughs.

"It just seems like a good opportunity." With his stomach feeling queasy it suddenly doesn't sound like a good idea to Paul even though when he voiced the idea it sounded like a good one. A good roll in the hay. After all, sex with Sophie is the only time he feels like a man around her.

Sophie stands up. "All right, then," she says. "If you want."

Paul looks at her. He smiles.

She begins to remove her shirt. Pulls it over her head. Her flat breasts in a bra that could be a bathing suit. It is brightly coloured, flowers on it. Lace on the straps.

"Here?" Paul looks around.

"Why not?"

"Where?" Paul looks at the couch, the rug, the leather chairs, the recliner, the coffee table, the cat, the side table with the candle flickering. He looks at the TV. He notices dust.

Sophie unclasps her bra in the front. It dangles on her shoulders looking very much like a gun holster.

She starts to step out of her pants.

"Oh," Paul says. When was the last time they had sex, let alone in the living room? He suddenly wonders if Sophie's anger can be seen as a good thing. For the cause. If she's angry all the time then the make-up sex will be good. Right? And he'll take one for the team.

The raccoon again. The second garbage can falls down.

Paul is concerned. He feels limp and soggy. His knees are weak. Too much wine. Red wine and white wine churning in his stomach. A cognac after dinner. More wine now. That bay leaf.

"Okay, yeah," he manages to say. "Okay." He clears his throat.

Sophie is naked. Standing there completely naked. Not looking at him. She is studying something on the wall behind him. Just over his shoulder.

"Let's go," Sophie says. "Hurry up, I'm cold."

Paul giggles. He can't help himself. A small giggle starts at the back of his throat and moves up slowly until he is laughing.

"What?" Sophie covers her breasts with her hands. "Why are you laughing?"

"I'm not laughing at you. I'm nervous." Paul giggles. "Sorry."

Sophie says, "Fuck you, Paul. Smarten up."

"No, really, Sophie." He can't stop laughing. He feels like he felt in high school when he would smoke pot with his friend Tommy in his parents' basement rec room. When they would sit together on the couch, passing the joint back and forth, and giggle. That's all they did. One would say, "Mauve," or something just as funny and the other would start to choke up with laughter. High-pitched, girlie laughter. Paul's mother would call down from the kitchen, "What's going on?" and Paul would hold his breath until he stopped laughing just in time to stop her from coming down the stairs. Just in time to shout up, "Our homework is funny," or something equally stupid.

Paul hasn't smoked pot since he was sixteen but somehow this situation – his naked wife in front of him looking horrifically angry, scowling, her arms wrapped around her chest, fire shooting from her eyes – somehow this is just as funny as the word mauve.

It must be the wine.

It isn't until a few seconds later, still chuckling quietly, being glared at by Sophie, that he realizes (as does Sophie) the living room curtains haven't been shut. That everyone out there on the street and at the side of the house can see into their lighted room, can see him laughing at his wife while she stands there buck-naked, her clothes in a pile at her feet. And then it seems to Paul that the whole world isn't asleep right now. They are up and watching.

"Shit," Paul says. "The windows."

Sophie looks at the openness around her, gasps and runs out of the room.

8.

A garbage can falls. Allan cuts his hand on the brick on the side of the house, rubs it raw. But there is Sophie. Stark naked. Small breasts, round shapely stomach – looks like she does sit-ups, it's toned – and no pubic hair that he can see. Raw. Like his kid. Allan stares.

He just wanted to see what they were doing, if they were cleaning up or leaving the dishes for the morning. He wanted to see what they looked like when no one was around, when they were by themselves. Allan wondered if Sophie lightened up then, if the scowl on her face disappeared when there were no guests around, nobody to disapprove of. But now Allan sees that Sophie obviously disapproves of Paul as well. She's glaring at him.

God she looks good, though. Allan rubs his hand. It's bleeding slightly. Sophie is facing him. Paul's thinning hair, his back to the window. Allan is outside, crouched behind the garbage cans at the side of the house and Sophie is standing there looking over Paul's shoulder right at him. Paul's shaking shoulder. Is he crying? But surely she can't see Allan? He wonders for a moment whether the whites of his eyes might show. He is wearing black leather, his coat. His hair is dark. Can she see him?

Paul is standing there. Such patience, Allan marvels. Wouldn't you just grab your wife and squeeze? Wouldn't that be what he would do right now? He feels himself growing hard again. Like a kid.

A spy, he thinks. A peeping Tom. That's what he is. He wants to laugh but he feels funny. This is funny, though, right? Or maybe not. Maybe it's not that laughable to be staring at your dinner hosts as they get naked in their living room.

But they left the curtains open. It's their fault.

Will Paul get naked? Hopefully not. Allan has seen him naked in the showers at the squash courts and he doesn't need to see it again. Although watching them have sex might be interesting. In a clinical way. When Allan shot his last commercial, the Canadian Tire one in July, with the fake snow all over the front lawn and in the trees, he caught the prop man with the costume girl in the trailer. He walked in on them. It was interesting to see, the guy's bare ass sticking out, his balls thumping away, but it didn't turn him on. There's something about watching, Allan likes strip clubs, for example, and porn, but it's never as good as getting it yourself. And seeing a man's crazy thrusting isn't a turn-on. It's the naked woman, not the man. Now having someone else watch him? That might be good.

A dark shape passes by his foot. A fucking rat? Allan squeals and kicks out. When he looks up again Sophie is gone and Paul is standing there. He hasn't moved. Paul's shoulders are shaking still, but when he turns Allan sees that he's laughing. Not crying.

At what? Sophie was more sexy than funny, Allan assumes. Actually, he can't imagine her being funny at all. Ever. She's too severe.

Maybe if she dyed her hair red. Then she'd be funny. Just a bit lighter, sparklier. Lucille Ball funny.

Maybe. Maybe not.

It's a fucking raccoon. Allan wants to shout. Scream. The raccoon is coming back at him, ambling along, hunchbacked, coming towards the garbage cans.

Rabies. That's all Allan can think. The thought invades his head and knocks out anything else. Everything else. Sophie's nakedness, his car at the curb, his wife walking home by herself, the kid, his hard-on, the guy who just passed him on the street with the dog, his bleeding hand. Rabies.

He doesn't want to die.

"Go away," he hisses and the raccoon stops and looks up at him. As if he wasn't there before and now the raccoon finally sees him. Allan bares his teeth and hisses some more. Maybe he can scare the bugger off. But the raccoon keeps coming. There's no way he's letting Allan get his dinner. Allan turns and runs from the side of the house towards the back. There's nowhere else to go. Maybe he can go around the house the other way. The raccoon settles itself at the base of the garbage can that Allan knocked over and begins to delicately pick through the spoils. The smell of raw chicken permeates the air. The raccoon twitters and chirps. Another raccoon joins in.

Allan is at the back of the house. A motion sensor kicks in and the entire backyard is lit up. Allan freezes.

9.

Inside the house, still giggling, Paul reaches for what he thinks is his drink and instead pulls the candle in the cup on the side table up to his mouth – the candle he just blew out – and takes a large gulp of the hot liquid wax.

10.

Up the front steps, across the porch, Helen is banging on the front door. There are no lights on inside her house. No lights on the front porch. It is completely dark.

"Damn it, where is she?" She is afraid to wake the baby, but also afraid the babysitter has fallen asleep and she'll be left to sit on the porch in the cold air until Allan comes back.

Speaking of Allan, where is he?

He's been gone for a long time. It shouldn't have taken him this long to go back to Paul and Sophie's and get the car and drive home.

Maybe they invited him in for one more drink? Doubtful, but better than thinking he got mugged. But she didn't get mugged. Surely he wouldn't either. After all, he's a big man in a black leather jacket. But he's also the kind of man to provoke a mugging. He'd swagger and saunter up to someone and poke them on the shoulder or something.

And Helen would get chopped up by someone like Patrick Bateman in *American Psycho*.

Funny that book. Funny in a horrific way. Her student Max didn't understand it when he chose it for his independent studies paper, thought that poor Bateman was a product of advertising. But why was he turning hair gel into an excuse for murder? Today everyone brings their Discmans to class. Their PalmPilots page them, or whatever the hell PalmPilots do.

Max had to be told about the unreliable narrator. Was Bateman fantasizing or was he really murdering everyone? Helen didn't like having to read that book. She took it to her department head and begged. But he said that she must respect her student's choices and, after all, a movie was made recently of the book so it must be important. She watched her back after she left class. But Max was harmless (and good looking) and his C+ translated into a B+ after he turned to more contemporary, less violent authors. Authors he seemed to understand better. Helen proudly got him hooked on Tom Wolfe and Don Delillo.

"This is good writing," she told him. "And you can look at the cultural representation of the character's physical style."

Now that she thinks about it, Helen wonders if Max, by choosing that book, was really calling out for help. Help with his clothing? He wanted permission, perhaps, to get a manicure?

Why is she thinking about Max? He will graduate this year and probably get a job working in a bank somewhere. His English degree will rot in his drawer.

Sometimes Helen feels so old. And yet she is only, on average, fifteen years older than these students. But fifteen years is an eternity in this culture. She thinks of the music she likes. She thinks of the music mentioned in *American Psycho*. Wasn't Bateman listening to the newest Huey Lewis and the News? For God's sake, Helen roller skated to it as a teenager. That's another thing – roller skates. Now they are Rollerblades. Or maybe just blades. Or maybe something new

46

has come along that she doesn't yet know about. Katherine will teach her all about the future. Or Helen will be like her mother and ignore it. Strap on an apron and smoke a cigarette while cooking meatloaf. Hand a martini to Allan when he comes in the door from work.

Helen sits down on the top step. She is suddenly very tired. She can feel all the energy in her body drain out through every pore. Her hands feel weak, her toes too. Ever since she got pregnant and then had the baby Helen's body seems to be collapsing on her, giving up. She remembers a time when it felt like she had batteries inside, batteries that a glass of wine or a cup of coffee or a chocolate bar would charge up. Batteries that lasted all night, dancing or making love. Now her batteries are dead. She puts her head in her hands. Her legs are splayed. Her skirt rides up. Anyone walking up the street would be able to see her bikini underwear, but she doesn't care. She's too tired to care.

She's wearing bikini underwear. She's not that old.

And then there is someone there on the street. A boy. He comes suddenly out from the side of her house, his hoodie pulled over his head, his loose jeans practically falling off. He skips a beat in his stride when he sees her sitting there and then he takes off at a fast run down the street towards Bloor.

Helen stands.

"Hey," she shouts.

Her babysitter had a boy over.

Just when she needs Allan to take control, to tell off the babysitter, he isn't there. Typical. Well, Helen thinks, she's told off plenty of her students, surely she can tell off a sixteen-year-old babysitter.

Helen walks across the porch to the front door and begins to bang again. A little louder this time. From inside she suddenly hears Katherine crying. Helen wants to cry.

Lindsay (or Lesley or Britney or Paris) opens the door. Her cheeks are flushed, her eyes are bright. Too bright for this late at night. She looks stoned. Helen pushes past her and runs up the stairs to Katherine's room. The babysitter stands at the bottom of the stairs adjusting her bra, clearing her throat, cupping her palm in front of her mouth to sniff her breath. Her homework book is there, where she left it when she came in, on the entrance table. Helen sees her pick it up and study it, look at the picture of the fox on the front and the word Math.

Down the street, the boy jogs off towards home.

11.

Oh god, his mouth is burning. Paul swallowed some of the wax, he actually swallowed it and it hardened in his throat on the way down. What if it thickens up quickly and chokes him? Paul struggles to pull the wax out of his mouth. Good thing his mouth is warm as the wax seems to be staying in a fairly liquid form. But is there wax in his stomach? The burning sensation on his tongue, like drinking hot coffee or burning his mouth on soup, is excruciating. Hot coffee or soup he can spit out, this is wax. It sticks there. Paul rushes into the kitchen and digs into the freezer for ice cubes. But then he doesn't want to suck on ice because it will harden the wax.

"Thit," he says. "Thit, thit, thit."

Scraping his tongue with his fingernails. With a breadknife. Picking at his teeth.

"Thit."

He is peeling hot wax out of his mouth, off his tongue, crying slightly from the pain of the burn, when he sees the backyard light go on. His entire backyard is lit up. He thinks, Raccoons, but can still hear them at the side of the house, in his garbage can. There's a fucking flock of them, he thinks. And then wonders what a grouping of raccoons is called. A pack? They are like wolves or hyenas. Scavengers. Paul wouldn't put it past a raccoon to drag a small baby off into the park and eat it slowly, from the belly up.

His tongue aches. The sides of his mouth are burned. He doesn't know whether he is peeling off skin or wax. His eyes water even more. His nose runs. The ice cube melts in his hand.

His wife is upstairs, probably passed out on the bed. Probably dressed in those huge PJs that make her look like a small child. Those PJs that are impossible to get off of her. Too many buttons. Not that he feels like doing anything anymore. His whole head is on fire from the wax. Paul remembers that he has spilt some wax on the coffee table too (when he spit it out of his mouth and missed his wineglass). He should clean that up.

The light stays on in the backyard. Paul moves towards the back door but then he sees something from the front window and turns and walks towards the front of the house.

A man with a dog is out front. He's taking a crap on his sidewalk. Not the man. The dog. Paul wants to knock on the window but the man looks anxious and bothered (maybe he doesn't have a bag?) and he can imagine, with his luck, the man charging up into his house and siccing his dog on everyone inside. Dogs will definitely drag a baby into a park and eat them. Paul has never liked dogs. They smell. They drool. They always jump up on him and often pee on his feet. Just a little dribble. Like they are marking him, letting him know who is alpha dog.

"Fuck," Paul says, but it comes out waxy, like "Thuck."

The man out front doesn't notice Paul watching. He is looking across the street towards Sheila's house. Single mom. Her husband left her for his secretary. Sheila told Paul one day that she wouldn't have minded so much except that it was such a stereotype. She hated that her husband reduced her to a stereotype. Can you imagine? The things you worry about. Paul thinks they probably weren't happy together anyway.

Who is?

Allan and Helen?

Not likely.

He and Sophie?

Paul moves again towards the back – he passes by the side window (these damn Toronto houses are so slim, he thinks. You can walk a straight line and see everything laid out before you like a tunnel, you can touch both walls on either side of the house, you can touch your neighbours' houses. Open your arms wide enough, Paul thinks, and you can lift your house off the foundation). He sees the raccoons digging through his open garbage cans. Open and knocked over. One raccoon has a chicken bone in his mouth.

"I hop ya toke," Paul says, still peeling the wax and occasionally spitting into the handkerchief he has found in his pocket. There is a baby raccoon rummaging through the bag of baby diapers. Good God, thinks Paul, imagining the mess in the morning. He hopes beyond hope that the raccoons will just eat everything up and he won't have to deal with it. He realizes, though, that he'll be hungover (on a Tuesday!) and perhaps spitting blood from the wounds in his mouth, as he tidies up shitty diapers (dog crap too out front probably) and chicken bones. The thought makes him suddenly very nauseous.

"What are you doing?" Sophie is standing in her nightgown on the stairs. She is whispering to him, but it sounds more like an angry hiss.

"The raccoons," he says, pointing towards the side windows.

"What's wrong with your mouth?" Sophie peers down at him.

The windows are under the stairs and so she can't see the millions of raccoons foaming at the mouth out there.

"I burned it."

"I can't understand a word you are saying. And don't shout. You'll wake the baby." Sophie starts to walk back upstairs. She turns. "Are you coming to bed?"

And Paul sighs. He turns off the living room light. He glances once more at the motion light in the backyard, lighting up his porch, the shrubs, the bird feeder, but decides it's the raccoons that have set it off, and heads up the stairs behind Sophie thinking that maybe her nightgown is a sign. Maybe her nightgown means sex. It's surely easier to take off than those damn PJs?

But Paul doesn't feel like sex. He just wants to go to sleep.

12.

Allan stands completely still in Paul and Sophie's lit up backyard. A raccoon is circling his feet, smelling him.

He's completely forgotten about seeing Sophie naked.

"Away," he growls. He kicks.

The raccoon hisses.

Allan wonders if rabies shots are part of the regular immunizations. He's not sure. He wonders if his kid has had a rabies shot? She gets her immunizations all the time, it seems. Seems every time he has something important to do at work he's taking her to the doctor for a shot. Hours in the waiting room with kids climbing all over him and the chairs. And then holding Katherine down while a doctor shoots her up and makes her cry. Pacing all night, terrified that deadly fever will strike her down.

Helen always seems to be teaching when they've booked the doctor appointments. Funny that. Allan thinks again, like he always does, about the fact that she went right back to work, right back to teaching, refused to take maternity leave. She worked until the end of May, and then had the baby, and then hired the nanny and took the summer off (researching and reading and getting her implants). But then she went right back to teaching at the beginning of September. Helen said that since she couldn't breastfeed she might as well go right back to work. She blames everything on her failure to breastfeed. But Allan knows that Helen knows that their Filipina nanny actually does a better job raising their child than she does. Grace is kind and attentive. Grace is like Helen is with her students, listening to their problems, helping them through learning issues. Women today, Allan thinks, complain about staying home with the kid – look at Sophie! – but maybe if they were paid for it? . . . Given a salary and benefits? . . .

And then again, it's not as if Grace is ecstatic to be a nanny. Allan remembers she has her own kids back in the Philippines whom she never sees. That can't be fun. He's aware of the irony – Helen is too – that Grace spends her days taking care of Katherine while someone else back home raises her own daughter.

He kicks again at the raccoon. The world is fucked, Allan thinks. The raccoon ambles off, across the grass, towards the other side of the house. Great, he's surrounded on all sides by raccoons. He wonders if he can climb the fence to the neighbours behind Sophie and Paul's? Sneak out the side of their house and then circle around and come back to get his car?

Allan wonders if Helen has even bonded with their child? Isn't that what women are supposed to do? Take time off work and bond with their kids?

Allan moves towards the back fence. He steps in something wet and sticky. Dog shit? Raccoon shit?

One leg up, Allan pulls himself over the fence and falls into the neighbours' backyard. He is drunker than he thought he was and so he lands loosely and doesn't hurt himself. But what is it that he has landed in? He smells something horrible coming up from below him. Then he realizes that he is about three feet off the ground; that he is lying on something incredibly soft and warm. An animal?

Compost.

He's landed on the neighbour's compost pile.

The light in Sophie and Paul's backyard goes off. Click.

Allan wants to jump up, jump off the pile, but he's frozen to the spot. The filth of it. The disgusting smell. The eggshells crunching below his arms. His hands feel something like coffee grinds.

He gags. He can feel dry chicken and sticky rice coming up his throat but he swallows quickly and breathes through his mouth.

How will he get back in his car like this? Covered? How? He'll have to leave the car there and walk home.

Allan sits up.

A squelching noise. Then another odour releases itself into the air. He jumps off the compost pile. Haven't these people heard of those compact compost units, the plastic ones with lids? Allan stands and stares into the darkness at the contraption he was lying in. A screened-in box with no lid. Then he sees the lid beside the box. Left open.

Just his luck. Why aren't the raccoons eating over here?

Wiping himself off, Allan surveys the neighbours' backyard, sees his escape down the open side and heads off towards the street.

This would be funny if it wasn't happening to him. This would be hilarious if it was happening to someone from work. Or Paul. This would be great if it were happening to Paul and Allan was up in Paul's bedroom with an angry but sexy Sophie. Allan wouldn't laugh at her. No sir.

He limps across the lawn. The side of the house is narrow. He has to climb over more garbage cans (no raccoons over here) and around several locked up bikes. He wipes his dirty hand on the brick wall. Why wouldn't the raccoons just feast from the compost at the neighbours'? Why bother with the garbage cans?

Chicken, Allan thinks. They are after the chicken bones.

As Allan comes around the front of the house he sees the sad man with the poodley dog coming out of the yard on the darkened side of the house across the street. The man bends and wipes his hands on the grass in the front yard. Then he straightens up, sees Allan and quickly pulls his dog along behind him. He scurries down the street.

Allan smells his hands, looks at his pants, squints at his shoes (which are covered in something sticky) and confirms that he will walk home. There is no way he's getting his car dirty.

He'll have to pick up the car tomorrow and be late for work.

Helen, once again, was right.

13.

Paul and Sophie are in bed. Sophie has turned away from Paul but he's trying to massage her back lightly, trying to get her in the mood even if he's not in the mood. His mouth aches, even after he brushed his teeth, after he gargled with Listerine (which burned horribly) and flossed out some wax and skin. Sophie can't stop thinking about tomorrow. She just fed Rebecca with some frozen breast milk and now she thinks about how Rebecca will be up crying by six – if she's lucky. Maybe by five. She will need to feed again, to have another frozen bag heated up, and then she will cry some more and burp and need a diaper change and Sophie will need to pump out all the wine in her breast milk for the day and dump it down the sink. And Paul will leave her and go to work and she will have to tidy up from the dinner party (pack the leftovers, clean the dishes that Paul just put in the fridge uncovered, vacuum up the crumbs under the dining-room table, hide all the bottles in the blue box, etc.). And then she will be alone. Alone with her daughter. And so Sophie lies in bed, barely registering Paul's touch, and scowls into the darkness, scowls at the wall and the drapes and the dressers.

Paul gives up, feeling thankful, and rolls over and falls asleep.

Helen is talking to the babysitter. Letting her have it. The babysitter is going to cry. She clutches her math textbook and keeps saying, "I'm so sorry, I didn't let him in. We just talked on the back porch. I'm so sorry." But Helen doesn't listen. And the girl looks stoned. She yells at Lindsay (Jessica, Janet, whatever the hell her name is) until Katherine wakes again and continues to cry. Helen packs the girl up and shushes her out of the house. She tells the babysitter she will pay her another time, when she gets her purse back, and makes her walk home on her own. Helen doesn't want to go out there again and the baby is crying. She feels a twinge of guilt but then reasons that if the babysitter is old enough to have a boyfriend and to be high on something, then she is old enough to find her own way home at one in the morning.

And where the hell is Allan?

Helen screams. In her head.

Allan is walking across the bridge for the third time tonight. Towards home. He is smelling his hands and staring at his dirty shoes. They are ruined, his shoes, his perfectly good shoes. So is his leather jacket. Although he may be able to get it dry cleaned. He picks off something stuck to his elbow and wonders what he must have in his hair.

He can smell coffee grinds and rotting vegetables and eggshells (whatever they smell like) and cheese, he swears he can smell old cheese. Allan didn't think you were supposed to put cheese in a compost. But what does he know? A homeless man is wandering around the empty streets and sees Allan. He approaches. Allan says, "I got nothing," and continues walking.

The homeless man says, "You stink. I've never smelled anything so bad."

"Fuck off," Allan says, and pushes on towards home.

14.

Sophie dreams that she is falling off a cliff. She dreams she is in Paul's office building, taking the elevator up and up and up and then suddenly the elevator hits the roof and keeps going and the elevator is glass and Willy Wonka is beside her. But then she falls off a cliff into the Grand Canyon. Up and down. Sophie wakes with a start at four in the morning and watches the ceiling spin around. She crosses her eyes, trying to focus them. She stretches. Sophie turns to look at Paul and he is lying beside her, on his back, also staring at the ceiling.

"Is it spinning for you?" Sophie whispers.

"Yeah." Paul rubs at his eyes and then turns and looks at Sophie.

"You have to work today," Sophie says.

"Whose dumb idea was it to have a dinner party on a Monday night?"

"I assumed we were old enough now, responsible enough now, to stay sober."

Paul laughs.

"Shhh, keep your voice down."

"I have a meeting at nine," he sighs.

"With who?" Sophie says, but she doesn't really care. "I have a hair appointment at eleven but I don't know how I'm going to do it with the baby."

"Can't she sit on your lap?"

Sophie glares, but it is fairly dark in the room and so Paul doesn't see the look clearly. Sit on her lap while she gets her hair cut? A three-month-old? What the hell is Paul thinking? But that's it, isn't it? He doesn't think. Not about her, not about her feelings and how she's stuck here in this goddamn house with a little baby who cries and wets herself all day long.

It's not that she doesn't love Rebecca. She does. And she wouldn't give her up for anything in the world, but if she could just have a break. If she could just get her hair done without having to take Rebecca with her to the hairdresser. She wonders how Helen does it. Her hair is dyed blonde, streaked, so it must need highlights often. And highlights take a long time. Sophie knows. The one time she tried it, streaking her dark hair with blonde (looking, in the end, like Elvira), it took about four hours.

And then Sophie remembers that Helen has a nanny.

"Damn her," Sophie says.

"What?" Paul shakes awake again. Sophie wonders if he sleeps with his eyes open. "Why does my tongue hurt?" he says.

"You burned it, I think."

"Oh, yeah. The wax."

"Wax? I thought you burned it on the chicken."

"No. I drank candle wax."

Sophie shakes her head. Paul must still be drunk.

"I thought the candle was my wine."

Sophie rolls back and resumes staring at the drapes, the dressers and the wall. Remember when I was Sophie Campbell? she thinks. Remember when I used to smile and laugh a lot? Remember when I wanted to be a veterinarian or a movie star or a nurse? Remember when I was sick and my father came home with a plastic doctor's kit for me and said that no daughter of his would be a nurse, she'd be a doctor instead?

And what is she now? A homemaker. A household engineer. A stay-at-home mom. A woman with breasts full of milk. A cow.

Sophie wants to cry but she's too angry, the world is too spinny, for her to cry. Her tear ducts have dried up with hate.

Before she had Rebecca she didn't work. Well, she worked on the wedding, she worked on the house (redecorating), she helped a friend sell some costume jewellery she had designed. But it's not like she gave anything up to have Rebecca, to be married to Paul. In fact, they've made her life more interesting, really. Now she has something to talk about at the hairdressers. Something to complain about. So, if she gave nothing up, then why does she feel like she has left something behind? Far behind. She left Sophie Campbell behind somewhere. Buried her under the bricks of her existence. Phooey, Sophie thinks. Blech.

Sophie thinks she'll go visit her mom and dad today. Maybe they'll take the baby for an hour while she gets her hair done? Of course her mother will have to check her schedule. And if Rebecca has any sniffles, any loose snot or a tickle in her throat, her mother will refuse to get close to her. "We're travelling next month," she'll say. "We don't want to get sick." And her father will be at his office, seeing patients. He can't juggle Rebecca on his lap while his patients complain about their schizophrenic behaviour, or whatever the hell they complain about. Sophie knows that even if the baby is completely dry of drool her mother will probably have a hair appointment herself. Or a nail appointment. Or pedicure, or eyebrow wax, or electrolysis, or massage, or a meeting with her own damn personal shopper at Holt Renfrew.

"Eeerghhhh," Sophie growls. She sticks her head in her pillow. "I wish," she says. "For once, I wish that I had something normal to worry about."

Paul grunts. He's fallen asleep again. Sophie rolls over to look at him and stifles the urge to punch him hard on his shoulder, or to pinch him, or pull out the hairs on his chest one by one.

The backyard light is on. Sophie can see it through the drapes suddenly. Has it been on all night or did it just go on? She hates the motion sensor. The raccoons set it off all the time and then a sliver of light comes through the drapes and blinds her.

Raccoons. She remembers a few hours ago. She remembers Paul looking blankly out the windows at the side of the house. She remembers the sound of the garbage cans crashing and she remembers that she stood naked in the living room while all the curtains were open. Sophie blushes. Even though Rebecca's room is right down the hall, Sophie suddenly hears snuffling and movement coming from the baby monitor that lives downstairs in the kitchen.

"Noooo," she whispers. "Please nooooo."

The noises stop.

Sophie rolls into Paul and snuggles up to him for warmth. She smells him because she loves his smell. Wrapping her arms around his torso, Sophie thinks, I love you, I hate you, I love you, I hate you, I love you.

And then Sophie thinks again about how she'll have to pump her breast milk all day and throw it down the drain and this thought angers her more than anything else. The waste of milk.

15.

After Helen heats up a bottle and comforts Katherine and puts her back to bed, after she paces the hallway downstairs and worries about the young babysitter walking home alone, things get quiet all around her and she realizes she's not as upset as she thought she was. It was just a boyfriend visiting, she tells herself. After all, they didn't have sex on her couch. But still she checks the couch to make sure. Touches it to see if there are any wet spots. Then she goes to the back porch and opens the door and sniffs to see if they were smoking cigarettes. Or pot. Or whatever. Lindsay did seem out of it. But everything smells cool and fresh and there are no butts in the garden that she can see. After all of this Helen puts on her jacket and her running shoes and walks out the front door. She is determined to find the babysitter and walk her the rest of the way home. Helen pauses on the step. She doesn't want to leave her baby alone. But she left some other woman's baby alone to walk ten blocks in the middle of the night through downtown Toronto, didn't she? The babysitter is someone's baby.

"Jesus, Helen," she growls. "You are so irresponsible."

Helen tries to picture the babysitter's mother. She can't remember the woman. Will she be the kind of mother who sits up at night waiting for her daughter's key in the door?

"What have I done?"

Surely she, of all people, should have taken better care of a young girl? What was she thinking?

When Katherine grows up, she will never babysit. That's for sure. Never. People come home drunk and want to drive the babysitter home. They let them walk – damn, damn, damn – home in the middle of the night because they are too goddamn angry. And the babysitters let boys in and screw them in strange people's living rooms. Don't they? Or they light cigarettes and possibly set the house on fire. Helen wonders why you don't hear of more babysitter mishaps. Surely it's a dangerous profession?

As she stands there on the porch, a figure comes out of the darkness on the street. She didn't notice him before. It's Allan. He walks towards her.

"Where the hell have you been?" Helen's voice is shrill. It's more a shriek than anything else.

"I walked home."

"Where's the car?"

"I saw Lindsay walking down the street. Why was she walking home?"

"You didn't walk her home?"

"I was at Sophie and Paul's."

"But you passed her on the street and didn't walk her home?"

"Why would you let her walk home? What are we talking about? Walk who home? I walked home."

Allan and Helen stand there staring at each other. And then they both begin again.

"She had a boy over."

"Who?"

"The babysitter. What's that smell?"

"Lindsay had a boy over?"

"And so I sent her home."

"But she shouldn't walk home alone."

"Why were you walking home? Where's the car? What's in your hair?"

"Who was the boy?"

"What boy?"

"The boy Lindsay had over."

"Stop," says Helen. "Stop a minute and listen."

Helen tells Allan her story.

"Why didn't you walk her home?" Helen says. "You passed her on the street and didn't walk her home?"

"I don't know," Allan says. "I thought I'd scare her if I went up to her. She was on the other side of the street and she was crying and walking quickly, almost running."

"God, Allan. You're so irresponsible. You forget the car. You walk past a crying girl and don't help, you . . ."

"But I fell in compost," Allan tries to explain. "I didn't forget the car."

Helen walks down the porch stairs. "I'm going to find her."

"No, I will."

"No," Helen looks at her watch. "She's probably home by now. Do you think she's home by now?"

"I don't even know where she lives, do I?" Allan says. He scratches his chin. There is noodle stuck to it. Or a maggot? Oh God, a worm. Allan shivers. He needs a shower; he needs to go to sleep. "It's Monday night, for fuck's sake," Allan hisses.

"Why would anyone have a dinner party on a Monday night?" Helen sighs.

"Why didn't we just say no?"

"Because we booked a babysitter," Helen says. "I can't believe we let the babysitter walk home alone."

Allan thinks Helen makes no sense (Why would they have to go out just because they booked a babysitter? Can't you cancel on a six-teen-year-old? It's not as if they have anything better to do, right?) but he's too tired to argue.

Helen and Allan walk up the porch stairs and back into their house. The baby is crying again.

"I couldn't hear her from outside," Allan says. "That's interest-ing. Remind me of that next time."

"Of what?" Helen is rushing up the stairs. "What do you mean you fell in compost?"

"Remind me," Allan says to himself, "to sit on the porch when she's screaming. So I don't have to hear it." Allan feels sick whenever Katherine cries. He feels helpless and hopeless. He usually wants to leave the house, to run away. A good part of him believes that when she starts to cry she won't stop and this terrifies him. What if she never stops? What if she cries forever, what if that piercing sound continues until the day he dies?

Allan climbs the stairs a minute later. He slowly peels off his clothes on the landing and throws them down the laundry chute at the top of the stairs. The nanny will see to them in the morning. He walks naked into the bathroom. Katherine stops crying. He can hear Helen singing to her. Allan listens before he turns on the shower.

She is singing and humming some sort of mangled version of Grace's lullaby.

Allan smiles. He climbs into the hot shower and washes the coffee grinds and eggshells out of his hair, washes the alcohol out of his pores, washes his ass and under his arms, scrubs at his face. God it feels good to be clean, Allan thinks.

Helen stops singing and places Katherine back in her crib. Carefully, carefully. She looks at the clock. One thirty. They will all be up in less than five hours. She has two classes to teach tomorrow/ today. It's today already. September 11th. Tuesday. It is only the beginning of first term and already Helen is tired. Introduction to American Literature and a tutorial on Contemporary Canadian Writers. She has to get Katherine a new soother and there are fall coats on sale.

Helen leaves Katherine's bedroom and falls into her own bed. She lies on the bed and takes off her clothes, struggling to unclasp her bra while lying down. Soon she is naked and under the covers and snoring. Helen dreams of brushing her teeth. She dreams of washing the makeup off her face, of flossing and of brushing her hair. She dreams of clean pyjamas and Tylenol.

After his shower Allan tries to wake Helen but she is like a rock, like concrete, like a statue – reclining nude – and so he gives up and snuggles down beside her and falls quickly and dreamlessly to sleep. Neither Helen nor Allan hear the telephone ringing in the kitchen. They have previously turned the ringer to low, so as not to wake the baby, and they have disconnected the phone upstairs. The phone rings off and on for an hour. A little later Allan dreams of the ringing and Helen dreams of cows walking across a field, their bells dinging cheerily. She dreams of fire then and alarms going off, and Allan dreams of screaming babies whose voices sound like doorbells. And at five Helen wakes from her drunken stupor and realizes that it is the doorbell. And someone pounding on the door and trying the knob and shouting, "Wake up, oh God, wake up."

Allan thinks the noise is his baby beginning to cry. Quietly at first, and then a howl.

Allan puts his pillow over his ears and reaches over to turn off the alarm clock, turn off the damn noise. He swats at it, knocks it off the table and falls back asleep.

The doorbell keeps ringing.

16.

You see in the newspaper that the incidence of bedbugs in fancy hotels has skyrocketed. People come home from vacation covered in itchy, oozing sores. Rich people. And you were worried about the dead prostitute stuffed into the box spring in a hotel, the one you saw in the movie *Short Cuts*. You have never once thought about bedbugs. But now you'll think of them every time you stay anywhere but home. You are relieved for a minute that your wife is gone. This is the kind of information she would have taken and run with, the kind of information that would have meant you had to pack your own sheets and pillows and pillowcases whenever you went on a trip.

But you don't go anywhere now. Not anymore. Not alone. Just walk the neighbourhood with your dog. And there are strange things in the neighbourhood, but not as strange as what you read in the newspapers.

If you ever do travel, though, you know that you will pack pillowcases.

There is also a cobra loose in Toronto in a boarding house. It is in the walls. A big cobra. Someone's poisonous pet. A man, Mike, has been hired to sit in the basement all day and listen for it. He is to call the people who will catch the cobra when he hears it.

"What does a cobra sound like?" someone asks Mike and you read that he says, "It sounds like a dead body being dragged across the floor."

You can imagine the sound. It haunts you at night as you lie alone in your bedbug-free, lonely bed and stare at the ceiling. As you listen to the planes headed to the island airport, coming in and taking off. The helicopters heading over the city. Constant traffic above you, around you. Noise that makes you tremble. Dead bodies being dragged across the floor.

You wonder if the dog you bought on the internet, Gibson, feels the same way you do. You wonder if there are bugs in his bed in the living room. It upsets you to think this and so you hum a bit and whistle to get the thought out of your head. And then you wash his dog bed.

Your wife hummed when she cooked. When she cleaned. When she bathed. Your wife was a hummer. A hidden musical genius. When she was young she would whistle. But whistling turned to humming. Then, when she got sick, the humming got quieter, more contemplative. And then it stopped altogether.

Sometimes you wish that something exciting would happen to you. Something that would take away your thoughts of your wife, of her death, that would temper your grief. You thought that by getting the dog you wouldn't be so lonely, but instead, his needs make you feel even more desperate and alone.

Tonight, when you took your dog for a long walk you saw some strange things – a man in his window scraping at his tongue with his fingers, looking out at you; another man sneaking down the side of the same house, going towards the back. The sightings of both of these men were enough to make you forget to pick up Gibson's poop, but they weren't exciting enough to focus your attention away from your depression. You and Gibson walked on and then Gibson broke free from his leash and ran into someone's backyard. He must have pooped again. He came out with his own excrement on his tail, you could smell it. When you went to grab him you accidentally touched his tail and got it on you and the smell of it made you gag. And then you wiped your hands on the grass, as carefully as you could, wiped hard and long, and then carried on, careful to hold tight to his leash, careful to wash your hands as soon as you got home. Nothing more happened tonight.

September 11th, 1:00 a.m.

Gibson went to sleep on his clean, bedbug-free bed.

You lay awake, staring at the ceiling.

17.

The babysitter is missing. This was inevitable, Helen thinks. She is being punished for staying out late on a Monday night, for not being able to breastfeed, for getting implants, for going back to work so quickly. For making the nanny work overtime too often. The babysitter is gone and the babysitter's parents are sitting in Helen's living room at 5:15 a.m., crying and shouting and arguing. Allan is making coffee and phoning the police. Katherine is sleeping through everything. Helen has checked on her twice.

"What time did she leave?" the babysitter's father keeps asking.

"I've told you, one or so? Ten after? Quarter to? I'm not sure exactly. Allan saw her walking down the street towards Bloor."

"Oh my God, oh my God," the babysitter's mother moans.

"She had a boy over," Helen says. "I was angry."

"No excuse," the father yells. "That's no excuse."

"What boy?" the mother says. "Maybe we should phone him? Was it Derek? Or Rick?"

"Derek," the father says. "That is his name."

"I don't know. I didn't ask." Helen sighs. "He had a hoodie on and baggy jeans."

"They all have hoodies," the father shouts. "All of them. Every fucking one of them. What kind of a person are you?"

"Calm down." Allan walks into the living room with a tray of coffee mugs and cream and sugar. He still feels drunk. "I'm sure there is some reasonable explanation. I'm sure she just . . ." Allan can't think of a reasonable explanation for a sixteen-year-old to go missing between his house and hers at one in the morning on a Monday night in the Annex of Toronto. Is there a reasonable explanation?

Except maybe the father – I mean, look at this piece of shit, Allan thinks, pudgy stomach, prematurely grey hair, nose hairs visible. And short. God, he's short. Wouldn't you run away if you could if this was your father?

"What?" the father shouts. "What possible reason? Why isn't she home?"

"Call again," the mother says, holding her cellphone to the father. "Call the house. Maybe she's home now."

The father takes the cellphone and walks into the dining room, scowling at it.

Allan looks at Helen. She looks at him. "The police said they'll be here soon," Allan whispers. He rubs his hands through his hair. Allan has to get his car and be at a film shoot at 7:00 a.m. Over in the warehouse district, on Eastern Ave. The company he's working for right now have booked a studio.

They are making another grief video. His fourth this month. He hasn't told Helen about these – she thinks he makes real movies and commercials – but lately he is getting paid good money to film dying people's last wishes. The last guy wanted some underwater scenes of him swimming in his pool. Strange, but that's how he wants to be remembered. Swimming peacefully. Allan used an underwater camera and followed behind him as the pale, sickly man swam laps in his indoor pool and surfaced occasionally to say something to the camera. He said things like, "I will miss you, but I'm happy now," "I'm not in pain anymore," "From the water of the womb to the water of the pool." That kind of thing. Allan wanted to say that he didn't think wombs were chlorinated. He had a hard time suppressing his laughter. He could feel it welling in his throat, creeping up quickly. Nervous laughter. Thinking of this Allan suddenly remembers Sophie's naked body and Paul laughing.

"She's not there," the father says.

"Let's go," Allan says. He pulls on his coat. "Let's walk around and look for her. Split up."

Allan and the father leave the house. Helen and the mother sit on the couch and stare at the coffee.

"We'll wait for the police," Helen says and the babysitter's mother starts to cry again.

Helen thinks that this is it. She's being punished for living such a good life. For being married and having a healthy baby girl, for being educated and having a good job and money and new boobs. She'll go to prison for recklessness, for letting the babysitter walk home alone. Not just letting her either, forcing her out the door and into the dark night. Oh God, Helen thinks. What have I done? Helen tries to cry but she can't. Nothing happens.

The babysitter's mother continues to cry.

Having a baby is supposed to make a woman more maternal, but Helen can't focus on anything long enough to feel anything. When she watches TV or reads a book it's with an empty feeling, a vacant feeling, her mind won't concentrate. Her babysitter is missing and all she can do is think nothing. Before she had Katherine, Helen didn't think it was possible for someone's mind to be blank.

But now, lately, hers is always blank. She stares at the mother – was her name Joyce? – and watches her cry.

And then the police knock lightly on her front door and Helen serves them coffee while they talk to the mother, while they ask her questions, while the one cop stares at her breasts and flirts. They put out an APB on Lindsay. They take a photo from the mother's wallet. They say, "Don't worry. I'm sure it's nothing," and "Kids today," and then they go out into the early morning. They will drive the streets, they say, and look for anything suspicious.

The mother cries some more and then falls asleep on Helen's sofa. Helen cleans up the coffee cups and puts the cream back in the fridge. She wonders what Lindsay's life is like at home. She never thought to ask her anything – about her family, her friends, her schooling, her boyfriend, what she's planning on doing with her life. A sixteen-year-old girl came into her house every couple of weeks to take care of her child and Helen never thought to talk to her. Just like she hasn't asked Grace, her nanny, anything about her life since the interview, since they hired her months ago.

Grace doesn't speak English well, though. Helen has that excuse.

But Lindsay? She spoke English.

And, after all, not speaking English well is no excuse at all – why couldn't Helen have asked Grace about her own kids, about her life back home in the Philippines, about what she thinks and feels. Grace isn't a robot. She's human.

Ridiculous white woman, Helen thinks. Sometimes she hates herself.

Helen's eyes water slightly. She climbs the stairs to her room and dresses for class even though she knows she won't be teaching today. The men still haven't come home. The baby begins to snuffle and coo. It is 6:30 a.m. Grace will arrive in about two hours.

Helen walks into Katherine's room and the minute her baby sees her she stops making noises and waves her chubby arms in the air and smiles. She is just beginning to recognize Helen. This is when Helen fully collapses. She begins to sob and can't stop. She picks Katherine up and holds her tight and cries until she feels empty again.

18.

Sophie is up with Rebecca. She is sitting at the kitchen table with Rebecca on her lap. She is trying to read the newspaper and listening for sounds of Paul out by the side of the house. Rebecca is cooing and reaching for Sophie's coffee, the newspaper, grabbing everything. Shoving everything she can find in her mouth. If she can find her mouth. It's usually just luck. The napkin, the placemat.

Then there is a scream and Sophie sees Paul run through the backyard and hop over the fence. She watches her husband, caught in his open bathrobe and awkward boots. Struggling. Sophie remains seated but stares out the back door from her chair. Rebecca continues to suck on everything she can. Sophie watches for Paul. He doesn't come back.

It is seven thirty in the morning. The television is on in the living room.

The scream stops. Sophie sighs. Rebecca coughs. The cat, walking by, looks startled but keeps walking.

Still no Paul.

Suddenly the stillness is broken by the increasing whine of sirens. Police. Ambulance. Fire truck. The noise breaks the air and Sophie stands and pulls Rebecca on her hip and walks over to the back door and looks out into the yard. She can see flashing lights coming from the street behind. Holding Rebecca tightly, Sophie looks back into her house, through the kitchen, the dining room, the living room. She looks towards the front window and wonders what is happening out there, without her, in the real world.

19.

Paul is outside, at the side of his house, at seven thirty in the morning, when he first hears the scream. His stomach aches. His head is throbbing. His throat is dry and his mouth tastes like stale garlic and red wine. Paul is ill. Staring at the mess the raccoons left makes him feel all the more sick. He tries not to gag. If he gags, he'll throw up. Paul straightens up, the black garbage bag in his hand, his wife's plastic kitchen gloves stretched tight over his large hands.

The scream comes from the street behind Paul's. From over his back fence. A loud, terrified scream; a scream that resonates up and down the street and echoes wildly. Paul looks around. Where exactly is it coming from? The scream doesn't stop. It's long and drawn out and panicked. Paul drops the garbage bag, peels the gloves off his fingers and steps over the mess of garbage and diapers and chicken bones and runs through his back yard and climbs over the back fence, avoiding the neighbours' open compost. (No wonder it always stinks in the backyard. Paul makes a mental note to talk to the neighbours about closing up their compost.) Paul runs down the side of the back neighbours' house. No raccoon damage to their garbage cans. He sees bungee cords holding the lids on, makes a mental note of that too. And then he comes out into the street and across the street and it isn't until he has located where the sound is coming from that he realizes he is in his PJs and bathrobe, that he is wearing his rain boots. His hair is sticking straight up.

There is a thin, tall woman standing in the front yard of a house wearing nothing but an off-white bra and underpants. She is pointing towards the front door of her house, which is standing open. The sound is coming from her. Paul runs up to her and takes off his bathrobe. He throws it over her to cover her nakedness.

"What's wrong? Are you okay?" Stupid question.

The woman won't stop screaming. "Inside. Inside."

Paul leaves the woman there, on the lawn, wrapped in his bathrobe, and runs quickly up the steps and into her house. A burst of adrenaline rushes through him. He feels nothing but determined. His head is clear suddenly and his stomach calm. Dead calm, he thinks.

He hears the woman following him into her house. She has stopped screaming but is breathing heavily. She is right behind him. He walks through the hallway and towards the kitchen where he sees the patio door slightly open and blackish stains running up and down the handles and the frame. Then he looks down and sees red smears and black drops on the linoleum. Paul's stomach lurches. He loses his courage. He looks back at the woman and she points, crying, shaking, to a small room off the back of the kitchen. It is dark inside. The curtains are drawn. Paul enters.

The woman flicks on the light behind Paul and he can't move. He is stuck to the spot. His legs turn rubbery. His mind seizes up. His stomach lurches again and he turns and vomits in the corner. And then he faints. Later Paul attributes his cowardice, his fainting, the paramedics reviving him, to the hangover. Later he tells Sophie that if she hadn't had a dinner party the night before he never would have fainted. Never.

And the strangest thing is, he remembers nothing but an image of the woman bending over him as he lay on her couch. He must have been moved there by the paramedics. He remembers her kissing his forehead. He remembers her soft lips, her swollen tear-streaked eyes as she kissed him. Just once. A small, delicate peck.

AFTER

1.

You are watching TV. The news. Carol Lin, the anchor from CNN, breaks the story, "Yeah. This just in. You're looking at obviously a very disturbing live shot there. That is the World Trade Center, and we have unconfirmed reports this morning that a plane has crashed into one of the towers of the World Trade Center. CNN Center right now is just beginning to work on this story, obviously calling our sources and trying to figure out exactly what happened, but clearly something relatively devastating happening this morning there on the south end of the island of Manhattan. That is, once again, a picture of one of the towers of the World Trade Center."

At first they say that it was an accident. For a little while everyone thinks that a small plane lost control and flew into the World Trade Center "by accident."

At first they say that your wife's illness is not real. They say that the cramping in her stomach, the constant gas and bloating, are nothing to worry about. "Take Pepto-Bismol," the doctors say. "Try to relax. Eat slower. Stay away from gassy foods."

When the blood comes, your wife stands up for her rights. She shouts her way down the hospital corridors until they decide to take her seriously. And they find it. The cancer. They find it quickly but it spreads even more quickly. Speedy cells.

She dies.

You are alone.

Announcements are made by officials in the undamaged South Tower that the "building is secure," and people may go back to their offices. This comes over the PA system. Some people hear it and ignore it and leave. Some people don't hear the announcement. Some people meet in common areas, such as the sky lobby on the seventy-eighth floor, to talk about what is happening. And then Flight 175 crashes at about 590 mph into the south side of the South Tower, banked between floors seventy-eight and eighty-four.

Millions of people see this plane crash live on TV.

"We're, we're involved with something else, we have other aircraft that may have a similar situation going on here."

"It's escalating big, big time. We need to get the military involved."

CNN's headline reads: "Second plane crashes into the World Trade Center."

At some point that morning, you can't remember the timing anymore, but at some point you see on TV the president of the United States in a classroom in Florida. He is reading a book to a group of kids. He is told about the plane hitting the World Trade Center and he stops reading and looks up into the blank air in front of his face. He looks a million miles away and there is fear in his eyes and a nervous smile on his face.

The thing you want to know, the thing that consumes you for a while until you find out the truth, is this: What was President Bush reading to the kids in the classroom, to the students at Emma E. Booker Elementary School in Sarasota, Florida? What book did he read? You think it would have been appropriate to read *Chicken Little*.

"The sky is falling."

Much later, on the internet, you find out that Bush was reading "The Pet Goat," the story of a pet goat who eats everything in its path: "A girl got a pet goat. She liked to go running with her pet goat. . . . The goat ate things. He ate cans and he ate canes. He ate pans and he ate panes. He even ate capes and caps."

The thing is, you loved your wife. But there were also times you didn't love her. She could be annoying. A pain. She was organized and controlling and bossy but that just meant you didn't need to think for yourself.

And now you do. Have to think for yourself.

2.

When the first plane hits the World Trade Center, Sophie is partially watching CNN on TV while she changes Rebecca's diaper on the floor and listens for the sound of Paul – where is Paul? – hoping he'll come back inside the house soon. She still doesn't know what that scream was and wonders what happened.

When the first plane hits the World Trade Center, Helen and Allan are taking turns holding Katherine as they sit on the couch in their living room with the babysitter's mother and father and the two police officers who have come back with a math textbook, a fox on the cover, that they found in a dark alley. The radio is on in the kitchen and the sudden energetic shouting of the news reporter hushes the babysitter's mother, stops her tears if only for a moment. Helen turns on the TV.

When the first plane hits the World Trade Center, Paul is being revived by a paramedic. He opens his eyes on the back room floor of this strange woman's house just enough to see the blood, the dead body on the bed in the middle of the room, the bound hands and feet. The face mutilated. And then he faints again and, lying on the floor, his body jerks quickly forward, and he pulls his back out. The paramedics wake Paul and carry him to the couch in the living room. A police officer walks into the house and says to anyone who is listening, "Did you hear a plane flew into the World Trade Center just now?"

Hours pass.

And the towers come down. One by one. And Sophie watches this live on TV; Paul sees it as he lies on the couch in the strange woman's living room talking to a paramedic; Helen and Allan see it on the TV in the living room that they've turned on, the police watching beside them, the babysitter's parents staring into the black box. Time seems to stand still.

One after the other. The two towers collapse. Almost in slow motion. People running. Dust enveloping the world. When the second plane hits the South Tower there is a gasp from everyone watching. And then the Pentagon. And then the plane crashes into the field in Pennsylvania. It is pure chaos.

Sophie feels like the world is about to end. It's not believable, she thinks. This isn't happening.

Paul wants to get home to his wife and daughter. His back aches from where he fell on it, his mouth is burned and raw. He has seen enough horror now for a lifetime. And then he worries about his office building downtown.

Helen is almost grateful for the distraction on the television as she steals looks at the babysitter's mother.

Allan stares, not understanding what he is seeing, forgetting for a time that there is a young girl missing and that her disappearance is partially his fault.

The babies squeal and try smiling and chew on anything they can get in their mouths. The babies shit and drink. The babies try to roll over, they do mini push-ups when placed on their stomachs, but no one is paying attention. The babies reach for their mothers and fathers. The babies note the flickering lights on the television, the commotion, the action, and do nothing out of the ordinary for babies. Katherine takes her bottle. Rebecca nurses.

3.

Helen is at school. It has been three days since the babysitter went missing and Helen is a wreck. She moves from class to class trying to focus on her teaching, on her students, seeing the babysitter's face in every student, every young girl smiling in the hallway or patiently listening as she lectures. She sees the babysitter's face in the books she is reading. Helen can't sleep because the planes that pass over the city, over her part of the city, seem louder than usual. Each time one comes over the house Helen suppresses the urge to duck and cover, to roll under the bed, to wrap herself in quilts and disappear. The babysitter's parents have been coming over with updates. The father still shouts at Helen and Allan, "You let her walk home alone!" and Helen feels all torn up inside, like her stomach has exploded and is shredded and raw. Her breasts ache and she wonders if the implants are leaking. Everything about her hurts. If she touches her temples, just lightly, a pain shoots through her brain and down her back. Wearing glasses to read is excruciating. Helen thinks she might be dying and this causes her more pain whenever she looks at her baby, whenever she leaves her baby with the nanny.

And thinking of the nanny makes Helen cry because this little Filipina woman, although she looks nothing like the babysitter, reminds her of Lindsay who then reminds her of the fact that Katherine will grow up soon and leave her and Helen can't bear the thought of all of this. A plane flies overhead and Helen ducks.

Her students watch her curiously.

They have been talking about September 11th. They have discussed it in all her classes.

Even if they haven't lost anyone in the attacks, these kids are feeling it deep down inside.

Or they are using it as an excuse not to do their work. Helen isn't sure.

But Helen has now moved on from listening to them talk about where they were when the attacks occurred and back to teaching American Literature. She has moved from Osama bin Laden to Raymond Carver and Flannery O'Connor and has bounced up to Rick Moody and David Sedaris.

Because she teaches American Literature Helen is expected to be an expert on September 11th. Her class enrolment has gone up in the last several days. There are people sitting in and auditing. As if Helen will tell them why. But Helen doesn't know why and American Literature isn't telling her anything.

"Maybe in twenty years," she says. "Maybe then we'll be getting the novels that tell us what we need to know."

"If we're still alive then," says one particularly sour student. All the students nod and roll their eyes at the same time. Agreeing or disagreeing? Helen isn't sure. These students are so incredibly malleable. Helen could mould them into little terrorists if she wanted to. No one seems to want to stand up for anything these days. She wonders what changes September 11th will bring. A new lexicon.

Helen sighs. She guesses it has always been this way, though. There are always topics people have to avoid in company. Helen thinks then of the dinner party at Sophie and Paul's the other night, before everything happened, and how Paul started to talk about cooking and how he implied that it was only women who could cook properly (giving himself an excuse for not helping and, at the same time, strangely complimenting his wife) and Helen thinks about how Sophie went silent and how she went silent herself and then Sophie rushed in and changed the conversation.

Among husbands and wives there are things that shouldn't be said, she guesses.

The dinner party. Oh God, she never phoned them to see if they were all right. She never phoned them to thank them for the dinner. The babysitter went missing. The planes hit the towers. And Helen forgot to thank Sophie and Paul for dinner.

"Read 'A Good Man Is Hard to Find' for next class," Helen says, suddenly. The students look up from their desks, their pads of paper. "Okay?"

"But we've done Flannery O'Connor," one student says.

"Have we?" Helen says, absent-mindedly. She shuffles her papers.

Allan will be home tonight. He isn't working. He will go out again and look for the babysitter. Helen will sit by the phone and wait. She will pray. She's taken to praying lately. Even though she is not religious. She will pray for the safe return of the babysitter. For all to end well. She will pray for happiness and peace. For teenage girls to go home to their mothers.

"I thought we were doing Hemingway next," a student says. "It says that right here in my outline. Hemingway." The student points to his piece of paper and Helen sighs again.

"Hemingway it is then," she says. "You are right."

The student smiles and looks at Helen's breasts. He is in the front row. He is always looking at her breasts. Helen thinks again that she shouldn't have had the implants. But then she looks around at all the perky young things in the classroom and realizes that implants were exactly what was needed. Who cares if a few male students can't concentrate? Who cares if her department head won't look her in the eyes?

Helen crosses her arms in front of her chest and begins to talk about Hemingway. But the students are getting up and leaving. They are talking amongst themselves. Helen looks at her watch. The class ended twelve minutes ago. She runs her fingers through her hair and says, "See you next week," but no one hears her.

The weather has turned. There is a chill in the air. Helen wraps her coat tighter around her body, hugs herself and begins the walk home. To Katherine and to Allan. To the nanny. She scours the streets for Lindsay the babysitter as she walks, but she is nowhere to be found.

4.

You go every day to work at the library and can't believe how quickly everyone else gets over it. You live with it all the time. Noise in your head, fear spreading through your bones. Your hands shake. But everyone else seems to move on to other things. Other things consume them. Their kids, their partners, their work. No one worries anymore about planes falling out of the sky, about towers collapsing. "It won't happen here," they say. "It won't happen to me."

But you, you can't sleep. You have trouble swallowing food. Everything sticks in your throat. Your stomach constantly hurts. Loud noises make you duck. And your co-workers are noticing this. Looking strangely at you. Rolling their eyes. Looking at each other.

"Besides," a co-worker says, trying to calm you one day, "look at all the safety measures they've now put in place. You can't whisper 'bomb' anywhere near the airport or you'll be immediately handcuffed and carted away. They check your bag for knives, for mace, for box cutters, for everything."

"You can't even wear your shoes on a plane anymore," another person says.

"And the lineups. They are checking everything."

But they've done planes, you think. What next? Surely they can't fly planes into buildings ever again. They succeeded so spectacularly with the World Trade Centers and the Pentagon that the next thing the terrorists do will have to be even more powerful.

"Bioterrorism. Poisoning our water. Our food," someone says, casually, when you mention this.

"Spraying diseases into the air. Can you spray bacteria into the air?"

"What do you think a sneeze is?" someone mentions.

It is as if there is a disconnect between what people are saying and how they are feeling. You can't be the only one worried. Are you the only one walking in the streets of Toronto with a cloud over your head? Finding it hard to breathe?

"Shock," they say. "You're still in shock."

"I don't know why," others say. "You weren't even there."

A nasty woman in the staff room takes ownership of the disaster and sidles up to you at the coffee machine. "You're blowing this whole thing way out of proportion," she says. "I mean, I knew someone who died there. You knew no one. Who do you think you are?"

You think she's from computer support. That's where you've seen her before.

5.

Paul has been lying in bed for three days. He can't move. He's been told he pulled his back out when he fainted in Vivian's back bedroom.

Vivian Middleford. The woman in her underwear and bra. The woman who touched her lips to his forehead when he was lying prone on her couch. The paramedics and police all around. She kissed his forehead. He thinks. Did she really do that or was he just imagining that?

Paul is on Robaxacet and Tylenol and anything else his doctor says he can take. Chicken noodle soup, which he can't bear to eat, and ginger ale – Sophie thinks he's got the flu, Paul guesses – and even a bottle of cough syrup.

The dead person in Vivian's back bedroom, murdered, and then the planes hit the World Trade Center and the Pentagon and the field in Pennsylvania, and Paul's back seized.

Every time Paul closes his eyes he sees the blood. Everywhere. He sees the bound hands and feet. He sees everything but can't make sense of it. That isn't what a human body looks like, he thinks. All cut up like that. It can't be possible. It could happen to him. It could happen to his baby. Or to Sophie.

And then he closes his eyes and sees Vivian in her underwear.

Paul watches the coverage of September 11th for days on the television. He watches those towers standing, then imploding, then standing again. The people running through the encroaching dust.

Sophie has called in to work for him. His cases will wait. The law firm understands. "How horrific," a partner says to Sophie. "A murder and September 11th. And his back. Paul's world will never be the same again."

Of course the police won't leave him alone. They question him about everything. Did he hear anything in the night? What did he see? What was he doing out so early in the morning? Is he happily married? Why was he in his pyjamas? Had he met Vivian before? Are they having an affair? What about his boots? And why was he hungover? On a Tuesday? Does he remember exactly what time he went to bed? Does he have witnesses? How many raccoons were in his garbage can? What precisely did they eat, the raccoons? The police come to his house and perch on the side of his bed and ask him question after question and then the police leave and Paul's back twitches and seizes up again. Robaxacet does nothing for him anymore.

Sophie comes into the room. The baby is taking a nap.

Sophie stands and stares at Paul in the bed. The floor is littered with Kleenexes.

"Christ, Paul," Sophie says. "When will your back get better." And it's not a question, really. And she looks nothing like Vivian looked with her lips pressing down on his forehead.

It, the body, the person, was Vivian's brother. He had flown in from Florida the night before and was sleeping in the guest room off the kitchen. Why someone would have a guest room off the kitchen makes no sense to Paul or Sophie, who spends one day working out floor plans in the middle of their king-sized bed. Why have a bedroom at the back of the house, behind the kitchen? Why have a bedroom with a floor-to-ceiling window right beside the screened patio door of the kitchen?

"It was supposed to be a TV room," Sophie says. "Is that it?" She shrugs.

It's as if the set-up of Vivian's house is the reason her brother was murdered. It's as if it's Vivian's fault, Paul thinks.

The brother's name was Richard. He was a construction worker in Sarasota. He had recently split from his wife and the police are trying to find her.

Four days later Sophie comes into the room and says, "If we lived in New York you'd probably be in the World Trade Center. I mean, your law firm would probably be there, right?"

He knows people who were killed in the terrorist attacks. One of his colleagues was actually there on business that day. Paul tries to rise from his bed to attend the memorial in downtown Toronto but the sudden movement of putting on his shoes seizes his back once more and he crumples down on the bed.

Everywhere Paul looks there is a mangled body. The police told Sophie that the brother was bound first. That he was drunk and probably didn't wake up. Sophie marvelled at the strength of the murderer. The brother had duct tape around his mouth and his hands and feet. Tight. Vivian didn't hear anything. Slept through it. The brother may have died of suffocation, the police officer said. Before he was stabbed.

Richard's body was cut up badly. But especially horrific was his face. As if the murderer wanted to get rid of every trace of human-ity in that face. Sophie thinks it will be good to talk about it. Her strange fascination with the details leaves Paul angry and confused. He doesn't need to know all of that. He saw it. Why does he need to know? Doesn't she understand?

A week after the murder, a week after the world changed, Paul re-members that Allan and Helen don't know about what happened that night. They haven't heard. In fact, Paul remembers that no one called Allan to cancel squash. He hopes his secretary looked at his calendar and called. Paul wonders if Allan stood in the squash court for fifteen minutes waiting. Once, when a client wouldn't stop talking, wouldn't leave his office, Paul was ten minutes late and Allan was in the court angrily whacking the ball against the walls. He played a mean game that day and Paul lost and went home with bruises on his shoulders from being forced into the walls.

"Did you call Allan and Helen?" Paul asks Sophie in bed. She is reading a *House & Home* magazine. She is commenting on the colour of their drapes and has been telling Paul that they should change them this year, that beige is "in" now and that their drapes are old fashioned.

"Didn't we change them last year?" Paul asks but Sophie isn't listening.

She puts the magazine down. "My God," she says. "I never called them. Did you?" She looks at Paul's pale face. "Of course, you didn't." She looks at her fingernails and pulls the quilt up over her legs. "You'd think they would have called to thank us for dinner."

"Not after September 11th. Not after what happened. Everyone would have forgotten about the dinner." Paul looks up at the ceiling. His hands are folded on his chest.

Paul sees on TV, in the paper, that man who jumped from the top of the World Trade Center and was captured on film. He sees the man in the white coat as he dove, headfirst, down to the ground. Selfish in a way, Paul thinks. What if he killed someone below? And then Paul wonders seriously if the man killed someone? Blood and guts and then Paul is thinking about brother Richard and Vivian and he can't get Vivian out of his head. He has to see her. Call her. Talk to her. Did she really kiss him? And if so, why? Paul tries to roll over and to look at his wife. She seems oddly unaffected by the events that have gone on lately. She hasn't reacted to the murder in their neighbourhood or to the terrorist attacks. Nothing seems to faze Sophie. Only the colour of the drapes. Probably because she grew up with her psychiatrist father. He probably coached her in calmness. Everything else, every other reaction, would be a symptom of emotional fallibility.

"I'll call them tomorrow," Sophie says. "We should go to bed now."

Yes, Paul thinks. Sleep. Paul craves sleep but when sleep comes all he sees is red blood and soft lips.

"Are you going to work tomorrow?" Sophie asks when the lights are out and the room is still and silent.

Paul doesn't say anything. He buries himself in the quilt and breathes heavily, faking sudden sleep.

"Because you really should go back soon, Paul." Sophie snags her fingernail on the quilt. "I need a manicure tomorrow. Maybe I'll see if my mom can take Rebecca."

6.

Helen and Allan are in a restaurant on Bloor Street. Katherine is with Allan's mother in her apartment on St. Clair. Now that they don't have a babysitter Allan and Helen have been using Allan's mother. She complains about it, she doesn't like looking after babies, but Allan begs like a child, says that his marriage needs together-time and his mother says, "Go on. Get out of here. We'll be fine." This is the second time Helen and Allan have been out for dinner in a week. Allan needs this because every time he looks at his daughter he sees Lindsay the babysitter and he feels off-balance.

At work he's been filming another living will video, a young woman who is dying of cancer and wants to leave something for her six-year-old son to watch when he's grown.

The police came to Allan's work yesterday, to the studio, and questioned him again about Lindsay. They questioned him away from Helen, alone. The details are becoming jumbled in his mind. Allan has nothing to lie about, but he was drunk that evening, he is a bit confused. Each passing day makes it all the more confusing. The police are tracing his every step but, for some reason, Allan doesn't tell them about seeing Sophie naked. He doesn't tell them about climbing through Paul's backyard. He doesn't tell them because it's humiliating. Also, because he can barely remember he did it. It seems so unlike his character. It doesn't seem like anything he would do. Spying on people. So he told the police that he walked back to Paul and Sophie's house, realized he was too drunk to drive, and left the car there and walked home.

That leaves some time missing. The police have it all down to seconds. When did he see Lindsay walking down towards Bloor Street? Why did it take him so long to walk from just over the Bloor Street Viaduct to his house after he went back for the car? Did he get lost, one stupid cop asks him. Did he see anything/anyone suspicious around Paul and Sophie's house? Allan notes the cops' looks, the intense glares and raised eyebrows, but he doesn't know what they want from him.

What is he supposed to do? Tell them he hopped around in Paul's backyard with a bunch of fucking raccoons and then climbed a fence and ended up in compost? He's a dad now; he's a husband. He's supposed to be responsible. If he tells them that they might suspect him of doing something to Lindsay. They might think he's capable of anything.

The woman he's filming is missing one breast and for some stupid reason she wants Allan to film her chest so that her six-year-old can see what she has had to go through. Allan thinks the six-year-old boy is going to grow up totally warped if his mother is flashing her one breast and her scar to a video camera in hopes that he'll see it when he's a grown man.

And then September 11th.

Everything seems to have happened in the last little while. The babysitter is missing. Two huge towers collapsed, killing thousands. Katherine is rolling over now and grabbing things. Helen looks like she's dead. Her eyes are ringed black from lack of sleep, from working too hard.

In the restaurant, Helen orders calamari.

Allan wonders if that's sensible, considering it's deep-fried and if Helen gains weight her breasts will just look like fat, not like breasts. Allan shakes his head. He has to stop thinking like this.

"What are you getting, Allan?" The waiter is standing there and Helen is poking him.

"A salad," Allan says. "And water."

Helen raises her eyebrows. "I'll have a glass of house red," she says. When the waiter leaves she says, "Why aren't you drinking?"

"I don't know," Allan says. "I just feel like being healthy."

"Red wine is healthy. Tannins."

Allan shrugs. He thinks of the woman with one breast. Her scar was long and hard and ridged. The other breast was nice, but not perfect. Not like Helen's. But then Helen's aren't perfectly real, are they?

"If you had cancer," Allan suddenly says. "In your breast. How would you feel it? Would you be able to feel it? The lump? Under the implant?"

Helen stops her hand halfway to her mouth, her water glass tilted towards her. She stares at Allan. "We talked about this," she says. "Remember?"

Allan shrugs. "I don't know. I don't remember. I was just wondering. Would you be able to feel it, a lump? And know it was cancer?"

"Fuck, Allan," Helen whispers. "What is your problem? We talked about this."

Allan sits quietly. Helen drinks her wine quickly when it comes. She orders another. Allan eats his salad. Helen, her calamari.

"I forgot to tell you," she says suddenly. As if she has forgiven him.

"What?" Allan is thinking Katherine did something great, or Helen's students did something stupid. But what she says next almost stops his heart, makes him suddenly understand what the police wanted from him.

"Sophie called." Helen tells Allan about the murder, about Paul, about his back and how he can't get out of bed.

Allan completely forgot they had booked a squash game. He didn't show up. At least Paul didn't show up too. Obviously.

Helen begins on the details of the murdered man.

"Jesus," Allan whispers. "Right there. In the street behind their house?"

And then Helen stops sipping her wine and looks straight into Allan's eyes. She begins to cry. "Oh my God, Allan. Lindsay."

Allan thinks. Murdered man. Lindsay missing. Someone out there.

"We have to tell her parents. The police," she says.

The police know the connections already. Allan is sure of it.

Allan remembers climbing the fence. He remembers lying drunkenly in the compost. He remembers heading out on the street right behind Paul's street. What if someone saw him and thinks he murdered the man?

"We can't tell anyone," Allan says. "It will just worry her parents. We don't know that there's a connection. Two different parts of town. Besides, the police will do that. Make a connection. If one needs to be made."

The woman with one breast smiles and waves at his camera. "Toddy," she says. "Just remember to treat your wife nicely, okay? Because all wives deserve that. Your daddy treats me nicely."

Allan climbed that fence to get away from the raccoons. He walked home from there. He didn't stop. He certainly didn't murder anyone. God, he thinks. But then his babysitter went missing. And he saw her on the street and did nothing. Walked straight past her. Didn't even say hello.

What if someone saw him climbing the fence? What if someone was watching from a window in the neighbourhood? He was lit up like an animal caught in the headlights of a car when he was in Paul's backyard.

"Are you going to finish your salad?" Helen has stopped crying and is forking Allan's salad into her mouth. She takes a sip of his water because hers is gone. She signals for another glass of wine and then wipes her eyes with the napkin. Her mascara has run. "Do you think that Lindsay was murdered? Allan. Oh God. I keep thinking she went off with a boyfriend; that she's hanging around in a boy's basement apartment, fooling around, drinking and stuff. Getting away from her mom and dad. They are so demanding and controlling. They are driving me crazy. I can't imagine what they'd be like for a teenager. Allan?"

Allan looks at Helen's eyes, at the mascara around her eyes, at her shapely nose and her straight teeth. He looks at her neck, so thin and lovely. She is a lovely woman. He desires her; he does love her.

"Allan? What are you looking at?" Helen picks at her teeth. "Do I have salad in my teeth?"

There was nothing out of the ordinary on that street behind Paul's street. Was there? Allan walked home. He saw some home-less people on Bloor but they were way too drunk to bother with murdering someone, with kidnapping a teenager. University kids coming out of the bars. The Danforth was less busy. The Bloor Street Viaduct had no one on it. Did it? Allan remembers hearing his foot-steps echoing and thinking someone was following him.

"What are you thinking, Allan?"

Was there someone following him? He can't remember now.

"We should call Paul and Sophie," Helen says. "Let them know we are thinking of them. Can you imagine? Can you imagine seeing a dead body like that? All bloody? God."

Poor Paul, he thinks. He guesses Paul won't be playing squash for a while.

Life used to be easy, Allan thinks. Before the kid. Before marriage. Before September 11th and the missing babysitter. Everything just seemed easier.

7.

You and Gibson are walking around the neighbourhood. Gibson is peeing on trees and romping through the grass. You pass the same houses you passed before September 11th but now they look sinister and evil. Everything looks evil. When you take the subway, when you walk anywhere and when you see people you think, They could kill me. Anyone could kill me. You knew this before, of course, but not in the same way. You have trouble near tall buildings now, which makes life awkward because your bank is on the ground floor of a tall building. Your lawyer's office is way up high, on the twenty-second floor of a building. And your psychiatrist. There are many things in tall buildings that you struggle to do. You certainly will never fly again. You've promised yourself this. You will never get into another plane. And if, for some reason, you have to fly, you will stay clear of any planes that have anyone who looks suspicious on them. You will wait for the next plane, maybe.

A colleague at the library where you work tells you that your feelings will pass. You will feel safe again. She says that all safe feelings are really fake feelings anyway, because no matter what you can never be safe. She says you weren't safe before and you won't be safe again. Even if nothing had happened on September 11, 2001, you still wouldn't be safe.

It's all a matter of perspective, she tells you. Think about it. This was just a blip.

But everything, not just the thick air, but everything seems to have changed. The whole world seems to have shifted. Moved slightly off axis. Tilted. Nothing will ever be the same again.

You say to the people you work with in the library, to your psychiatrist, "It's amazing this didn't happen before. A plane used as a bomb. It makes complete sense. Of course it does. Because isn't that what airplanes are? Steel tubes filled with combustible fuel moving quickly through the sky?"

And your wife is buried under the ground. You watched them lower the casket and you were wracked with grief. Now you are alone and the world seems to be falling apart.

8.

Sophie is with her mother and father at their house. Sophie feels fat. She always feels fat around her mother and father. Her father kisses her on the cheek and smiles warmly. He takes Rebecca from Sophie and unbundles the baby from her layers. He goo-goos and ga-gas. His noises bother Sophie more than anything. Because they are forced. They are the noises a grandfather is supposed to make when he plays with his new granddaughter. Nothing is natural anymore, Sophie thinks. But then she knows nothing has ever been natural with her parents. It's more about what is right than what is natural. And right can mean many things as long as right is smiled upon by their friends and colleagues.

"Darling." Sophie's mother comes into the front hallway. "Did you get your manicure?"

Sophie holds up her hands and Sophie's mother barely looks at them. "The girl at the front desk watched Rebecca."

"Now I told you she would, didn't I?" Sophie's mother gives a high, tinkling kind of laugh that makes Sophie cringe again. "I was just so busy this morning. Shopping. Wait til you see what I bought."

Sophie looks at the floor.

"Later. Oh come in, come in." Sophie's mother waves her hands and directs them all into the living room. Candles are lit. Mozart is playing on the CD player. The lights are dimmed. Sophie wishes, just for once, she'd catch her father wearing old track pants and watching football on TV, or her mother with an avocado face mask and cucumbers on her eyes. Sophie smiles to herself.

"Wine?"

"Sure," Sophie says. "Just one glass."

"And how is Paul?" Sophie's mother asks as she takes Rebecca from her husband and places her on the couch and surveys her baby clothing. She nods when she sees the Baby Gap label on Rebecca's dress. She approves of the tights – white with little red bell designs on them. Rebecca smiles and burps loudly. Sophie's mother looks away. Takes her wineglass and sips. Looks back at the baby. She's a specimen under a microscope.

"Paul's still not out of bed," Sophie says. She doesn't know why she is telling her parents this. Her father will get involved. Sophie has a habit of saying things to her parents that she knows immediately she shouldn't have said. Her foot is often in her mouth. Sophie looks at her heels. She looks at her new nails and admires the coral colour, the subtleness of it. These are hands, she thinks, that don't wash dishes. Then she says "ha" in her head. She releases air from her nose. Her mother looks quickly up at her. Disapproving.

"I should talk to him," Sophie's father says. "He should come see me." He takes out his PalmPilot and starts thumbing through his calendar. "I have an opening this Thursday at one o'clock. That would be good."

If Sophie were working she'd have a PalmPilot. She'd know how to use it. She thinks she should get one anyway. It would be nice to have everything with you at all times. Your calendar and phone book. That would be fun.

"I don't know, Dad," Sophie says. "I don't know if he wants to talk to anyone right now and he can't get up. He says his back really hurts."

"Nonsense." Sophie's father almost shouts. Rebecca pouts from her position on the couch. Sophie rushes to pick her up before she starts crying. Crying babies are like uneducated waitresses to her father. He can't stand them.

Sophie's mother says, "Happy hour. It's happy hour," in a singsong voice to Rebecca as Sophie grabs her and holds her tight. Rebecca kicks out and almost spills Sophie's wine.

"Have him come by next Thursday at one o'clock. I can give him an hour."

"He can't get out of bed, Dad. His back."

"I don't do house calls."

"I know, I'm just saying –"

"Listen, pumpkin. Your husband must need some professional help. He's seen a horrible thing. And then with the state the world is in right now – you should see some of my patients. What they are going through. It's outrageous. It's almost as if, for some of them, they were there, in the towers. I have this one older gentleman, mourning the death of his wife – he's taken 9/11 and made it into his own personal trauma. You should see him, Sophie. Jittery and nervous. Scared of airplanes. Has a very hard time coming up to the office."

"What happened again?" Sophie's mother asks.

Sophie and her father look at her.

"I mean, what did Paul see again? I know about the World Trade Center. Really, Frank." She smiles vacantly and looks wistfully at the bottle of wine. Sophie's father pours her another glass. "Thank you, Sweetheart."

"Paul saw a murder, Mother. Remember? He helped a woman whose brother or something was murdered." Sophie bounces Rebecca on her knee. Rebecca smiles at Sophie and grabs a fistful of her hair and pulls hard. As she untangles Rebecca's small hand from her hair, a nail breaks. "Oh, Jesus," she moans.

Her father looks at her. Again, disapprovingly. "Pumpkin, no need to swear."

Sophie puts the false nail in her pocket and puts Rebecca on the floor. Rebecca rolls to her stomach and does a small push-up with her pudgy arms. She pushes hard. She turns red in the face. Sophie picks her up again.

"What are you doing about that man, Dad?"

"What man?"

"The one whose wife died."

"Oh, yes. The murder. That was horrific." Sophie's mother is looking bored. Sophie knows her time there is running out. Her mother's attention span, when it comes to babies, or when it comes to Sophie, is very short. If Sophie were talking about golf or tennis, well, perhaps her mother would invite her to stay for dinner. Sophie isn't sure. Sophie realizes that happy hour really is only an hour in her parents' house. If it were to go beyond an hour Sophie doesn't know if her mother would stay seated. She doesn't know if her mother would just get up and leave.

"Nothing much," Sophie's father says. "Just listening. That's all I can do."

"I should go," Sophie says. "Rebecca needs her dinner." It amazes Sophie that her father gets paid to listen. She's always listening, she thinks, and not a penny comes her way.

"I think you should have another glass of wine, Lillian," Sophie's father says. He pours the wine. "You're welcome to stay, Sophie."

"No," Sophie says. "Thanks, though. I have to get home and feed the baby. I have to feed Paul."

"Surely Paul could make supper? Just because he's a man doesn't mean he should get waited on."

"He's in bed, Dad. I told you."

"Yes, but he's there, in the house, and you're here. He could put on a pot of water to boil pasta, couldn't he? Call him, tell him to get everything ready and then, by the time you are home, you'll have supper. Do that."

"No, Dad. I have to go."

"She has to go, Frank. Fill up a little, darling. Just a touch?"

Where Sophie's mother demands happy hour, her father could easily be comfortable with happy night. As long as his granddaughter remains quiet and his glass remains filled.

"Ah well. Thursday then." Sophie's father stands. He fills his wife's glass. Then his own. Then he sighs. He holds out his hand as if wanting to shake with Sophie. She feels puzzled and then sees him remember – she is his daughter. He pulls her close for a hug.

Sophie's mother walks her to the door.

"He'll be fine, Sophie. Really, honey. He'll be just fine. Your father is a miracle worker. You just let him do his magic on your husband."

Sophie shrugs on her coat, bundles Rebecca back up and walks out the door. It's his back, she wants to shout, not his head. Her mother blows kisses into the cooling September air. "Take care, my love," she calls out.

Sophie buckles Rebecca into her car seat in the back and then climbs into the car. She pushes the heated-seat button and waits for the heat to flow through her rear end and up her back. To comfort her. She is going home to her husband who is lying stiff in bed. Terrorists attacked the United States. But nothing else seems to have changed. Her parents certainly have not changed. Her daughter still needs diapers and breast milk and her husband will be hungry for dinner. Sophie looks at her broken nail and starts to get angry. And then the heat comes through the seat and she turns the radio on and Rebecca coos in the back of the car, playing with her little jingling toy, and Sophie cries a bit but is fine when she finally gets home.

9.

Allan is at work, filming the woman with one breast, when the police come in to see him for the second time. They enter the studio quietly at the point when the woman with one breast is crying. She is sobbing into the camera and Allan doesn't know whether to turn the machine off. Does she want this left to her son and husband or not? It's not an appropriate time to ask her, so he just keeps filming. He can edit later. Allan gets all the angles of her face; he films her wringing hands in her lap. He films the pile of Kleenexes that is gradually growing beside her chair. He films close-ups of her eyes, swollen and red-rimmed.

"Allan Baxter?" The police officer walks towards Allan, towards the woman. He has a quizzical look on his face. "Are you Allan Baxter?"

The one-breasted woman stops crying. She sniffles. She rubs her eyes and her nose with the back of her hand. She throws another Kleenex to the floor. And she quickly puts her shirt back on.

Allan turns. He sees the two police officers standing there. Different men from before – how did they get in? There is supposed to be security at these lots so that people won't interrupt the filming.

"I'm Allan Baxter," Allan says. Meekly. His voice comes out an octave too high. If that doesn't sound suspicious, Allan thinks, nothing will.

"We'd like to ask you some questions," the officer says. "About Monday, September 10th. About the dinner party you were at."

"I've already answered questions regarding the disappearance of my babysitter. I've been over it a hundred times."

The one-breasted woman looks at Allan. She gathers up her things. "Your babysitter disappeared?" she says. "Is that the one on the news?"

"No. Yes. Sit down. You don't understand."

"We aren't here about your babysitter," the officer says.

"Are you a freak?" the one-breasted woman says. Her voice is shrill. She stands. "Are you getting your kicks out of this? I showed you my breast," she shouts. "Oh God, why are you taking advantage of dying people?"

Allan thinks, technically you didn't show me your breast, you showed me your missing breast. Technically.

"I'm just doing my job," Allan says. "Wait."

The woman rushes out of the studio. Allan groans.

"You're filming her naked?" the officer says.

"No, just her breast. Just the breast that isn't there, actually."

"Mr. Baxter, I think you have some explaining to do."

"Is this about Lindsay? Did you find Lindsay?"

The officers look at each other. "The murdered man is Richard Middleford."

"What murdered man?" Allan is panicking. His heart has sped up. He feels sick to his stomach. He thinks he's getting an ulcer.

The officers are now standing with their hands on their gun holsters.

Allan says, "I don't know why you're here."

"We're here to ask you about the night you had dinner with Sophie and Paul Moore. There was a murder behind their house. Mr. Moore discovered the body."

"Oh, yes, that murder. So you aren't here about Lindsay?"

"I think you should come down to the precinct with us. I think we should have a talk. About Lindsay, and about Richard Middleford, and maybe about this woman here, the one who just left?"

"I think I should get a lawyer, shouldn't I?" Allan says. "I don't know, I've never been in trouble with the law before." Allan feels like crying.

"You're not in trouble with the law, Mr. Baxter," the officer says.

"Are you?" the other officer asks. "Are you in trouble?"

"But I should have a lawyer. They always have lawyers on TV."

"You can call your lawyer at the precinct."

"I don't have a lawyer," Allan says. "The only lawyer I know is Paul Moore."

"You can call him. Let's go."

Allan realizes suddenly that he has been filming this whole thing. He turns off the camera and follows the officers out of the studio. Maybe someone will find this film later, he thinks, and realize he's innocent. Maybe someone will find his dead body in a police cell battered by the cops or criminals. Maybe he'll be coerced into saying something he didn't mean to say and he can use this film to show a judge that he wanted to get a lawyer but didn't have one. He'll phone Paul when he's at the police station.

"Can I follow you down in my car?" Allan asks.

The officers laugh.

"But what about my car? They close this lot at 5:00 p.m. I won't be able to come back and get it."

"You'll have to figure that one out on your own," the officer says as he puts his hand on Allan's head and lightly pushes him into the back of the patrol car.

Allan burps a little – some bile. Is he going to be sick? And they drive downtown, towards the police station. If given only one phone call, Allan thinks, who should he phone? Paul or Helen?

10.

You are alone. There is a wide circle around you. You are a flaming building, going down. Everyone wants to stay away from you because you give off heat and anger and sadness. You are combusting from within. Slowly falling.

The picture that really got to you was the one of the man diving from the top floor of one of the towers. He was diving straight down, his arms at his side. A graceful dive, headfirst. *The Falling Man.* Captured on film. A still photograph of a man in uniform, a chef's outfit perhaps (he may have worked at the restaurant on top of the tower, they say later), as he dove purposefully to his death. That's the photograph that made time stand still for you. That's the photograph that made you want to stop everything, that made you want to climb into a shell like a hermit crab, burrow under the sand. Nothing, you think, will ever affect you the same way again.

And this makes you feel something because it shows you are alive still. It shows that there are horrors in the world that still bother you.

You are glad you bought a dog over the internet.

Gibson with his nose so wet and clean. Gibson with his warm ears. Most nights you curl next to him for warmth and listen to him breathe. Listen to him growl as he chases people or rabbits or squirrels in his dreams, while you are haunted by the solitary night.

This is what you'll get if you search the internet for strange news stories:

"Elmo Doll Used to Smuggle Drugs"

"Man Accused of Mailing Severed Cow's Head"

"Bush-Masked Bandit Steals Social Security Money"

"3 Indicted in Basement Liposuction Death"

"Woman Wallops Intruder with Cooking Pot"

"Florida Man Pulls Dog from Gator's Jaws"

"Man Dies After Lawn Mower Flips, Pins Him Under Water"

"Fart Goes Wrong"

Sometimes, when you see what is out there in the world, what is happening day after day, you say to yourself (not to anyone else, you wouldn't dare), No wonder those men flew planes at the World Trade Center. No wonder my wife died. No wonder her organs stopped working. No wonder those polyps turned to cancerous black marks and then spread like oil. So quickly.

The world seemed crazy before but it seems crazier now. You look around you. At the people around you. The people hurrying. Even in the library you work at. Everyone is busy. Everyone is moving so fast. But you know why they are doing that. They are moving fast so that they won't have a moment to think about the fact that they are going to die.

*

When the days bleed into each other, the news keeps piling on tragedy, and as you are walking Gibson in the park you run into her. A girl. She is stoned or something, sitting on a park bench, smoking a cigarette. Her eyes are vacant. You recognize her from the television and the newspapers. The other news that has been filtering through. "Missing Babysitter" right next to "Survivor Impact Statements." Gibson moves up to her and she pats him on the head.

You have been thinking about September 11th so much that it surprises you that you have registered other news stories on TV. The missing babysitter.

She sits, bundled in a blanket, her eyes completely empty. Her hair matted. She is barely recognizable but you have a way with faces and so you know immediately who she is.

You suppose she needs food. You suppose she is lost, she needs to go home.

Gibson sniffs her, recoils from her smell a bit, barks.

"Gibson."

The girl startles. Her eyes come alive.

"He won't hurt you," you say, but you aren't too sure of that. Gibson has been acting strange lately. You think it is time to get him neutered.

The girl gets up quickly and begins to walk away.

"Wait."

She stops. Then she begins to run, lopsidedly. The run of someone not quite well, not quite sober.

You are over nothing yet. You are scared most days and you are tired. You haven't slept solidly since September 11th. You haven't done anything properly. Work is punctuated by heart palpitations. No one will talk to you about the World Trade Center anymore. It's hovering there, in the blind spot of your eye. All the time.

The girl cries out. "Leave me alone."

"I can help you," you say. "I can take you home. You are missing. Do you know you are missing?"

"I don't want to go home." She stands there, looking at you. Looking at Gibson. The babysitter.

There is a line of blood under her nose, above her lip. You are stuck here in time, looking at her dark blood. It reminds you of your dead wife and the blood in her stools. Follow through, you keep saying to yourself. Wake up. Get out of it. Move forward. Help out. But you can't.

You are actually scared of the girl.

But she is more afraid of you.

"I can feed you. You can come home with me. I'll take care of you." It's like your wife is talking through you. You can hear her voice in your head.

"Yes," the girl says. Matter-of-factly. Her voice cracks. She cries. "I'm starving."

Gibson knows when he doesn't like something. He growls.

This girl, you think later, after you get her to come into your house, after you heat up a frozen lasagna and leave her in the bathroom with a towel and a robe, an old shirt of yours, your wife's old skirt, as you walk down the hallway, turning on all the lights in the house, as you bolt the front door and cover Gibson in his blanket, this girl, you think. You've saved this girl. She knows nothing about how lucky she is. Anyone could have taken her.

You couldn't save the people in the World Trade Center.

You didn't save your wife.

But this girl.

11.

Helen is in the middle of conducting a tutorial when her cellphone rings. One of her students giggles. Helen excuses herself and answers the phone. She would never usually answer the phone but it must be an emergency. No one has this number except her nanny. And Allan.

It's Sophie. She says that Paul got a call from Allan. That Allan has been taken to the police station to be questioned. Sophie says that Paul is still at home in bed with his bad back, and, besides, he isn't a criminal lawyer and there is nothing he can do. Sophie tells Helen that she didn't even wake Paul to ask him, but she knows what Paul would say anyway.

"Some good friend you are," Helen shouts. Her class, in the room beside her, stops talking. They listen. Helen whispers, "My husband is in jail and you didn't want to wake Paul?"

"Helen," Sophie says. "You don't understand. He hasn't slept in two weeks. Not really. Just catnapping. His back. Besides, there is nothing he could do for Allan. He's not that kind of lawyer."

"What about recommend another lawyer? We don't have a law-yer. Jesus, Sophie."

Sophie is silent.

"Do you know anyone? Can you give me a name?" Helen says.

"I'll wake him," Sophie says. "I'm sorry, I didn't think of that. I didn't think you wouldn't have a lawyer. Everyone has a lawyer, don't they?"

"Listen, I'm going down to the police station right now. Tell Paul to meet me there."

Sophie says, "Helen, he can't get out of bed. Physically. He can't."

"Okay, tell him to call me, to get me a lawyer who will meet me there."

Sophie begins to cry. "Oh God, I'm sorry, it's just –"

"I know. No. I know. Just tell him to call me as soon as he can." Helen hangs up. As soon as he wakes up, goddamnit, she thinks.

She tells her tutorial students to read something, she can't even remember what, tells them she has to leave, and then leaves. She forgets her briefcase in the room. And her coat. It isn't until Helen is halfway down the block on the way to her car that she remembers her coat. By the time she goes back to the classroom it is gone.

Her new coat. From Holt Renfrew. The suede one that was far too expensive and not warm enough, but that clung to her like a bodysuit, the coat that followed the shape of her shoulders, her breasts, her waist. That coat.

Her briefcase is there, though. She scoops it up and runs away, down the hall, outside the building, down the street, to her car, to the police station, to her husband.

Sophie didn't say what this was all about and Helen can only assume they've found Lindsay, the babysitter. Maybe they think Allan is involved somehow. She can only assume the news isn't good.

12.

Paul clears everything up with the police.

"In fact," Sophie says later, when they are all back at Sophie and Paul's house, having dinner, after Paul drove Allan back to the studio to get his car. "Your arrest, Allan, actually cured my husband's back. Got him out of bed."

"Well, I'm glad it did something for him. It did nothing for me." Allan is drinking out of a beer bottle. Sophie ignores this. Allan can't look at Sophie. The last time he saw her, through the window, she was buck-naked. He can't look at her now without thinking of that.

Helen stretches. She leans back in her chair at the dining-room table. The candlelight flickers. There is one too many buttons on her blouse open. Paul sees the bulge of her new breasts. He watches them rise and fall. He thinks of Vivian Middleford. His back aches – but it's a dull throb now, not the severe muscle-seizing cramps that seemed to spread through his bones.

Vivian came to his office today. Right after he dropped Allan off with his car. He went back downtown quickly to check on things, find out what he'd missed. Paul figured that once he was up it was better not to lie down again. Vivian walked right in, past his secretary, and shut the door behind her. She moved quickly towards Paul, who was sitting behind his desk, and she came around and touched his shoulders, massaged them, and said she missed him. She said she couldn't stop thinking about him, how they had shared this horrible moment and that it had somehow brought them together.

"Missed me?" he asked.

She kissed him then, her red lips. On his forehead again.

It was strange, Paul thinks, but lovely. Sharing something life-altering, like they did, changes the way you interact with people.

Missed him? Why would she miss him? He doesn't know any more about her than what he knew that morning – her dead brother in her house, her lips on his forehead, standing on the street in her underwear and bra.

Paul aches, though, when he thinks about it. She kissed him. And then left the office quickly. She was embarrassed. She apologized and backed out quickly. What should he do? What could he do?

"Jesus, Allan," Paul says, clearing his throat. Whenever he thinks about Vivian he feels as if Sophie can see straight through him, into him, like she's watching TV on his chest. Like Lady Macbeth, like her red spots, Paul has red lips on his forehead. He sips his wine. "I can't believe how scared you looked."

"There were criminals in there," Allan says. "And drunks."

"He was more afraid of the drunks," Helen purrs. "He was afraid that one of them would throw up on him."

"I'm grateful you came down, Paul," Allan says, for the sixth time in an hour. His eyes well up. He opens another beer – Paul has lined some up beside him – and sucks on the bottle.

"Yeah, well. I'm glad to be up and moving again." Paul pauses. "When I started practising law I thought I'd be a criminal lawyer," he says. "Isn't that why most lawyers go into law? And then we're tempted by the salaries of the corporate lawyers. It's all about wealth." Paul stands and goes over to the buffet to open another bottle of wine. He pours it out into the glasses and then sits down again. "It's all about keeping our wives happy."

"Ha," Sophie says. "If that was the case, you'd be making much more than you make now." Sophie plays with the takeout box of Thai noodles on the table. She pokes it with her chopsticks. She burps up a garlic taste. Rebecca is asleep in her tilted back high chair, her head nodding sideways. She looks uncomfortable but Sophie doesn't want to wake her to put her to bed. She's feeling tired and lumpy. Her stomach is soft. She pokes at it under the table.

"What did they want, really?" Helen asks. "What did the police want?"

"I told you," Allan says. "They just wanted to know what I was doing after the dinner party that night. Paul had just told them that we'd been at his house and that I had come back for the car. They wanted to know if I had seen anything suspicious."

"But why did they take you to the police station?" Sophie asks.

"Because of the situation. Because of our babysitter and the woman I was filming, I guess."

Helen looks at Rebecca. She thinks of Katherine at home with the nanny, who is staying late tonight. She thinks of Lindsay and she wonders if they will ever know what happened to her. Lindsay's boyfriend is being questioned, according to the police. He is a suspect. A drug addict, supposedly. He sells drugs. Supposedly he got Lindsay high a lot. Helen identified him today, at the police station. She pointed to a photo the police had of him. She pointed him out as the one she saw leaving her house. All the photos the police showed her of young teen boys were the same. They were wearing the same things: baggy pants and hooded sweatshirts. She thinks she got the right one. He was the one who looked the most angry. But there is no body. No Lindsay. There is no crime. Yet. How do you charge someone with nothing?

"It's been such a nightmare," Helen says. "Hasn't it? We had such a nice dinner party that night and then everything went crazy." She leans into Allan a bit drunkenly. Her breasts shift and everyone is aware. Sophie pokes at her soft stomach again. She kneads it with her hands. Before she had Rebecca her stomach was hard as rock. Sophie sighs.

"I guess we all should have got in touch sooner," Paul says. "We should have told you about the murder and you should have told us about Lindsay. It all seems connected now, doesn't it? But at the time it didn't."

"It's not connected," Helen says. "It can't be. A girl went missing. That has nothing to do with what you saw, Paul."

Paul shrugs. "I hope not." Why was Vivian Middleford in her underwear in the street? The room off the kitchen wasn't anywhere near her bedroom. Was she walking around in her underwear in the house? This thought turns him on.

"But it is weird that we were all connected to both things. You can see why the police needed to talk to me, really," Allan says. He remembers jumping into the compost. He remembers coming out of the side of the house behind Paul's house. He remembers walking home covered in compost and seeing Lindsay walking down the street crying. Jesus, why didn't he do anything?

"Tell me about your new filming job, Allan," Sophie says. "That's the thing I don't get. I thought you filmed TV shows and commercials. Not people who are dying."

Allan shrugs. Helen sits upright in her chair. "Yes, Allan, tell us about this. This woman with one breast."

Helen saying "breast" makes everyone turn a slight shade of pink. They all look at the tablecloth. Sophie sips her wine. Paul clears his throat.

"It's just something I got into on the side. They are called grief videos. There's a whole market out there, supposedly. The local funeral home approached me on a commercial shoot one day. It's big money."

"Big money? Really?" Helen says. "I don't see any big money? Where?"

"Well, it's money. When the industry is low, it's something that I can do to keep us afloat."

"Honey," Helen says. She is a bit drunk. "I'm the one who keeps us afloat. My salary. You don't even own a life jacket."

Paul clears his throat again. "So what do you do? Get them to talk about dying?"

"No. They talk about whatever they want to talk about. Sometimes it's just videos of them saying goodbye, saying the things they would like to say to everyone at their funeral, that kind of thing. Sometimes, like with this one guy, they want you to follow them around for a couple days so that their family gets a sense of them moving and living."

"Creepy," Sophie says.

"This woman. The one with breast cancer. She wanted to show her chest to her son and her husband. So they wouldn't forget."

"Oh, now that's really bad."

"That's mean," Helen says. "That's mean to make them remember her by seeing her maimed."

"She wasn't maimed."

"Sure, she was maimed. Her breast cut from her. Dying."

"God, that's not maimed," Sophie says. "I can't imagine having everyone see that. I can't imagine wanting my kid to remember me that way. Suffering. Sure. But that's not maimed. That's life."

"Well," Allan says. "Everyone is different, Sophie. Everyone has different relationships with their kids and their spouses. Everyone sees their lives and deaths differently."

"You sound like my father," Sophie says.

Paul grunts. He'd tried to get out of his bed that Thursday to go and talk to Sophie's father, but he couldn't do it, and the man called and berated him for wasting his time. His father-in-law actually said that he could have been playing squash but was now sitting in his office for an empty hour, waiting for Paul. An empty hour. He thinks of his life in time segments of empty and full. Paul didn't tell Sophie. What was the point? He's sure Sophie's mother said something. The way things are going on around here, though, Paul thinks, it's not as if he and Sophie talk about her parents. They don't talk about much, really. Just whether the cat has been fed. Whether Rebecca could possibly be cutting a tooth so early or just drooling and crying for no reason. Whether there is anything good on TV.

But now Paul is up. He's up and socializing and back to work. He'll go tomorrow all day, if he's not hungover. He pours another glass of red wine. The colour makes him pause, makes him think of the blood he saw that morning. Everywhere blood. But he channels his thoughts quickly to something else. To Helen's breasts. He stares at them. That's a good distraction, he thinks. He just needs good distractions around him at all times. Vivian's kiss. Especially in bed at two in the morning when Sophie is breathing heavily beside him and the street light from outside is shining through the drapes and all he can think about is the condition of Richard, the way his body was attacked, his face, as if someone was so incredibly angry with him they couldn't help it.

"God," Paul says aloud.

"What?" Sophie is blowing out the candles. They have burned down to the end. Wax is dripping on the tablecloth. "Oh, do you want to hear something funny?" she says.

Helen looks across the table at Paul and then looks at her husband. She can't think of anything funny, anything that would make her laugh. Her husband was questioned by the police today. He's been withdrawn lately. Quiet. Sneaking around with this new job. Not talking to her very much. Sick at dinner the other week.

"The night you guys came over Paul drank wax." Sophie laughs. "He took a sip of the candle wax. It was stuck all over his tongue. Burned his mouth."

"Really?" Allan perks up. Puts down his sixth bottle of beer. Burps. "That would fucking hurt."

"It did," Paul says. "My mouth was a mess for about a week. It still hurts a bit. All burned up. The worst was you couldn't swallow the wax because it hardened by the time it got down your throat. I spent a long time trying to peel it up, scratching at my tongue." He laughs. "I'm glad I was drunk."

Rebecca startles in her high chair and cries. Then she stops and goes back to sleep. Everyone whispers.

Allan remembers himself caught in the backyard light, remembers all of that night. But he can't tell anyone about it. Especially because of what happened to that man. He imagines the police would have a field day if they knew he was sneaking around behind houses covered in compost, spying on his friends. Allan opens another beer. Helen kicks him under the table. He ignores her.

"We should have some dessert," Sophie says. She stands. "I've got ice cream. And a mango."

"Sounds good."

"What about the next day?" Helen asks. "How did you all handle the next day? The World Trade Center?"

The room goes silent. Helen looks at Sophie as she pauses between the dining room and the kitchen. Sophie looks at Paul. Paul looks at Allan. Allan looks at the floor.

"Sorry," Helen says. "I shouldn't have brought it up. We have enough to think about."

"No, that's okay," Sophie says. "Let me get dessert." She leaves the room.

"Honestly," Paul says, "the murder was just so present that the planes didn't seem real."

"Yeah," Allan says. "We had the babysitter's parents in our living room and everyone was crying. It was bad."

"You could have filmed it, Allan," Helen says. "One huge grief video." It angers Helen she had to find out the same time her friends found out about Allan's new filming business. She is his wife, isn't she? But she wonders if she's also angry because these kinds of silly home movies seem so much below Allan. They aren't art. Neither are his commercials, though. But what's the difference between filming someone's wedding and filming grief videos? Anyone could do it. And art is just that – something that not everyone can do. That's why it's art. It's hard to do, or hard to conceive, or hard to implement.

"That's not nice," Sophie says, laughing. She comes in from the kitchen with ice cream in bowls, with mango on top.

Allan is looking at his wife and thinking, This is why I didn't tell you. This is why I don't tell you anything.

"When do you think we'll be able to joke about it?" Sophie says. "About September 11th?"

Everyone is silent.

"I'm just kidding," Sophie says. "Of course, you can't joke about it."

"New York," Helen says. "That's far enough away."

"It doesn't matter," Paul says. "The whole world is different now. Everything has changed."

"Someone will start making jokes about it. Movies even. Soon enough. You wait." Allan gets up and goes to the bathroom.

"I don't know about jokes," Helen says. "Movies maybe, but not jokes."

Rebecca cries again. Paul takes her from her high chair and says, "I'll put her to bed."

"There's breast milk in the freezer." Sophie nods lazily from her chair at the table. It is dark in the dining room now that the candles have been put out. Sophie is drinking more red wine. She splashes some on her ice cream. It curdles slightly.

The men are gone. The baby is gone.

Helen and Sophie look at each other.

"What a crazy couple of weeks," Helen says.

They raise their wineglasses. And clink them together.

"I hope you find the babysitter," Sophie says. "That's such an awful thing."

Helen nods.

"Imagine how her parents must feel. Just imagine." Sophie's eyes water.

Just then Helen's wineglass tips – by itself – onto the white tablecloth that is already splattered with wax. The red wine pours out across the table. Sophie looks at the stain. Studies it. Helen pours salt on it quickly. "I'm so sorry."

"Doesn't matter," Sophie says. She stares at the stain. "It looks like something."

Helen looks at it from all angles.

"A snake?" Helen asks. "A fish?"

"No," Sophie says. "Blood. Spilled blood."

13.

The world looks different after the girl comes into your house. It's brighter, somehow. More distinct. Everything seems to glow, to have a purpose, a reason. The world was dark, even a bit fuzzy around the edges before. Now everything is sharp and colourful.

United Airlines Flight 175

American Airlines Flight 11

American Airlines Flight 77

United Airlines Flight 93

It looks like a poem. You study the numbers wondering if there is meaning in them. After all, 9/11 has meaning.

When the Taliban bombed those statues in Afghanistan should you have known that the world would change? It seemed like only a blip in the papers one day. The statues were there. Then they were gone. The news moved forward. Now you watch the news like a hawk – hoping to find the next thing before it happens.

Post-traumatic stress disorder. Your psychiatrist tells you he thinks this is what you have. PTSD.

But you weren't anywhere near the World Trade Center. You were in Canada. You were just getting ready for work. Watching the news on TV.

It is that your whole view of life has changed. You still struggle through, you check out books for people, you re-shelve and you try to smile, but nothing is the same anymore. Children in the park aren't just children in the park. Now they are potentials. Little potentials. Potentials for good. Or bad. You aren't sure about anything these days. Even the library regulars seem fraught with danger. You aren't surprised by anything anymore.

On the internet you can find out how to make a bomb. You can find out what you need to buy – what kinds of fertilizers – you can find out the exact measurements. You also notice that there are instructions on how to kill yourself and on how to dance the mambo or make a cherry pie. There are live broadcasts of the planes hitting the World Trade Center and the Pentagon and you can sit and watch them hit again and again. And you do. If you watch the planes hit enough times then maybe you won't wake up every night sweating. Maybe you will sleep through the airplane noises as they pass over your house on the night routes towards Ottawa or Montreal. The rush and boom of sonic engines. Maybe you will be able to make decisions again. You used to know just what to do and you used to do it quickly and efficiently. Now you are out of control. And aging. Sixty-one. And nothing to show for it. Except a dead wife.

But then you got a dog. And now a girl. In your house. That's not being greedy. You just wanted to stop being lonely. The buildings collapsed and then you found her in the park and you will save her from the things she is afraid of. But now you don't know what to do with her. Your purpose here is twofold – loneliness and rescue. She will rescue you from your loneliness. You will rescue her from the drugs. She curls up on the couch with a blanket wrapped around her shoulders, her eyes dead. She watches TV.

You can't keep her forever.

She isn't locked in here. But she doesn't want to go home.

She is confused and craving more drugs. Coming off them. Agitated and anxious.

She claims her father beats her and that's why she doesn't want to go home. You are not sure you believe her. She looks up and to the left when she says it and you can't remember if that is the way people look when they lie or when they tell the truth.

She needs you.

She needs you to help her get sober.

It has been a long time since someone needed you.

You'll take books out of the library and you'll help her and then, when she is all better, you'll send her out into the real world. There can't be anything wrong with that, can there? A few more days? A few more weeks?

Sometimes, though, you still feel as if you have shit on your hands from the night before September 11th.

You've taken to walking around and around the block with Gibson, your eyes peeled to the sky. You've taken to thinking that planes are going to fall out of the sky. You mention this one night to the girl and she laughs.

"Planes out of the sky?" she says. "Not again."

Soon the girl begins to eat. She lies on your sofa and watches TV and eats everything you have in the house, fills up the hole that is empty from the drugs. You are a bit relieved. She might just take care of herself. She might just get up and go one day and you won't have to do anything. As long as she doesn't turn you in.

She sees the very few newspaper stories in the back pages about her anxious parents; about how she is considered missing; about the teenage boy, Derek, her boyfriend, who is questioned and released; about the man she babysat for the night she disappeared. She sees them all on TV. She lies sideways on the couch with Gibson. She sees the planes. Over and over. The infernos falling from the sky. The buildings collapsing in on themselves, floors disappearing below people's feet. She sees all this and the ceiling. She doesn't react. She pets your dog.

You envy her. Almost. Some kind of drug-induced trauma that helps her deal with the world as it is now.

But then you wonder what she really saw when she disappeared from her family. Where did she go? She won't talk about it. It must have been bad for her to be the way she is now.

She has an awesome ability to forget reality. To not see it. Or to see reality but ignore it.

You'll have to look this up at the library. You are sure it has a name.

But you want to keep her this way. This girl who stopped your fear.

And you also want her to go away.

When you go to your psychiatrist's office you don't tell him about this girl. You feel viciously guilty about it. But you tell him that you are feeling lighter. Happier. You tell him that looking out his window doesn't bring your heart to a stop. You tell him you don't feel so lonely anymore, now that you have a dog.

Your doctor laughs.

"Good," he says, his fingers steepled together to hold up his chin. "Great. I'm so pleased for you."

14.

Sophie's father is not at his desk. His receptionist says he's visiting patients in the psych ward at the hospital. She says he'll be back soon and she gets Sophie a cappuccino and Sophie bounces Rebecca on her lap and sips her cappuccino and looks at the beige walls and glass coffee table. She looks across the room at the windows that look upon downtown Toronto. Way up. They are way up. Too far up. It must be scary working up here now, Sophie thinks. After everything.

It amazes Sophie that her father listens to people complain all day long. It amazes her because he never listens to Sophie.

The receptionist talks quietly on the phone and then begins to type something into the computer. She smiles at Sophie every so often. She hasn't once looked at the baby.

A man comes in the waiting room. He is older than she is, but younger than her father. He is impeccably dressed. Sophie admires his suit, his tie, his polished shoes. He sits across from Sophie and picks up a copy of the *New Yorker*. He smiles at Rebecca. Sophie smiles at him and then notices his hands are shaking and so she looks away.

What is he here for? Sophie wonders. She can't help but think about all the things this man must be telling her father, all the things that are private and strange. Her father sometimes tells stories about the people he treats. After he has stopped treating them. Sometimes after they have died. Like the one man who jumped from an overpass over Highway 401 and landed in traffic. Her father told about how he couldn't look up when he walked, this man. He was so scared of life, scared of everything around him, that when he went outside he couldn't look anywhere but at his own feet. Sophie was a child when her father told her this and she often wondered if the man fell off the overpass by accident. Maybe he was looking at his feet and he just walked the wrong direction. But her father laughed and said the man had to climb up over the edge, he had to balance on the rail, before he went over. It was deliberate, her father said. And Sophie was to learn from it. She was to learn that looking up and out, having straight posture, facing the world head-on, was preferable to being run over by trucks on the 401.

Now Sophie is in the office waiting for her father who has summoned her to talk. And this lovely, kind-looking man across from her – manicured nails, hair greying perfectly, aftershave smelling delicious – is waiting too.

Here he comes. Frank. Dr. Campbell. Her father.

"Sophie, darling," he says. He nods to his patient, takes a pile of notes off his receptionist's desk and ushers her into his office. His inner sanctum. As Sophie takes her coat off, her father cuddles Rebecca who begins to whimper and fuss.

"Here." Sophie takes her daughter from her father. He looks relieved.

Frank sits behind the desk and motions for Sophie to sit in front of it. Doctor/patient.

"You wanted to see me?"

"Darling," Frank says. "Don't be defensive."

"What?"

"You sound like I'm about to accuse you of something."

"I'm not really worried about you accusing me of anything, it's more I'm worried about you psychoanalyzing me."

"You don't need that," Frank says. He swivels his chair towards his windows and looks out. "Do you?"

"Dad, what did you want? I've got to go and you've got a patient." Sophie signals out towards the waiting room.

"Yes, yes, I know." Frank swivels back, puts his hands on the desk. Locks eyes with Sophie. "How is Paul?"

"What do you mean?"

"Is he back at work?"

"Yes. He went yesterday. First day. He's doing better." Sophie looks down at Rebecca. She looks so much like Paul. Bald like him, ears sticking out slightly. She has his deep-set eyes.

"Good. I like to hear that. You know, he didn't show up for our appointment."

"Oh?" Sophie had forgotten all about that. She told Paul to go see her father, but then she erased it from her mind. "I didn't know that. His back. He couldn't even get here, Dad."

"And we had a little talk on the phone."

Sophie wonders when? When she was out buying groceries one day? Or in the shower? Wouldn't she have heard Paul on the phone?

"Well, I'm sorry he cancelled your meeting."

"That's just it, Sophie. He didn't cancel. He just didn't show up."

"Oh." Sophie wonders if her father is going to charge her for it? Is that what this is about? Paul missed an appointment and didn't give twenty-four-hours' notice? Surely not.

"I think that's irresponsible, dear, and I just wanted to make sure that he isn't letting any of his other responsibilities slip too."

"Oh God, Dad, that's ridiculous. His back. Have you ever had a seized up back? It's horribly painful, I've heard." You can't have sex anymore, Sophie thinks. You can't even snuggle. In fact, forget talking to your wife, or even looking her in the eyes.

"People deal with shock in different ways. But most people need help to get over it."

"Shock? No. Paul is fine now. He's back at work. He isn't having nightmares anymore." Sophie isn't sure of that, really. Last night, for example, she opened her eyes and saw Paul staring at the ceiling, sweating. There were huge beads of sweat on his forehead. He was blinking rapidly, as if he was trying not to cry. Sophie merely closed her eyes and went back to sleep. She figured there was nothing she could say or do that would comfort him. Maybe he does need her father? Or someone else? Someone to talk to.

"You know, Sophie," Frank says, "the police have a pretty good profile of the person they think committed that murder. They are quite certain that they are close to pinning it on the wife. She was some sort of athlete in school. Strong. And he was drunk or something so that could happen. A woman could murder a man. It's not unheard of. They just need more evidence. They are matching things up right now."

"How do you know this?"

"I have friends in the police force. From the hospital. After all, the person who committed this crime will most likely end up there. In the hospital. It was the act of someone completely psychotic."

Sophie nods. "She must have been incredibly strong," she says. "I can't imagine having the strength to kill Paul. Even if I was an athlete in school."

"I think that when they catch the killer," Frank sighs, "Paul will get some closure. I think he'll feel better when that happens."

"Sure, yes. Why wouldn't he?"

"But until then, darling." Frank's voice is soothing. "Until then perhaps he should see someone. Talk to someone."

"Oh."

"And if he doesn't want to talk to me, I completely understand. It might be awkward to talk to your father-in-law. But I can recommend doctors, of course."

"Of course."

Frank writes something down on a pad of paper on his desk. He rips off the paper and hands it to his daughter. The baby grabs it from his hand and Frank looks angry. Just for a minute. There is a slight twitch in the set of his mouth. Then he smiles.

"Silly granddaughter," he says. "Here. Let me kiss her."

Sophie stands and puts on her coat while her father cuddles her daughter.

"I'm just making sure my baby is fine," Frank says, handing back Rebecca. "I'm just protecting you."

"I know. Thanks." Sophie reaches up and kisses him on the cheek. "Say hi to Mom."

Frank waves.

Sophie leaves. On the way out she smiles at the man reading the *New Yorker*. The man smiles back and then looks quickly down at his polished shoes, searching the floor for a way out. Sophie hopes that her father will cure him, whatever is wrong with him. Tell him to look up, look up at the sky.

15.

Allan is listening to the Ramones' "I Wanna Be Sedated" on the car radio as he drives quickly down the street. He is singing along out loud when suddenly he sees the sad man with the dog walking directly ahead of him, crossing the street.

And then he remembers.

Allan remembers the man with the dog coming out from behind the house across the street when Allan came out covered in compost. The newspapers now say that the police think it was the wife who killed the man, but Allan can't believe that. He was there, after all, around the same time. He remembers the man leaning down and wiping his hands on the grass. The dog sitting patiently beside him. The dog looking at him. The man looked at him too. He remembers clearly and quickly and he pulls over and watches the man make his way down the street, the dog marching happily beside him. Tail wagging.

Then he remembers he saw the man earlier that night too. He saw him in front of Sophie and Paul's house, walking his damn dog. Just before Allan snuck to the side of the house. Just before the raccoons attacked him. Just before the motion detector light and the compost and then coming out and seeing the man again, wiping his hands. Wiping what off his hands? Was he wiping blood off his hands?

"Oh God," Allan says. "That's it."

The man disappears around a corner. Allan follows but the man and the dog are gone when Allan sees a break in traffic and turns left. Allan drives around and around the block for a while and then around the neighbourhood, until he gives up and heads off towards his new grief video job. He's got to tell someone about the man with the dog.

But who?

Who would believe that he just walked innocently home that night when he is tied to both incidents – the murder and the babysitter? It's bad enough he has no alibi for the time he is missing, but the police seem to have let that slide.

No, Allan can't tell anyone. Not yet. He has to think this through. He has to make sure the house the man came out from is the house where Paul saw the murdered man.

How do you bring this up casually, Allan wonders? During a squash game? During drinks at a bar? "Hey, Paul, show me the house where the man was cut to ribbons."

Allan is sweating even though the temperature has dropped considerably. He opens the window and lets the breeze from the city cool him off. Cool him down. Freeze his mind.

16.

It has been a while since Paul drank the hot wax but he still has a sore on the inside of his cheek. Just on the left side, towards the back. He works it with his tongue, opening the flap of skin and closing it. His cheek bulges in and out. Like he's chewing gum.

Paul keeps looking out the window of his office. He is thinking about Vivian's kiss that morning. He looks down, to the small people on the streets below. He watches. Her lips were hot on him. Her hands hot, too, on his shoulders. Paul is grateful that his office does not face Lake Ontario. It does not face the island airport. If it did, he would have to move. Or quit. He would have to get away from the building and its closeness to air traffic. As it is, his office faces uptown and so the only planes he sees are way up there. So far up in the sky, actually, that he reasons he could take the stairs down before one made it to this floor of the building. He would see it coming. Yes, he knows he would. Paul stares out his window all day. But then he thinks about his back, how stiff it still is, and wonders if he'd make it down the stairs.

It has occurred to him in the past few hours that when he woke from his faint on Vivian's floor, the paramedics and police surrounding him, walking him to the couch, Vivian was dressed in jeans and a T-shirt. She wasn't in her underwear and bra and his bathrobe anymore. In fact, he was in his own bathrobe and it was speckled with blood.

When did she have time to change? When did she put his bathrobe on him?

Paul sighs. What has he accomplished today? His assistant comes in two times and asks him just that question.

"Do you need me," she says, sarcastically, "or can I go home?"

He turns and looks at the files on his desk. He looks at the messages his assistant has written on pink Post-it Notes and thrown on his table in the corner. Paul looks at the cup of coffee from this morning that he didn't even drink. Did he have lunch? Paul's head aches and his vision seems clouded. The inside of his office looks so dark compared to the light from outside. His eyes tear up. Cataracts? He wonders if he's losing his eyesight.

"Are blind people allowed to drive?" he remembers his brother's kid asking him once when they saw a man with a white cane on the street. As if it were only a matter of getting a licence.

And if he was blind then the world would be dark and all he would see was his memory of the dead man in the house that horrible morning. At work all he can see is the planes hitting the Twin Towers.

"Get over it," he tells himself.

A colleague in New York was having breakfast in the World Trade Center restaurant on that morning. His wife watched the planes hit from her New Jersey office, she watched the buildings fall. She knew her husband was in there, eating eggs Benedict, his favourite, three cups of black coffee, a freshly squeezed orange juice. Paul imagines she could picture him there, in his suit just back from the dry cleaner. And now she's a thirty-four-year-old widow with two preschool kids, still working an office job in New Jersey.

What about the hundreds of thousands of refugees in Darfur? Or the limbless in Sierra Leone? Or the grandmothers taking care of generations of children whose parents have died of AIDS in Africa? Paul knows how he should feel and how he shouldn't feel. Watching those buildings collapse after seeing a man cut to ribbons tied to a bed seems to have looped Paul's mind in knots.

He thinks he should see someone. It's time to see someone. To talk.

Not his father-in-law. Never.

He tried to talk with Allan when they met for squash yesterday but Allan was obsessed with the babysitter missing and with a man with a dog, and was babbling on as if he were drunk. Maybe he was. It was near dinnertime. Maybe Allan had stopped for a beer on the way to the squash court.

Paul has not tried talking to Sophie. There's really no point. Sophie doesn't want to talk about anything. She made that clear when he was stuck in bed. She wants her husband to be strong and invincible. What would he tell her anyway? Would he tell her that he thinks he may be falling in love with Vivian Middleford? That she appeared out of nowhere and kissed him on the forehead and he forgot everything else?

He does want to talk to Vivian. Vivian, who wore his bathrobe over her underwear. But Paul knows that seeing her again will do more harm than good. He's like spun glass. Fragile. She might break him. Upset the delicate balance of his life, his work, his soul.

And Sophie may be right. What's the point of talking? You just go over and over the same things. Nothing anyone can say, nothing Paul can say, can possibly take away what he saw, what flashes in front of his eyes again and again.

"Get over it," Sophie says to him at home that night. "Get on with your life. It's been two weeks, Paul."

Paul holds his daughter close to his heart while he watches the news on TV, about September 11th, about the missing babysitter, about the murder; he listens to her squeals of delight as she clutches her stuffed giraffe. The police haven't found anyone responsible. The news says they are looking at Richard's wife. They seem to be asking a lot of questions about her. But they haven't found anyone responsible yet. For anything. No one is responsible and Paul's cheek is still sore.

17.

You know about some things. Because you work at the library you read lots of books. You know about art collectors and stamp collectors and antique collectors. You know about those people who collect figurines and ceramics and little owls or chickens or pigs. You know that Gibson collects pebbles because when you come home from your walks he drops them from his mouth, pebbles from the lawns, and piles them on the front porch in the corner.

You have never been one for collecting. In fact, you often throw more out than you bring home. Your house is minimally furnished. Only the necessities. A table. A chair. A reading lamp. A bed. And after your wife died you got rid of all her figurines and her knick-knacks.

When she was alive and her friends came over they would laugh at how you straightened the few coffee-table books that you would put out, how you would make sure the angles lined up effectively, how the candle on the mantle balanced the painting above.

It's not that you are particular, or strange, or set in your ways. You just prefer order to mess. There are lots of people like that in the world. You were like this as a child and your mother appreciated it. Your father would leave things everywhere – his tie on the dining-room table, his briefcase in the living room, his coat on the floor – and you and your mother would lock eyes. You would be aware that your father wasn't doing it right. He wasn't obeying the rules of the house.

Your wife appreciated this, you think. But you don't really know. She never once mentioned it, your fastidiousness. She laughed with her friends but you just thought she was being polite.

So when you bring the girl home it baffles you. You do not collect things.

What are you doing, you ask yourself.

What is going on?

When you finally begin talking to her, you talk yourself hoarse. And, because she is stoned, she listens. You aren't used to this. A girl who listens to you talk. By the time she starts up, talking to you, telling you about herself, you don't need to talk anymore and are happy to listen. The more this girl tells you about her life, her secret life with a boyfriend who supplied her with drugs, her parents who know nothing, her father who beats her (again, the eyes go up), the more you know you did the right thing bringing her home, getting her clean. Helping her. And she is grateful. She tells you this one night over a meal of spaghetti and garlic bread. She still seems so shaken; she won't mention the night she disappeared. She won't mention what happened to make her spiral out of control. Before she had kept everything secret and in balance: school, parents, boyfriend, drugs. Why, you ask her, did you take off that night? What was the catalyst? Why did you disappear?

But she goes silent. She shrugs.

She is still stoned. She has drugs hidden on her, you assume – in her pockets, tucked into her bra?

You haven't touched her. That's not the point. You haven't kidnapped her. She is free to go. If she wants to.

You aren't a bad man. Really. You used to be married to a kind woman. A beautiful woman. A woman whom you adored. You went to college and you have a job and you make money from it and you save that money for retirement. You used to go, with your wife, to the occasional dinner party and cocktail party and drink martinis and whiskey sours, and had a few friends who would say, "Come again. We love seeing you two" and "It's been too long."

This girl in your house. This babysitter.

Sometimes you think she is a figment of your imagination. Sometimes you have to knock on the guest room door to reassure yourself. Remind yourself that she is living in your house. That she is missing. That the police are looking for her and her parents are searching.

You are becoming more nervous. Lately you've felt as if someone is following you. Every time you take Gibson out you think you see the same vehicle on the street. Sometimes parked. Sometimes moving.

But then you go to work and you forget most things and you focus on what you think is important. The fact that you haven't felt sad in a while. That the girl has made you feel human again.

You've seen how suddenly everything can change. You've seen it on TV. You saw it in the hospital. So focus, you tell yourself. Focus on the here and now.

18.

At a café in Yorkville, Sophie and Helen are having lunch. It is a brisk Saturday and they left their babies at home with their husbands. Helen is buying lunch to thank Sophie for getting Paul to come to Allan's defence at the police station.

Helen says, "There is nothing. The police have found nothing. No evidence. Only her math textbook and a drugged-out boyfriend. I'm starting to think I imagined her. Was there really a girl named Lindsay who babysat for us? I can't believe I hired a girl who dated someone on drugs."

"Uh-huh," Sophie says, her mouth stuffed with chèvre and roasted apple panini.

"But then I see her parents on the news and I know it was all real." Helen sits back in her chair. She picks at the crust on her panini and rolls it into balls. She's lost her appetite lately. Good for her figure, she thinks.

Sophie, on the other hand, can't stop eating. "Do you want that?" She takes Helen's picked-at panini and starts to eat it. "It's the breastfeeding," she says. "I can't stop eating." It's Paul, it's Paul, she wants to shout. She hasn't wanted sex very much lately, but he doesn't want it at all.

"Hmm." Helen looks down at the floor. She looks up and sees one of her students sitting on a stool by the window. Her student is reading a book that is assigned for next month. That's encouraging. Someone reading ahead.

"Paul's back is fine now," Sophie says, her mouth full again. "He's back at work and loving it." He's not, Sophie knows, but she doesn't know what else to say. Whenever she is with Helen Sophie remembers that they have nothing in common. But when they are apart Sophie always thinks it would be fun to have her over for dinner, or to go out for lunch with her. Helen is buying, Sophie thinks, so she's going to get a cappuccino and biscotti for dessert.

"It's amazing that so much happened that night."

"Yeah, it's like our dinner party was cursed."

"Really," Helen says. "Think about it. Our babysitter disappeared and your neighbour's brother got murdered and then the towers and the Pentagon and Shanksville . . ."

Sophie nods and finishes off the sandwich. She washes it down with her Diet Coke.

"And the only connection to two of the crimes is us. The four of us," Helen says. "We are the missing link."

"Good thing the police don't suspect us of anything."

"Well, Allan," Helen says.

"Yes, but they don't suspect him. There was no evidence that he was in that woman's house." Sophie looks at Helen's shocked face. "I mean, of course not, Helen. Of course not. He was with you. He was walking home." Sophie swallows. "At least we aren't responsible for the planes and the towers."

"There is that hour that he can't account for," Helen says. She remembers that Allan was covered in garbage when he came home. Why was he covered in stinky vegetable peelings? He said he fell in compost. But she didn't ask him anything else. He showered immediately too. Getting rid of evidence? And the next day she had to pick all kinds of crap from his pants before getting the nanny to put them in the laundry.

"We all can't account for an hour here and there when we've been drinking." Sophie laughs.

"Yes." Helen looks again at her student. The girl hasn't even turned her page. She's staring out the window at the people going past. At the men going past.

"Are you getting dessert?"

"I know he's innocent. Of course, he is. But it's amazing that the police think that too. If you think about it. We are the one connection to Lindsay's disappearance and to that man's murder. Me, you, Paul, Allan."

"I know. You said that before. And you don't have any connection to the murder, really. Neither do I. Neither does Allan. The police were careful. They looked into all of it." Sophie wipes her mouth on her napkin. "I'm having a cappuccino. A bowl. And a chocolate almond biscotti. Do you want anything?" Sophie gets up and carries her plate to the counter. She orders and then sits down again. "You're lucky you aren't breastfeeding," she says. "It really makes you hungry."

"Yes, well." Helen feels so angry suddenly. Sophie is an idiot, she thinks. Sophie is like a cow, chewing her cud, staring wide-eyed and innocent at the world around her. Not taking anything in. Helen wants to shout, "I couldn't breastfeed, you fucking idiot." There isn't a topic of conversation that would interest Sophie, Helen reasons – besides food and clothes.

"So, I bought a Gucci bag at Holt Renfrew the other day," Helen says, testing her theory. "It was marked down."

Sophie sits up straight. Her eyes light up.

Ah, Helen thinks. I'm right – food and clothes.

Two businessmen walk past their table.

"Whoo, ha," one of the men says. He stops dead in his tracks and looks down at the women. "What have we here?"

Sophie smiles nicely.

Helen says, "Two women trying to have a private conversation."

"Well, don't let me stop you. I'll just admire your mouths while you talk."

"Go away," Helen says. She's not in the mood to flirt.

Sophie giggles.

Helen looks at Sophie and realizes that she has packed on the pounds in the last little while. Sophie's face is quite round now. She's lost that small, angular beauty that she regained right after the baby was born. She's a tiny woman and this new weight shows on her.

"Let's walk," Helen says. "Let's go."

The man moves on, acting chagrined. He puts his hand on his heart and closes his eyes. Pretends they've injured him. Pretends he is crying. His friend scowls at him and moves to their table.

"I want my coffee," Sophie says. "And my cookie."

"Get it to go."

Outside Helen takes Sophie's purse for her while she negotiates her large cappuccino and her biscotti.

They walk through Yorkville, the air chilly around their necks and heads. They talk about their babies. Helen tells Sophie about one of her students and how he argues with her at every class no matter what she says. She tells Sophie about the other students who seem depressed and obsessed with 9/11. She tells about the time she saw a student late at night at Robarts library staring at her computer and when she got close she could see that the student was watching the towers fall over and over again.

"There was so much going on that day that I don't really remember how I felt."

"You didn't process it, I guess," Helen says. "Me too. We watched it happen and then we went back to looking for the babysitter."

"What do you really think happened to her?" Sophie asks. She stops and sips her cappuccino.

"I don't know." Helen faces Sophie. "I don't like to think about it. I like to imagine she took a bus somewhere south, maybe Florida. I like to imagine she's down in Florida on the beach with a hot surfer. Maybe she needed to dump her druggy boyfriend. I like to think that maybe she's glad she's away from her mother and father." Helen pauses. She takes off her sunglasses and wipes her eyes. She worries about her mascara running. "But I know that's not true. I know something bad happened to her. I can feel it in my bones."

Sophie stops sipping. She looks at Helen. "I think Paul is going crazy," she says. Then she tries to laugh.

Helen focuses on Sophie. "I thought you said he was okay."

"I lied. I think that maybe everything, the murder – I think everything really screwed him up. And he won't see anyone. He won't talk to my father. He won't talk to me. I feel like all I do every day is hold my breath, hoping he doesn't crack up. Do you know?"

Helen takes Sophie's arm and leads her forward. "I know." Helen thinks of Allan and how he's never where he says he is anymore. She called him on his cellphone the other day and he was in his car when he said he was in the editing studio. She knows this because she could see his car from her office window. She could see him sitting there, parked, with the engine off, talking on the phone, right outside her window.

"That night," Sophie whispers. "I wish we could do it all over again."

"Do it again? You mean you wish it never happened?"

"Yes, I guess that's what I mean."

Sophie and Helen keep walking. Around and around the short blocks of Yorkville and down to Bloor Street and into Holt Renfrew. Sophie is going to look for a Gucci purse for herself. And Helen needs a new coat.

19.

There are news reports about the missing girl. You avoid looking at them. She avoids looking at them. She tells you to forget her name. Call her something else. But you still think of her as Lindsay, the babysitter, and you hate to be reminded about who she is and where she came from. All you want to do is get her cured and then send her back out into the world. She has been listless lately. Suffering withdrawal symptoms, you suppose. Her hands shake. She sleeps all day. You put speakers in her room and run a wire under the door to the CD player. Tight squeeze, but you manage. Mozart. Bach. The music calms her, you think. Calms the savage beast inside of her. Your wife would play this music while she cooked. You would read your newspaper in the chair by the television set. You would eat together, quietly, listening to the music.

Lindsay.

She was pretty. They show her pretty face in the papers.

Now she is rough-looking. Older. Her eyes are wild. It looks, you tell her, like she's seen a ghost.

She is sixteen years old. She has a mother and a father. A little brother. A cat named Muffles. A boyfriend who supplied her with drugs. The boyfriend who is not talking to the media. Merely scowling. As boys do. His pants pulled low. His hooded sweatshirt covering his head. A chain hanging from his belt. A skateboard under his arm.

You look away from your computer whenever you see her on it. But sometimes you don't look away fast enough. Sometimes your fingers just type her name in and you can't stop yourself. Sometimes you type in "World Trade Center" and watch the planes again and again.

And sometimes the phone rings and you startle and jump. She startles and jumps. But it's mostly telephone sales. Trips to Hawaii, rug-cleaning supplies, donations to Diabetes Canada. You sometimes wish you could take her out. To the ballet. To the symphony. Or the art gallery for a show and dinner in Chinatown or Kensington Market. You'd like to take a cab there. Unlimited excitement. Clever conversation. Beautiful women and men. You would wear a tie and your cashmere coat that you ordered online now that you know how to do that. You could even polish your old leather shoes. The days are getting shorter. It is getting chilly in the evening.

You manage to forget that the girl should be going home. You manage to forget that her parents are worried. You justify this – when she is free of drugs you will walk her home. You will reunite her with her parents and her brother and her cat. You manage to forget all of this and laugh with her as you watch TV and your life goes on. Moves away from the day you led her towards your house. From the day she made you stop thinking about the Twin Towers. From the day things changed and shifted.

It is one of those days when you are purposefully not looking for stories about her on the internet that you see a picture of a man you recognize from somewhere. A man who seems vaguely familiar. This man, the article says, is the last person to see the girl alive.

The girl was babysitting for this man and his wife. You know him from somewhere. You study his face, the cut of his leather jacket, the scowl on his lips.

Where have you seen him before?

Outside your house. Just the other day. He was sitting in a car just outside your house and he was looking straight at you when you came out to walk Gibson. He was scowling, like in the photograph. This man who is connected to the girl in your house. The girl who is having nightmares, who wakes screaming in the early morning.

You know there is no excuse for your behaviour. You are intelligent. But you also know that you were sad and she needed you. And you needed her. With or without 9/11. You took her away from the danger she was in – the boyfriend, the drugs. You didn't mean to go so far. You didn't want it to go this way, your life. This life after your wife.

You are getting help from a psychiatrist. Changing your ways. Trying not to think about how sad you are. Your psychiatrist even told you that he was happy with your quick progress. Only three months, he said. You are getting over your wife quickly. But he is pretentious and keeps looking out his window instead of at you. And now you are stuck with this girl who makes you feel complete but who should be home with her family, and there is a man out there somewhere in a car watching you and you really don't trust him. What does he want? And you wonder if this girl is telling you everything she should be telling you.

20.

Helen and Allan are in bed. They are wrapped in a post-coital embrace that is warm but embarrassing. The more years you are married, Helen thinks, the harder it gets to snuggle after sex. Or anytime, for that matter. She remembers lying in Allan's arms when they were first together and feeling completely comfortable. But now she is aware that her elbow is in the wrong place, her hip is falling asleep, her toenails need cutting. She is aware that Allan's breath is a bit rancid, smells like gin and onions and toothpaste, and that he hasn't shaved his neck lately. Helen wonders why he was sitting in his car outside her office when he should be working?

"How are your classes going?" Allan asks.

"So-so." Helen rolls away from Allan, relieved to have an excuse to spread out her arms and legs, to open up.

"Are they still talking about the World Trade Center all the time?"

"They are." Helen sighs. "But they seem to be able to relate it to literature a little bit. One student connected Shakespeare's *Richard III* to Osama bin Laden."

Allan laughs.

"I know. It doesn't work. No matter how you look at it. But it made for an interesting essay."

"What'd you give him?"

"Him? Oh, her. I gave her a C-, I think. I can't remember. I think she was the one who needed work on her grammar. Spelled everything wrong. Commas in the wrong places."

"Aren't these university students? Shouldn't they know that stuff by now?"

"You'd think." Helen sighs again. Allan takes her hand. They lie, side by side, on their backs, looking up at the ceiling fan. The light. The baby is asleep in the next room. Helen can feel Allan's sperm running down her thigh and wetting the bed. She'll have to get the nanny to wash the sheets tomorrow. God, so embarrassing. She hates sharing her personal life, but she hates a dirty house more. And what does she really know about the nanny? What does the nanny think of her? What does she say to her friends?

"Do you ever think about Lindsay?" Allan says. His voice is meek and quiet.

"What do you mean, do I think about her? Of course I think about her. All the time. Don't you?" Helen is sitting up now. Her perfect breasts barely move with gravity. "Jesus, Allan, I can't stop thinking about her. She's probably dead somewhere and it's our fault."

"It's not our fault."

"Okay, it's your fault." Helen feels weary suddenly. She lies back down.

"It's not my fault. I didn't do anything."

"That's it, Allan. We didn't do anything."

"How can that be our fault? How could we know? Listen, Helen, she was dating a drug addict. There was more to Lindsay than we knew."

"One minute," Helen says, "everything is normal. The next minute the world has fallen apart for Lindsay, for her parents, for us."

"The world fell apart that day for thousands of people, Helen." Allan is still speaking quietly, but Helen can hear the anger in his voice. His defensive voice.

"Why are you so defensive?"

"What are you implying?"

"Well, you seem so defensive about it. Like you're involved somehow."

"I'm not involved. You just said we're involved. What the hell do you mean, Helen? Do you think I did something or that I didn't do something? Which is it?"

"I don't know."

Helen rolls away from Allan. Allan rolls away from Helen. They listen to the heat go on, the pipes make noise as the water travels through them.

"Where were you for that hour, Allan? That night. Where were you?"

Allan, facing the wall, is silent.

"What are you keeping from me?"

Still, Allan is silent.

21.

Vivian comes into his office and it takes Paul a moment to gather his thoughts, to look up into her face without wanting to rush into her body. His assistant leads Vivian in, gives her a cup of coffee and leaves the office with a curious look on her face. Paul stares at Vivian, wondering if she'll come around the desk again, wonders if she will kiss him, this woman in front of him. Seeing her he thinks of her red lips and the blood on the floor of the guest room in her house.

Vivian is in Paul's office, holding her coffee. She smiles at him. Who is this woman? Paul thinks.

"Hello, Paul," she says. Paul rises up to shake her hand but she ignores him. He sits back down on his desk chair. The chair squeaks. Vivian looks behind her and then sits in the chair directly in front of Paul's desk. They are separated now by a large expanse of polished wood scattered with pieces of paper and Post-in Notes, a computer, a phone.

"Hello," Paul says. He clears his throat.

Vivian says, "I was wondering if we could go somewhere. You and me. We could talk about Richard, about what you saw that morning. I have no one to talk to about all of this."

"I'm so sorry," Paul says. What else is there to say? What should he say? He shuffles some of the papers around. Visions of Richard's gruesome body dance in front of his eyes.

"Yes. Me too." Vivian looks around the office. "Quite a view up here," she says. "You must have been nervous after September 11th."

Paul nods. Still nervous, he thinks. About Vivian. About the planes. His colleagues told him that for days after September 11th, while Paul was at home in bed, there were air force jets whipping around in the skies over Toronto. Guarding the buildings. His assistant said that she would look out and see a small dot in the sky and then the jet would come closer and she would hold her breath, waiting for it to be a terrorist attack. But it wasn't. Instead it was the air force swooping low over the city. The planes aren't there anymore, though. Who will protect him now? Paul thinks. From ruining his marriage. Because that's what it looks like right now, with Vivian crossing her legs, uncrossing her legs, letting her long legs show.

"I think," Vivian says. She is quiet. "I think I should have come to talk to you sooner. I'm sorry. I just am having such a hard time. And I certainly –" Vivian blushes. "I certainly shouldn't have kissed you. I'm sorry."

"Me too," Paul says. "I should have come to you. To talk to you."

"I know about your back. Your wife told me. Your back gave out. Are you okay now?"

"Sophie?"

"I went by your house this morning. She said that she didn't think I should bother you, that you've just now got better again, that you are finally sleeping at night."

"I'm not sleeping at night," Paul says. "She doesn't know." God, he thinks. She saw Sophie. And what did Sophie think of that? Paul is sure he'll hear about it later. Vivian with her long legs and long hair.

"It's easy to fake it, isn't it?" Vivian sighs. "I've been staying at my friend's house over near High Park. I pretend I'm sleeping every night while she checks on me. In and out, she comes in and out of the guest room and peers at me. I keep my eyes closed."

"I know," Paul says. "I know exactly what you mean." He leans his elbows on his desk and puts his head in his hands. He takes her in. Vivian. She's lovely.

"I can't go home," Vivian says. "I can't face my house."

Paul feels so many things right now. He is consumed by emotion.

"The rest of the world is talking about September 11th," Vivian says. "And all I can think about is what happened to us that morning, what happened to my brother."

"Do the police have anything?" Paul asks. "Anything at all?"

"Nothing really. They can't find his wife. There are no leads. They questioned me. They talked to you, I guess?"

"Yes."

"No one was out that night. Or no one has come forward saying that they saw anything. And I am, or I was, a heavy sleeper. I didn't hear a thing. How could I not have heard anything?" Vivian begins to shake. Her hands shake. She puts her coffee mug down on Paul's desk. She stands and looks out the windows. She looks down at the streets below. "He was gagged, I guess. He made no noise." Vivian's shoulders shudder. "You know, I keep picturing the scene as if I were there when it happened. I picture Jennifer attacking him. I picture the way she cut him, the way she bound him, the way he struggled. Jennifer is large, kind of chubby, or she was last time I saw her, it's been years. She used to be on the rowing team at school. Big upper arms. But I just don't get it. I can't stop trying to see it.

"Sometimes I wonder if I was there. It seems so real. Maybe I was there, watching. What do you think?" Vivian turns and looks at him.

Paul stands and walks over to her. He wants, suddenly, to be close to her. He wants her to kiss him again. A strange woman. A woman of strange passions. She is hiding something, though – he can feel it. "You weren't there. You were asleep. It's over now. There is nothing you can do."

"I heard about that missing girl, the babysitter, and I thought that my brother was lucky, really. If you think about it. At least we found him. At least we know where he is now. How it happened. Why it happened. Sort of –"

Allan's babysitter. Vivian is talking about the babysitter. Paul feels like he's having a hard time processing this. He feels as if he's running in water. The world is so connected.

Vivian moves towards Paul but he chickens out and sits back down. Vivian follows and perches on the corner of Paul's desk. She looks into his face. Her eyes, he thinks. So deep and blue.

"Everyone keeps telling me to get on with my life," Paul says. "I have a baby daughter. A wife."

"Yes."

"But I can't figure out how to do it. How to get on with life."

Vivian says, "Maybe if they find Jennifer, Richard's wife. Maybe if they catch her and prove it was her? Do you think they will catch her? Or whoever did it? Maybe the babysitter? Could it have been the babysitter?"

"I don't know. How could that be possible? Allan and Helen live across the city. Do you think his wife did it?"

"I don't know anymore." Vivian begins to cry. "I don't seem to know anything anymore."

"Your two o'clock is here." Paul's assistant is suddenly in his office. He didn't hear her come in. Neither did Vivian. They both start.

"Oh, thanks," Paul says. He notices Vivian's tears on her cheeks and he resists the urge to wipe her face.

Vivian stands. "I'm sorry to have bothered you at work," she says, suddenly businesslike and brisk. "I just thought it was easier. I thought that maybe your wife wouldn't want to hear us talking about it."

"I think that was wise." Paul looks at his hands. He holds out his right hand and shakes Vivian's hand. Her hand is moist and warm. Vivian leans up and kisses his cheek, right near his lips. Her red lipstick again on his face. He wants to lick it off. Taste it. Like he did with Helen's glass of wine.

"Can we talk more? Can we meet somewhere and talk? It might be good for both of us," Vivian whispers.

"Yes."

She smiles.

Paul imagines he sees himself in her smile, in her eyes.

Vivian walks out of the room and Paul's two o'clock appointment comes into his office and sits down heavily in a chair. He wonders if his client can feel what he just felt, looking at her leave. Can his client feel the lightening of his heart? Can he smell her? Paul breathes in, deeply.

Can he?

Paul suddenly, inexplicably, imagines quitting his lawyer job and moving to the country to live with Vivian Middleford. He imagines holding her hand as they walk through the cornfields far away from Toronto. Far away from Richard and Sophie and his little baby and his life as he knows it. Paul knows this is ridiculous. He isn't thinking straight. He loves his wife. He loves his baby. He loves his job.

Doesn't he?

Paul takes a deep breath, wipes the lipstick from his cheek and sits down behind his desk. He glances out the window briefly, stares at the empty blue sky. An empty hour, he thinks. His client begins talking non-stop and Paul does all he can to tune in to the man's one-sided conversation.

22.

The man has been snooping around the neighbourhood. You've seen him get out of his car and walk around the block. You've seen him through your front window as you peer between the slats of the blinds. He is a tall man, muscular. He wears a leather jacket. The girl hasn't seen him. She thinks you are imagining things. She tells you to come back to the TV, watch the shows, laugh with her.

Her shaking has become less noticeable but she is still biting her nails raw. She is still waking up screaming each morning. But she is laughing at the occasional TV show.

One morning you heard her say, "I didn't do anything," loudly and you thought she was awake; they were so clear, her words. But when you went in the room you saw she was sound asleep.

But this man. Outside your house.

You told her that he is the man she babysat for – the night she went missing.

She doesn't believe you. She hasn't seen him. She won't look out the windows in case someone sees her. "I feel safe here," she says, her eyes glued to the TV.

Gibson has been barking at the man since early last night. The man comes and searches around your property and then he goes away in his car. Gibson barks. Gibson growls and lunges at the window. The man comes back. Gibson begins to foam at the mouth. Even you are scared of your dog. The anger you see in his eyes. It is pure animal anger. Even the girl is a little afraid. She says that she wonders if the dog sees her father out there. She wonders if the dog will turn her in. She panics and locks herself in the bedroom. Even when you reassure her about her father, that it isn't him out there, even then she won't come out of her room.

The girl moans all night and Gibson hears her. Lying on the foot of your bed, his ears perk up. He growls. A low rumble.

"Mommy," the girl cries.

When the man finally stops walking around your house, he looks up at the front porch. He looks at Gibson's collection of pebbles. He looks at the basement windows, boarded up. You see him through the blinds.

You want to shout out. You want to shout, "Leave us alone."

You know there are freaks out there. You know that some people get an idea in their head and they can't let it go. Look at Osama bin Laden and the World Trade Center buildings.

Your world is falling apart. Free fall, like the man in the chef's uniform. In the background you hear nothing but Gibson ripping into the sofa cushions, desperate to get outside and bite the man who creeps around your house.

Why did you bring her here?

And now she won't go home.

What would your wife do?

"I'm just a librarian," you tell the girl. But she curls up in front of the TV and won't leave. She says she wants to stay. She feels safe with you. She says she won't tell anyone she was here. Ever. She won't get you in trouble.

And the police are searching, searching, searching. Getting closer. What should you do?

"Safe from what?" you say. "What do you feel safe from?"

The girl doesn't answer. Won't answer.

You touch Gibson's warm, soft head. Gibson. Your dog. Your soulmate. Your companion.

And then he bites your hand hard. You bleed. You hit him on the side of his nose, just as hard as he bit you. Gibson looks guilty, puts his head down into his paws and lies on the floor for two hours while you look out the window for the man who creeps around your house.

23.

Allan has it in his head that this must be the man who killed the man in the house, the man Paul saw bound and stabbed. This man with his dog.

But how does he go about proving this without implicating himself?

For days now he's been worried. Ever since he saw the man on the street, ever since he found the man again and followed him to where he lives. He looks at the pile of pebbles on the front porch, a collection, and looks at the basement windows all boarded up. There must be something in that, Allan thinks. But then he notices that this man's neighbours' basement windows are all boarded up too. In fact, most of the houses on the street have boarded up basement windows.

But the man sneaks around. He is nervous about something. Even when the man is at work in the reference library, Allan watches him move stealthily around the shelves, talking to no one. Quiet, reclusive older man. Allan hears someone say his wife died recently, that he hasn't been the same since.

The dog barks incessantly. The dog won't stop barking.

Allan has been watching. Allan has watched the man's house, followed him to work.

Even if the man isn't the killer, he is the only one who saw Allan sneaking around backyards that night, the night the man was murdered. The night Lindsay went missing. Or Lesley? Lindsay. Allan sometimes forgets her name and he worries that this means something about his age, or his attention span, or his ability to process information. How can he forget the name of the girl who went missing just after he saw her? He's blocking it out. That awful night. But if this is the only person who saw him then Allan must do something about him because one day this man will recognize him and maybe come after him. He will eventually tell somebody.

Unless this man has something to hide?

If Allan told Helen, maybe? Told her everything? But Helen suspects him as it is. Ever since she found out about the grief videos, she's been preoccupied with where Allan has been. "Where have you been? Why are you late?" Every night she confronts him at the door. She says it's because she is worried. She says it's because she loves him and is suffering some sort of post-traumatic stress after 9/11, but Allan wonders about this. Lately, he sees something in Helen's eyes. A mistrustful squinching of the eyebrows. She bites at her lips. She stares at him all the time. He can feel her eyes on him.

Right now Allan is sitting in his car double-parked in front of the man's house. He can hear the dog barking. There is a honking car behind him and Allan signals and shouts, "Go around me," and gives the guy the finger. "Jerk."

What if he just walked up the front steps and knocked on the door?

The man couldn't stab him, could he? Allan looks at his leather jacket. He's not invincible, he thinks. Even though he is wearing leather. But a man wouldn't stab just for the sake of stabbing. He wanted something from that man he killed, didn't he?

Allan's cellphone rings. He jumps.

"Yeah?"

"Where are you?" It's Helen. She is between classes, in her office. She wants him to pick up milk on the way home tonight.

"Why can't you pick it up?" Allan sees the man's curtain move slightly. The man is looking out. He knows I'm here, Allan thinks.

"I've got class until five and then I'm going to the gym."

"Yeah, well, I'm working late."

"Did you call Grace to tell her that?"

"No, did you?"

"Yes. I said you'd be home at six. I said I'd be home at seven."

"Helen, I've got to go. I'll get milk later. I'll try."

"What are you doing, Allan? Where are you? She's not our slave. Maybe Grace has something else to do."

"I'm at work."

"No," Helen says. "No, you're not. I saw you drive past my office ten minutes ago."

Allan pauses and looks out his window at the street. The day is dark and cloudy. "What?" he says.

"I saw you. I saw you drive past here."

"So? I had to get something for our set."

"Are you doing another one of those car commercials? Or another grief video?"

"Commercial. I needed something for the set."

"What?"

"What what?"

"What did you need?"

Allan looks again at the man's house. Allan hasn't had much work lately. He spends a lot of time in his car. Allan looks around him in the car and takes note of all the fast-food containers and old Styrofoam coffee cups.

"Basketballs." That's all Allan can think of, although he has no idea how to connect that to cars.

"Oh." Helen doesn't sound convinced. "For cars?"

"I've got to go," Allan says. "If I'm going to pick up milk on the way home I should go now."

"Call Grace," he hears Helen shout as he hangs up.

He shuts off his cellphone, opens the car window and begins to dump all the garbage from his car into the road. He ignores the honking of the cars passing. Allan ignores the two women walking across the street who glare at him.

When he has emptied his car he pulls out and heads over the Don Valley and down towards the studio district to see if he can find another job. Something that has nothing to do with death. In any form.

24.

Sophie worries constantly about Vivian Middleford. The woman has come by the house two times in the last week and Paul went out with her once and came home smelling of alcohol. The woman is sexy and sly and controlling. She is a woman who doesn't like women. And Sophie doesn't like her at all.

Sophie lies on the floor looking at the specks of sunlight shining through the blinds. Every so often she watches Rebecca's eyes light up and her lips smile as she takes in the TV shows that flash across the screen. *Teletubbies.* "Again. Again," the Teletubbies say.

Paul is better. But he is also not better.

He is here now; he is present, not stuck in his nightmare world, not seized up in bed. But he is also not here. He is vacant and distracted.

Sophie has no one to talk to about this.

Is her husband having an affair? An affair with the woman whose brother was murdered?

Ridiculous.

But is it? She's heard worse from others. Husbands who disappear on kayak trips and then move out with the woman whose kayak was blue and who took the rapids fearlessly. Husbands who sleep with office colleagues in their cars in the underground parking lots below their buildings. Husbands who just leave. Take off. For no reason. "I don't love you anymore," they say. Or "I never loved you."

Sophie reaches out for the bag of potato chips on the coffee table. It is nine thirty in the morning. This is her second bag of chips so far today. Rebecca gurgles and coos.

Sophie has hours and hours before Paul will come home from work. Hours in which to do nothing but change diapers and feed the baby, comfort her while she cries, put her down for her nap. Maybe Sophie will crawl into bed herself then. Give in to the overwhelming heaviness that is weighing all of them down.

Sophie's whole world seems to have changed after that dinner party with Allan and Helen. After she almost cracked Paul's grandmother's butter dish. After she appeared naked in her living room for the whole street to see. It seems that her life has spiralled down since then. Paul, with his murder. Paul, with his time off work. Paul, and his new girlfriend (he calls it "grief counselling" when he goes for a drink with her). Sophie's father actually thinks it's beneficial for Paul to spend time with this Vivian woman. Vivian Middleford. What kind of a name is that? It sounds like a name from one of those historical Harlequin romances Sophie read before she was married. It sounds made up. Sophie imagines the butler coming into the drawing room and announcing that Vivian Middleford is "waiting in the foyer, sir." Or walking on the moors.

Sophie rolls on to her stomach to get rid of the chip crumbs. She wipes her fingers on the rug. The cleaning woman will be here tomorrow.

"I must do something," Sophie says suddenly. Rebecca looks at her and smiles. She coos and a line of drool comes out of her mouth and trails across her bib. Then Rebecca puts her fingers in her mouth and looks up again at the TV. "Again. Again," the Teletubbies shout.

School. She could go back to school. Or get a job. Or join an exercise group. Or do something with the baby – take her shopping or swimming or for a walk in her carriage or something. A baby music class. No. Sophie must do something herself. For herself.

If her husband is going to leave her for a sexy, improbably named woman with blood on her floors, then Sophie has to have something of her own. A job. A better education. Night classes. Continuing education. The Annex Learning Centre. Sophie has seen those newspapers on the street corners. Advertising business classes and paralegal courses.

What is a paralegal? Sophie's been told many times but she just can't remember. Why does this always happen to her – she feels so stupid all the time.

She wants to cry. Sophie wants to cry and then call her father. She wants to talk to him. But she's afraid of sounding as weak as she feels. She's afraid of what he'll say, of what he always says, "You're blowing this all out of proportion, Sophie love." That's what he always says. For a psychiatrist who blows everything out of proportion himself in order to get clients – "You're feeling sad? You must be depressed." – Sophie's father has always played down everything that has ever happened to her. Everything. When she binge ate and then became bulimic in high school her father just laughed the whole thing off. He said she was just rebelling to make him angry and that she would grow out of it.

She did, of course.

It wasn't fun sticking her finger down her throat. But what if she hadn't? And what about his reaction to Sophie's mother's drinking problem? He encourages her. He eggs her on. He doesn't think there is a problem. Only the outside world has problems, Sophie thinks. Not my father's family. Besides, Sophie acknowledges, people do have more problems than she does. She's aware of this and it makes her sad and angry both. And confused. How can one person's problems cancel out another person's problems?

Sophie has no right to complain.

Sophie's father has been extraordinarily busy since September 11th. He hasn't had more than a moment to talk to her. Sophie's mother says he hasn't been home until well past dinner in weeks. This causes Sophie's mother to drink more. And to call Sophie and complain about Sophie's father.

Sophie gets up and walks into the kitchen. She goes straight to the freezer and pulls out the vanilla ice cream. A spoon in one hand, the carton of ice cream in the other hand, Sophie goes back to the living room and lies down on the floor on her stomach. Rebecca reaches out for her mother, but Sophie rolls away slightly.

"My ice cream," she says. "Not yours."

And then Rebecca begins to cry and Sophie's morning has begun.

Changing and comforting her baby later, Sophie looks out the upstairs window and sees Vivian Middleford coming up the front walk.

Again, Sophie thinks. What does she want?

Surely the woman knows that Paul is at work? It's eleven thirty in the morning on a weekday. What day is it? Sophie wonders. She's lost track of time. God, she's bored. And did she ever put the ice cream away?

As she rushes into the living room, sees the mess all over the rug, the cardboard container having collapsed in upon itself, the ice cream leaking in a puddle and river down towards the centre of the room, the doorbell rings.

"Hello, Vivian," Sophie says, holding Rebecca in one arm, like a football, trying to stop the cat from escaping with her foot.

"Hello, Sophie. I'm so sorry to bother you again, but I was wondering if . . ."

"He's at work."

"No, I know that." Vivian looks around, peers behind Sophie into the house. "I was wondering if, perhaps, we could talk about Paul. Please tell me if I'm stepping out of line, but –"

Sophie glares.

"Yes, I just. Well, last night, when we met for coffee, Paul said something that intrigued me. He said something about a friend of yours, an Allan, I think, and how he and his wife lost their babysitter the same night Richard was killed? The babysitter that has been in the paper? The police asked me about her, of course, but I didn't realize there was a connection to you and Paul."

"Come in." Sophie kicks the cat back inside and adjusts Rebecca on her hip. Vivian looks at the puddle of ice cream in the living room.

"Oh dear," she says, pointing. "That will stain."

"It's pure fat," Sophie says. "I'm sure it will stain. There'll be a mark there. A fat mark." As she says this, Sophie self-consciously crosses her arms in front of her stomach. She's been gaining some weight lately, but Sophie reasons to herself that she always gains weight during stressful times, or in the fall – as if her body needs the fat to get her through an Ontario winter. She begins eating in November, usually, and peaks around Christmastime. Then in February the weight starts coming off. This year, with the stress of everything, Sophie has started earlier. She hopes that means she'll lose the weight earlier. Then she thinks of stains on rugs and wonders if Vivian's rug has been cleaned or merely discarded.

She looks at Vivian's body in her tight jeans and fitted jacket. Her long legs. Long hair. Long everything. Although Sophie bets her breasts aren't long – like Sophie's are now that the baby pulls and pulls at them.

Sophie sighs and sits down. "I really don't like talking about my husband," she says. "I don't really know you."

"I know. This is strange." Vivian sits down across from Sophie and stares at the ice cream on the floor. "Would you like me to help you clean this?"

"No. I'll do it later. It's not like it'll get any worse than it already is."

"It's not really Paul I want to talk about," Vivian says. "It's his friend, the one who –"

"Yes, Allan. Who lost the babysitter. Lost her. Like she was a toy or something. Did Paul really say, 'lost'?"

"I don't know. It might have been my word."

"She disappeared. They made her walk home alone. No, Helen made her walk home alone. But Allan saw her walking alone down the street and, well, he didn't do anything. He just went home. Or so he says."

"Don't you think," Vivian says, carefully. Sophie can tell she is picking and choosing her words with great skill, tiptoeing across the English language. "Don't you think it rather odd that he was here, at your house" – Vivian opens her arms to signify the entire house – "and then he went home –"

"Both of them were here. Both of them went home. His wife too."

"Yes, but he came back to get his car, right? He was alone at night near your house. Then he saw the babysitter."

"So?" Sophie scratches behind her ear. She fiddles with her earring. Connections, she thinks. So what?

"I think it's odd, that's all. How well do you know this man?"

"Oh, we've known him for years," Sophie says. Then she thinks, how long have we known them, Allan and Helen? And she can't remember when they met. Surely she's known Allan for a while?

It seems like a while. It seems as if he's been driving her crazy for a good long time. With his beer and his cologne and his squeaky leather jackets. "The police didn't make a connection between your brother and the babysitter," Sophie says. "I would trust what they say. Allan is a good man. He would never do anything to hurt anyone." Sophie thinks of Allan lining up the beer bottles in front of him at her dinner that night. She thinks of how he always has to kiss her on both cheeks, like he's some Frenchman or something. She thinks of his cologne and his leather jacket. She thinks of Helen's large, new breasts. What kind of man makes his wife get breast implants? Sophie can't understand it.

"I'm sure I'm completely overthinking things," Vivian says. "It's just that I'm looking for answers. It seems the police aren't doing anything. Or they aren't telling me anything. And I can't stand being at the house." Vivian looks again at the ice cream. "I can't go into the room off the kitchen. I just keep seeing Richard all tied up there. Covered in blood."

"Yes, right." Sophie hates listening to this story. Paul talked about it and now Sophie sees it when she closes her eyes at night. The papers she reads tell her about the knife wounds and marks. "Really, Vivian," Sophie says. "I'm sure there is no connection between these two events. I mean, seriously, if you think about it, you could connect all of these things to September 11th, too, couldn't you? They all happened within almost the same time. I mean, maybe the terrorists came here first and kidnapped the babysitter and killed your brother." Did she really say that aloud? Sophie was just thinking it, she didn't mean to say it.

Vivian stares at Sophie for a minute. Her eyes widen.

"I suppose you are right." Vivian stands. "I won't bother you again about it. It's just that one of my neighbours, an older woman who is often wrong about things, her eyesight isn't that great, well, she remembers seeing a man in a leather jacket coming out from the backyard directly behind your house that night. She remembers seeing him come out in the front yard and he was wiping himself off as if he was covered in something."

"The house directly behind ours?"

"Yes. That house is directly across the street from mine."

"A leather jacket?"

"Yes. My neighbour says that she saw that and when Paul told me Allan wears a leather jacket, well, I just wondered."

"Why would Allan have been in our neighbours' backyard?"

"Maybe my neighbour is wrong. She really does have poor eyesight. That's why I haven't said anything to the police, actually. I don't want them to get off track when it comes to looking for Richard's murderer. They need to find his ex."

"Yes, but . . . Allan does wear a leather jacket and I know he was wearing it that night. I remember asking him to hang it in the closet, not on the back of his chair."

"But it could have been someone else, right? It's just that your friend had to come back for his car, so maybe, well, maybe he went into the backyard, into your backyard." Vivian begins to move towards the back of the house. She stands in the kitchen. Sophie follows her. "And from your backyard he would easily be able to get into their backyard." Vivian points a finger at Sophie's backyard neighbours. "And from there, well, he could certainly get to my house." Sophie follows Vivian's finger.

"But why? Why would he kill your brother?"

"Why did Lindsay disappear?"

"It's Toronto. It's a big city. These things happen. The police said that the two weren't related at all. In fact, they were questioning the babysitter's boyfriend, I read that. And, besides, they already questioned Allan and they released him. They had nothing." Sophie is talking quickly now. She's nervously scratching behind her ears. "I'm sure your neighbour saw someone," Sophie says. "But I'm also sure it wasn't Allan. He's a nice man." Sophie thinks of how angry he makes her when he drinks. Annoying, chauvinistic, often arguing every point she makes. "He wouldn't do anything to hurt anyone. He has a baby. A daughter. The same age as Rebecca. And a wife."

Vivian turns and looks at Sophie. Then she walks towards the front door. "I'm sure you are right," she says. "Thank you for talking to me about it. I hope they find the babysitter."

Sophie lets her go, this Vivian Middleford, this stranger with the Harlequin name. This annoying woman who may or may not be sleeping with her husband. Surely not, Sophie thinks. She watches Vivian walk down the street towards the Danforth. She thinks, Why doesn't she just jump the fence out back instead of going all the way around? But then she remembers that Vivian can't stand being at her house. Not with all the blood, the memories, the fear.

Allan? Could he? Would he? No, it's not possible. And there's no reason. There has to be a reason. Right?

Back in the living room Rebecca has managed to roll over for the first time and now she is lying in the melted vanilla ice cream.

"Ick." Sophie has to bathe her now. Rebecca's downy hair is covered in ice cream. So is her sleeper and her hands, which, to Rebecca's delight, have managed to find their way into her mouth. She's a perfectly happy baby, sucking on her sweet creamy hands.

25.

She is gone. You sense that immediately when you come in from work, from shopping downtown. You put the French loaf and bottle of wine you've purchased on the kitchen counter. You stop and listen. There is no sound. But there is never any sound. Except the TV. And that is off. Gibson is lying on the floor in front of her room when you go up the stairs. He growls at you.

You did nothing to her. You saved her, really. Took her away from the world outside. There is no reason she should want to turn you in. You did not violate her. You did not beat her, of course. You did not even speak to her meanly when she was withdrawing from the drugs. You played music for her and gave her food and water.

But will anyone believe this?

You left the door open, never locked. You told her she could go home anytime she wanted.

You know nothing about teenagers but you've heard they aren't stable emotionally. They sniff glue. They kill themselves with drugs and starvation and sex.

This reminds you of the time you had a goldfish. You did everything for that goldfish. A clean bowl, food, little plants. But still the goldfish died.

And your wife died. No matter what you did, who you talked to at the hospital. No matter what you said.

What didn't you do for the girl?

You can take care of a dog. Gibson hasn't died. So it's obviously not your fault. Right? Although Gibson is starting to look mangy. He's got a look in his eyes these days. He used to be such a nice puppy and now he's turning into something mean.

When was the last time you fed Gibson?

It's all about composure. If the police come knocking, you will be calm. You will smile nicely.

There is no proof that she was ever here. Is there?

And now you compose yourself before you open the door to her room. It's funny how you know without seeing it that she is gone. It's as if you always knew exactly how long someone would stay with you. Like you knew the night your wife died.

Now what are you going to do?

Are you going to go back to worrying about planes and tall buildings? Are you going to go back to just seeing your psychiatrist and talking about your dead wife and your intense loneliness? You know you are going to worry about the girl.

The door is now open and Gibson is sniffing at her bed, he's circling it like a vulture. His teeth are bared. Fangs showing. He is growling quietly. We are all animals, you think. Even Labradoodles can turn into pit bulls.

The world fell apart when your wife died and you were alone, and then suddenly, without meaning to, you had company in your house. There is French bread and wine waiting downstairs and she is gone.

What will you do now? What will you do?

You think of sealing off the room. There must be fingerprints and hair and toenail clippings in there. Things the police could use to convict you. Just lock it up, cover up the door. How bad would that be? You aren't sure. The man who is watching you all the time might suspect something if he sees you bringing building supplies into your house.

You remember that Edgar Allan Poe movie *The Black Cat*, about a man who seals his wife up in the wall. Alive. And the cat gets in there somehow and howls so much the police break down the wall and find the dead woman.

Your poor wife with her eyes wide open.

But it's not your fault. You know that. It's Osama bin Laden's fault. You blame it on 9/11. A man is watching you. You had shit on your hands one night and then a few days later a girl was in your house and now she is gone. You can't walk your dog anymore because he is beginning to lunge at people on the street and you aren't sure if it's a happy lunge or an attack.

For now, though, you must think. You lock the door and go back downstairs. Gibson follows behind. You feed him the French bread like a bird, crumbly bit by bit, and you drink the wine out of the bottle. Shivers move up and down your spine as you think of the poor girl out alone on the street. And you think of the man on the street outside watching your house. Did he see her leave? Or did he take her? Gibson digs into the bread as if it's flesh.

26.

Paul and Vivian are lying side by side on the empty floor in the empty room off Vivian's kitchen. They are not touching. They lie there, looking up at the ceiling. The carpet has been removed, the furniture is gone. The room is bare.

"This is the first time I've been in this room again since that morning," Vivian says.

Paul doesn't move.

"Oh God, Richard. Imagine. Just imagine. What a horrible way to die." Vivian sobs.

Paul rolls over onto his side, away from Vivian. Lying on his back made him think too much of Richard, of how he was taped – his legs, his arms – to the bedposts. Paul is suddenly so glad that his bed is a Japanese design, low to the ground, and has no bedposts. It's all solid wood angles. Nowhere to tie anyone up.

"I don't know if this is working," Paul says to the wall. His back is towards Vivian. Vivian rolls towards him. Touches his shoulders. "I feel nothing but pain."

"Do you think," Vivian says, "that this has anything to do with Richard anymore? With his wife? Jennifer? Do you think it's bigger than Richard? Bigger than his death? Maybe it has to do with what's happening in the world out there. If you think about it. Richard. That babysitter, what about her? What about 9/11?" Vivian points towards the high window, but Paul doesn't see her. "Everything is bigger than both of us."

"I'm not sure I know what you are talking about." Paul has noticed that Vivian mentions Allan's babysitter a lot. Questioning him about her, wondering where she is, worrying about her.

"I mean that everything has become so much more complicated lately. Convoluted. The news. Afghanistan. Missing teens. Abusive men. Everything that is happening."

"What does that have to do with your brother?"

"Oh, I don't know. I'm just wondering."

"No," Paul says. "I think it's about Richard and about the fact that we witnessed it. The world has always been scary."

"Well," Vivian says. She sits up. Looks at him. "We didn't actually witness anything. Did you? I didn't."

"You know what I mean. We saw him. Like that. Bloody and such."

"But so did the ambulance guys and the police officers and the fire department. Do you think they are all feeling like we are feeling? Why won't anyone tell us anything?"

"Probably some of them will remember the scene. How could you forget?"

"I think they are thinking about other things by now. Other things that they are seeing every day. I bet the police have forgotten all about it."

"Maybe," Paul says. He rolls towards Vivian, who is lying back down, and, because she has moved towards him, they are suddenly touching. Their knees touch, their calves, Vivian's face is close to Paul's. He looks at her fine eyes, her nice lips. He kisses her. Vivian kisses back hard. Paul can feel the place where the hot wax scarred him the night Richard died. He can feel Vivian's tongue on the spot.

They roll apart.

"Why did we do that?" Paul asks. He thinks about Richard's wife, the one Vivian told him about. Supposedly she burned Richard with her cigarettes. She was always drunk. And very violently drunk – throwing plates and glasses at him. Then he thinks about Vivian's ex-boyfriend, Ted, how he was gay. Vivian told Paul all about her past before they came here to the house. How could you be gay and be involved with Vivian? Look at her. It's beyond Paul's imagination. Vivian told him how much Ted and Richard liked each other. Not "liked" with air quotes, but just liked. They would tease Vivian when Richard would come to visit. They became good friends. And then Ted left her for another man. Vivian was heartbroken. Now Richard is dead. Vivian is a mess. Jennifer is gone, and so is the babysitter.

Vivian leans up on her arm and looks down into Paul's face. "Oh come on," she says. "It was going to happen no matter what. We both want it to happen. I need it to happen. I just got out of a bad relationship."

"I have a wife. I have a child."

"Your wife is miserable," Vivian says. "You don't seem to want to do anything with your wife or your baby." She kisses Paul again. "I want you. I want you to make me forget Ted. And Richard. And you've been wanting me. I know that." He kisses back. He pulls her towards him, on top of him, and she lies there, her body light and warm.

It occurs to Paul that the last time these walls saw two people touching they were touching in a horrific way and so he pulls away from Vivian. But she pulls back.

"Sophie, Rebecca," Paul says. "I can't."

"Yes, you can," Vivian says. "I need you to. You need to."

"Do you think this will make anything better?" Paul's voice is hoarse.

Vivian kisses him again. She reaches under his shirt and touches his chest, his stomach, the hairs above his ribs. She is experienced at this. Seducing a man. "Yes," Vivian says. "This will make everything better. This will give us something much better to worry about." Vivian is crying. He can feel the wet tears on his cheek. He can taste their salt. "I didn't protect him, Paul. I told him it was fine to leave his wife, to leave Jennifer. I said I would protect him and I didn't. I couldn't. I went to sleep. I said everything was okay, that he could get on with his life now that he left her."

She's right, Paul thinks. Maybe it's that he has nothing else to worry about in his life, nothing bigger than he is, nothing bigger than work or his child or his wife or his money or his friends or his health. He needs something larger than that to take away the image of Richard all cut up.

Paul begins to take off Vivian's clothes. Slowly. He peels off her sweater, then her shirt, her bra. He remembers her in her bra the day it happened. He remembers her underwear and, as he takes her pants off (she moves her hips up to help), he wonders if she will be wearing the same type of underwear. They were off-white, boring. But, no, she is wearing bikini underwear and they are purple with small daisies on them. Paul stops and looks carefully at her under-wear. He looks at her skin; he kisses her belly button and remembers that she was dressed when the police came. And when Vivian is naked Paul finally realizes that he is doing exactly what he was supposed to do, what everything has led him to do. He is fulfilling some sort of destiny. This is exactly what Sophie has thought he was doing all along. And now he's doing it. All Paul can think of at this moment is that it serves her right. This all serves Sophie right. This is what she gets for not feeling sorry for him, for not taking care of him after he pulled out his back. Sophie. She was once the love of his life. His wife. And then everything changed. Or nothing changed. They just got married. That was it.

And then Paul looks towards the wall, where the bed used to be, and he sees a spot of rust. A mark on the wall. Blood. Richard's blood.

Of course there is blood there, Paul thinks. Nothing is ever cleaned up.

27.

Allan watches the man come out of his house, look around, go back in. Then the dog comes out. Barks at a passerby. Allan gets out of his car. He is going to confront the man. But the dog rushes at him. Sees him across the street, getting out of his car, and rushes down the steps, though the rain, and lunges/jumps/attacks. Allan struggles, knocks the dog off his ankle, kicks the fucking beast and climbs back in his car. He starts the engine, his heart pounding. The dog howls and growls and barks furiously at the window, its wet fur stuck to its face, its lips foaming. Is it rabid? Allan thinks. Oh God. He escaped the raccoons only to be bit by a rabid dog?

Allan drives off down the road. His leg aches. He doesn't want to look down, to see the blood. When he passes the man's house he looks in his rear-view mirror and sees the man peering out from the front door, beckoning the dog back in with one long finger. He sees the dog put its head down and hump slowly back up the porch and into the house. Cowering slightly. The man looks around again, peers outside, watches Allan's car leave and then closes the door behind him.

Allan drives straight home. Shaking.

That's it, Allan thinks. He's definitely the one who killed Paul's neighbour. Who else could it be? Mad dog. Long finger. Boarded up basement. Pebbles on the porch. He's really weird. Now Allan has to report all of this. He has to tell the police about his snooping the night of the dinner party, about seeing Sophie naked through the window. There's no other way around it. First, he should tell Helen. Then the police.

But first he has to wash his ankle. Get rid of the rabies germs.

When they arrest the man they will kill his dog and Allan will find out if the dog is rabid. Allan rubs his stomach, imagining all the needles, the long needles, going into his stomach lining, his tight muscles. Why does everything have to happen to him?

There are no more grief videos to make. The company he worked for, doing this freelance, went out of business. They just told him. The woman whose one breast he filmed didn't pay because she said Allan took advantage of her, and she died shortly after the filming.

That's the problem with having dying clients, Allan thinks. They feel no responsibility to pay up. They have much bigger things to worry about.

Allan dropped off the video he made of that woman to her son and her husband a couple of days ago. He thought it was the nice thing to do. He didn't worry about the payment, told them that if they wanted to they could pay the head of the company that financed the video. The man was red-eyed and sad; the boy was listless. Allan hoped they like the video. Even the part with her breast exposed. He hoped it was just what they needed.

Limping into his house, Allan sees Helen sitting in the living room. She is drinking red wine and staring at the empty fireplace. Allan looks at his watch.

"Where's the nanny?" Allan says. He looks at his leg. The dog didn't puncture the skin. But there will be a bruise there.

"Out for a walk."

"In the rain?"

"Yes, babies don't melt. There's a cover for the stroller."

Allan looks at his watch again. Figures it out. "What are you doing home? Don't you have a class this afternoon?"

"What are you doing home?" Helen snaps. "Don't you have work this afternoon too?"

"I got bit by a dog," Allan says.

Helen turns towards him and looks down at his ankle. "Were you filming a dog?"

"Huh?"

"How did you get bit by a dog?"

Allan pauses on the way up the stairs. Now is the time, he thinks. He can wash his ankle later. He walks back down to the living room and sits next to Helen.

She says, "Is there blood? Don't get blood on the couch."

"Do you remember the night Lindsay disappeared?"

Helen looks at Allan as if he's crazy. "Do I remember it?" She leans back into the couch and takes a deep swallow of her wine.

It suddenly occurs to Allan that Helen is drinking in the afternoon. This is not like her. Everything seems off suddenly, everything seems odd.

"Do you remember how I went back for the car?"

"Yes, of course. You don't remember though, if I'm correct."

Allan begins to tell Helen everything. He feels such relief: the raccoons, Sophie's nakedness, his peeping Tom activities, the compost, the man with the dog coming out from behind the house, wiping his hands on the grass. Allan tells Helen about seeing the man again, about following him now, about thinking that this man, yes, this man with the dog, the dog who bit him just now, this man must have killed Paul's neighbour's brother. He's acting strangely, Allan says. Peeking out from his windows. Looking suspicious.

Helen sits still and listens.

Allan tells her that he didn't tell anyone, the police, her, because he thought they would suspect him. Because if he's capable of looking into windows (Allan laughs, nervously) then surely he could also murder a man or kidnap a babysitter. Right?

Helen breathes deeply. Allan watches her new breasts move up and down. The sense of relief, the weight lifted off his shoulders, he wants to hug Helen. And so he does.

Helen shoots away from him, lurches away from him, in disgust. She throws her wineglass towards him, misses, the wine splashes out over the couch, the rug, the floor. The glass shatters as it comes to a stop near the radiator.

"Jesus, Helen." Allan moves towards her again. "What's wrong?" "Don't you touch me." Helen's eyes are huge. Allan looks at her carefully. She is hunched over on the couch, arms wrapped around her large chest. "Don't you fucking touch me."

"What?" Allan notices that his ankle has stopped aching. He rubs at it with his finger. He licks his finger and then rubs at it. "You're making no sense. I just told you everything and now you're mad?"

"Mad? You're fucking mad," Helen says. "You lie to everyone. About your job. And now this. How do I know?" Helen stands. She shouts, "Where were you that night? What did you really do?" and then she runs out of the living room, into the hallway. She stops at the bottom of the stairs. "Did you take Lindsay? Did you kill her?"

"What the hell?" Allan stands up. Stares at his wife. "What?"

"Leave me alone," Helen says. She begins to cry. "Just leave me alone." She rushes up the stairs and slams the bedroom door.

Allan sits again on the couch. He nurses his ankle. What the hell is she on about? he thinks. It amazes him that his wife could think these things about him. He thought the police might, especially as they've already questioned him and he didn't tell them the truth the first time, but his own wife? Allan doesn't know what to do now. If his wife reacted this way, what will the authorities do?

Allan looks at his hands, his elbows resting on his knees. He studies the wine stains around him.

A door opens upstairs. "I'm getting my breasts done again," Helen shouts. "I'm getting them back to the way they were before." Slam.

Allan leans back and looks at the ceiling. The nanny and his baby come in the front door, the nanny dripping wet.

She is singing, a Filipino lullaby he has heard her sing before, the one Helen was attempting to copy a while ago.

Allan realizes he has no idea what she is saying. Sometimes he even forgets her name. And this woman is raising his child. This woman, Grace, that's it, is loving his Katherine, taking care of her. More than he is. He feels so sick.

He wonders if he has rabies.

He wonders if his wife is going to leave him.

He wonders if he should try to find out what that song says. What it's about. Maybe Grace is teaching Katherine a song that says, "Destroy your parents."

"Hello, Mr. Baxter," Grace says when she sees him there, a large smile lighting up her face. He suddenly realizes she has a pretty and kind face. "The rain, she comes down hard now."

28.

You have thoroughly cleaned her room. Dusted, vacuumed. Evidence, you think. There can't be any evidence. You think you can fool the police. All signs of life, of her life, will be gone from your house. It's her word against yours. A quiet librarian. Your psychiatrist will vouch for you. He'll say you've been so sad over the death of your wife. He'll say you've been stressed about 9/11. He'll say that you couldn't possibly have let the girl come live with you.

You realize you are crying. You wipe the tears from your cheeks.

"It wasn't your fault," you say aloud – to Gibson, to the vacuum – "she came here to get clean. You were good. She left because she was ready. It isn't your fault. She told you that her father abused her. She told you these things and she screamed hysterically in the night. She had nightmares she couldn't control – surely a nightmare is real proof that something was wrong. Something was frightening. She was crazy. God, she was probably crazy."

Sometimes you forgot she was missing and thought of her

as another companion, like Gibson. Someone to eat dinner with. Someone to sit quietly in front of the TV with.

You don't want to go to jail.

She may be dead out there. Overdose. Murder.

You'll be eaten alive in jail. Definitely.

It is late. It is dark. It is raining hard. There is no one around outside. The man's car is gone. You want to take Gibson out for a walk, but a plane roars by, overhead, way up in the sky, and the noise terrifies you. Once again. Here we go again, you think. But you leash the dog and head out into the world.

You leave wet footprints on the sidewalk.

When you were a small boy there was a fire in the neighbour-hood. Just down the street from your house. In the middle of the night. The story went that a young man fell asleep, drunk, his cigarette glowing. He set fire to his bed, to his sheets, his pyjamas. Awake, burning, the house on fire, he jumped out the second-floor window, went through the glass, cut off all his toes and limped, bloody-footed, down the street, until he lost consciousness and died in the grass two houses down.

As a child you would study what you thought were those foot-steps burnt into the sidewalk – black, raw, toeless. Footsteps stained with blood.

And then it rained and they were gone.

When you were a small boy your neighbour put a dead dog out in the garbage. Overnight the raccoons got into the garbage bag and tore the dog apart. You remember seeing tufts of fur and bone out on the street. Black and white fur. And leg bone, although, at the time, you didn't know what it was. It wasn't until your mother told you the neighbour's dog died that you fully realized what you had been poking with a stick and moving around on the ground.

No wonder, you think, as you walk down the sidewalk and into the rain, as Gibson tugs on the leash, no wonder everything frightens you. No wonder you are worried about the girl.

No wonder you are all alone.

29.

Paul and Allan are playing squash. This was the only way Allan could think of to get Paul alone, to tell him about seeing Sophie naked, about creeping through his backyard, about the man with the dog, before the whole story comes out. Allan has spent the last twenty-four hours thinking that he is guilty. A good part of him feels as if he killed the man, as if he stole Lindsay from the street. Helen has not come out of the bedroom. She has locked herself in. She has locked the connecting door from the ensuite bathroom out to the hallway. The nanny is confused but she barely speaks English and so she just shrugs to Allan when he passes her in the kitchen and the dining room. The baby is happy. Grace makes sure she is happy. Gurgles and coos as if nothing is going on. As long as Grace is there, and her formula, Katherine is fine.

Is anything going on? Allan doesn't know. He did nothing wrong.

But he was so drunk he can't remember most of that night. That's what bothers him. The police will question him and confuse him even more. Allan thinks that if he talks to Paul, tells him every-thing, then that may solidify the night in his mind. Besides, Paul's a lawyer and can give him advice he may need. Free advice.

Since he hasn't worked in a bit, Allan needs free advice.

Helen.

Christ, Allan thinks as he bashes the squash ball into the wall, as he watches Paul whip it back at him, Helen locked in their bed-room (Allan slept on the couch, wet still with wine). All Allan needs right now is support. He needs a stable, calm, confident wife to walk with him into the police station while he gives his story. If the police see that Helen is upset, maybe they won't trust his story.

"Ah," Allan shouts as he misses the ball.

Paul swings his arms around. Almost hits Allan with his squash racket by accident. "I'm feeling goooood today," Paul drawls.

Allan does what he always does. He starts to get mad. Whenever he loses, Allan gets angry. This usually helps him win. His opponent feels his anger and begins to back off. Just a little. This gives Allan the upper edge.

Today the upper edge doesn't work. Paul wins the game. Paul is gleeful in the locker room.

"You're such an idiot," Allan says. "Stop getting in my way."

Paul snaps at him with his towel. Like a kid, Allan thinks. Like a goddamn kid.

"I won, I won."

"You've won before. What's the big deal?"

"I don't know." Paul sits on the bench, dries himself off with his flicking towel. "I just feel great today. Like a new man. My back feels good."

Allan looks at him. He hasn't known Paul that long but some-thing is different. "What's up?"

"Nothing. I'm just not thinking about the murder anymore. In fact" – Paul grins – "I don't even want to mention it again. Ever again."

"Oh." Allan senses something in Paul's look. He suddenly says, "You're having an affair. Aren't you? That's what it is. I've seen that look in men before."

"What?" Paul stands. Almost falls over. "What? Why would you say that?"

"No, nothing. I guess I'm wrong." Allan looks down at his feet. His big feet in his big running shoes. "I just thought . . ."

Paul is silent. Twitching a bit. Nervous.

He is having an affair, Allan thinks. Who really cares? Although suddenly he feels better because some of that night now makes sense to him – Paul laughing at his naked wife. That works now.

"Listen, I have something I have to tell you," Allan says. "About that night."

"What night?" Paul is drying himself off. His back is stiff, but not seizing up. "I don't know why you'd think I was having an affair. Why would you think that? Just because I won and I'm happy about it?"

"The night of the murder. The night our babysitter disappeared. Your dinner party."

"I know," Paul says thoughtfully. "The chicken was dry. The rice was sticky."

"Ha." Allan swallows. "No, really, I came back to your house to get the car, right?"

"Listen, Allan," Paul says. "I've got to head back to work. Work. Not an affair." Paul looks up and to the left. "And I don't really want to talk about that night anymore, okay? I want to move on. Forget it. I need to get my life back on track. I've got other things to worry about."

"Yeah, but –"

"No, really." Paul is severe. Direct. His voice is loud. Allan stands. Paul moves backwards, towards his locker. He places his squash racket, his towel, his running shoes and shorts and T-shirt in the locker. Then he locks it.

Not sure what to do now, Allan sits down on the bench and stares after him as Paul leaves the locker room.

Later Allan is standing in front of the house of the man with the dog. Just standing there. Hoping the dog doesn't come out again and attack him. His ankle aches just looking at the house.

People watch. People walk past. Someone asks him if he's lost. It is raining lightly. Allan is getting wet.

Finally he climbs the steps to the house and knocks on the front door. Loudly. He can see into the front hall from the hazy curtain in the door window. He sees modern furniture. Not much of it. A small table. Glass and iron. A mirror. A candlestick.

And then the dog comes running and growling towards the door. Barking like its life depended on it. In the background, beyond the haze, beyond the hall table, Allan can see a figure moving about, coming closer to the door.

"Yes? Can I help you?"

He stands there, the chain on the door keeping the dog from getting out, keeping Allan from getting in. The man looks nervous. The dog attacks the door, chews at it. The dog's nose comes in and out through the crack in the door. The man says, "Hush," in a quiet voice. A high voice. "No bark."

The man is nervous. Nervous about his dog, about the intrusion. His sweater is on crooked, the buttons done up wrong, he is wearing slippers and is unshaven.

"I'm sorry," Allan says. Shouts. The dog is still barking. "I don't mean to bother you."

The man looks concerned. Afraid. The man touches the top of his barking dog's head and the dog snaps up at the man's hand.

"My dog is upset," the man says. "Are you selling something?"

"No, I just wonder if –" and then Allan stops talking. Wonder if what? What is he going to ask this man? Did you kill a man recently? This man who looks so sad and forlorn, this man who looks lonely and confused. This man whose eyes are terrified, whose mouth quivers. This man whose long fingers come around the door, holding it slightly ajar.

"I'm sorry, did you want something?"

"No, sorry." Allan is suddenly upset at himself for even thinking this could be the man. "Sorry, I've got the wrong house. I thought my friend lived here."

The relief on the man's face is palpable. Allan can feel it come towards him like a wave. Carry him away. It's a rush of relief.

"Oh, no problem, that's no problem at all. Stay, Gibson." The man shuts the door behind him and his dog and Allan watches through the hazy curtain as his figure heads back down his hallway, past his glass table, his candlestick.

How, Allan thinks, could this man do any harm to anyone? Not this sad, old man. Sure, his dog could kill someone, but not this man. Allan stands on the porch and looks around him at the street, the cars parked along it. He looks at the rain falling quietly and he listens to the swish of car tires as they pass.

Driving home, towards his angry wife, Allan suddenly thinks that something was odd in that house. The man was too nervous. As if he was hiding something. Or is Allan just imagining that? There was the sharp, bitter, tangy smell of fear about the man. Maybe he's just afraid of his dog, though. Allan drives home with his eyes to the ground, watching the lines on the road and trying to stay within them.

30.

"You what?" Sophie screams. "You what?" She wants to throw something at him. A vase. The baby. Anything. They are in the kitchen. Rebecca is nestled on Sophie's hip. Crying. Sophie made her cry by screaming. "No. I can't believe this. No."

Paul shakes his head. He looks at the floor.

"How could you?" Sophie thinks suddenly that this is like TV. She sees herself from above now. She sees the gradually expanding waistline, the mother with babe on her hip, the hair that is unbrushed, the husband in his suit and tie having just come back from work . . . or . . . having just come back from fucking his new girlfriend.

Vivian, Vivian, Vivian.

Sophie cries. "I can't believe this, Paul. Not us. Look. We have a baby. Look at her."

But Sophie can believe it. Didn't she, in fact, know this was happening? It seems so obvious now. The late nights, the smell of alcohol on his breath, the sudden happiness – of course that should have given it away – he was suddenly very happy.

"I'm so sorry, Sophie. I don't know how to explain this to you."

"You're leaving me? Us? Is that what you are saying? For that Vivian woman? For the woman whose brother was murdered in her house? Is that a turn-on or something? Women who have murderers come into their houses and murder their brothers? Is that what it is? Something that turns you on?" Sophie picks up a spatula from the container on the counter and whips it at Paul's head. She misses. She picks up a soup spoon and does the same. It hits.

"Sophie, calm down. Ouch."

"You," she screams. "You tell me to calm down. You come home, you tell me you are fucking –"

"Don't say that word in front of Rebecca –"

"You are FUCKING another woman," Sophie shouts this in Rebecca's ear and Rebecca cries even louder. "And you want me to calm down? Calm down?"

"I just –" Paul stops talking. He sits down. He rubs at the spot on his head that was hit with the spoon.

"What are we supposed to do? What will Rebecca do? A no-good father. A scum. A shit."

Sophie throws another spatula at him. Her aim is good. What would my father do? What would my father do? What would my father say and do? This is all Sophie can think and this thought infuriates her even more.

Rebecca won't stop crying. Sophie shakes her. Paul stands.

"Give me the baby. You'll hurt her."

"I don't care anymore, Paul. I don't care." Sophie pushes Rebecca at her husband. He takes the baby quickly and shushes her, rocks her in his arms. Rebecca holds her arms out for her mother, but Sophie turns from her. "I don't care about you. I don't care about Vivian or Rebecca. I just don't care."

Sophie cries. She doesn't mean this. Or does she?

Suddenly Rebecca stops crying and the silence in the room is eerie. All Sophie can hear are the cars passing on the street outside. She can hear the rain on the skylight over the porch. She can hear the spaghetti sauce bubbling in its pot. Sophie is out of spatulas to throw. She looks around for something else.

The funny thing is, Sophie thinks, she doesn't want to break anything permanently. She doesn't want to throw a dish or a bowl or a glass. Hurt Paul. Yes. She wants to hurt him. But she really, actually, if she thinks about it, doesn't care enough about this to break something for good. This shocks her. She really doesn't care enough about this. Sophie says this to herself a few times. Does she care?

"All the support I gave you," she hisses, "when your back gave out. When you just stayed in bed all day like a slug. You're a slug. And all you can do to repay me is to have an affair?"

"I fell in love with her, Sophie. I couldn't help myself. It's not an affair. It's love. I know that's no excuse."

"You're damn right that's no excuse." Again – a television show. Sophie sees herself in black and white. The old soap operas. She remembers her nanny watching those when she was little – sobbing into her handkerchief. "Little Sophie," the nanny would cry. "Julian is leaving Tina for Melissa." And Sophie would watch, fascinated. Her tough nanny crying, crying, crying.

"We haven't been happy, Sophie. In years. You haven't been happy in a long time."

"Ever." Sophie turns on Paul. "We've never been really happy. I hate you. I've always hated you." Sophie wants to shout, "I've never loved you, Paul," but can't bring herself to do it.

"We were happy when we first got married, weren't we? You haven't always hated me. That's not fair."

"No. No, we weren't happy then. Think of the day of our wedding. My dress ripped going up the church steps and I remember feeling just plain pissed off through the whole ceremony. I remember worrying about the damn dress and not caring about what we were doing. It was all about the dress."

"It's always been about the dress for you," Paul says, quietly. "Or the house. Redecorating. Shopping. Sometimes I think you only married me because I have the potential, as a lawyer, to make money."

"Don't you blame this on me," Sophie shouts again. "Don't you ever, ever, ever blame this on me. This is all your fault."

"But, Sophie, it's not. It's our fault. Together."

"No." Sophie storms over to Paul and begins to hit him on his back as he turns from her. "You believe that? That crap? Together? Did I go out and fuck someone? Did I?" Rebecca cries again. Holds her arms out for her mother. "No, no, no, no, no. This is all your fault. It will always be your fault. Don't you ever forget that."

Paul moves from Sophie's punches. He takes Rebecca into the other room.

The spaghetti sauces spills over. The pot of water for the noodles boils until it is foam and then it spills over too.

Sophie follows Paul into the living room. She remembers taking off her clothes in here, with all the curtains open. And now they are fighting in the living room and the curtains are open still. The neighbours will see. Again. They will see her life. The breakdown of her life. She remembers Paul laughing, giggling, laughing at her. Oh God, was that the beginning of the end? When he laughed at her standing naked in her living room? The curtains open for everyone to see?

Sophie closes the curtains. "When you laughed at me, here, in the living room. When you couldn't stop laughing, were you sleeping with her then?"

"Sophie, I didn't even know her then. I didn't know her until the next day."

That was the last time she was naked in front of her husband, wasn't it? Strange that she hadn't realized that until just now. Now another woman has been naked in front of him. Sophie doesn't fit into her jeans anymore.

She sits on the couch and begins to cry. Paul, with Rebecca on his hip, sits beside her. He has the nerve, Sophie thinks, to put his hand on my shoulder. To touch me. She pushes him off.

"Go away. Don't touch me."

Paul stands. "I'm going to put Rebecca in the bath. Then bed. Then we'll talk more. Okay? I don't know what to do, Sophie. I don't know what to say to you. I don't know how to explain."

"You should have thought of that before you told me. Or before you slept with her. Think, Paul. That's all you had to do. Think." Sophie's shoulders fall, her spine curves in, she wants to disappear into a snail shell.

"I know."

"Why did you tell me anyway? Why did you bother? I would never have found out. We could have gone on. We could have faked it."

"But I want to leave you," Paul says. "I want to be with Vivian."

Sophie sinks into her chest even more. Paul begins to take Rebecca up the stairs. He turns. "I really didn't want to hurt you."

"Too late for that," Sophie says to her chest.

"I'm so sorry. I guess I thought you'd be relieved."

Silence for a minute. Sophie laughs. She nods her head in her snail shell.

"What should I do about your dinner? Do you want your dinner?"

"I'm not hungry, Sophie. I'll just put the baby to bed."

Sophie listens to him mount the stairs, Rebecca making snuffling noises like she's about to cry, and then Sophie moves back into the kitchen and turns off the burners on the stove. It's a disaster. Sauce and boiled water everywhere. Of course, he'd tell her this news when she was cooking. Of course. Typical. She dishes a huge helping of spaghetti and sauce onto her plate, piles all the grated cheese for two onto it and begins to eat. Standing at the counter she shovels the spaghetti in with a spoon, wrapping it around and around, until her mouth is red and raw, the front of her shirt speckled with sauce. Sophie eats until she feels as if she is going to vomit. Until bile rises in her throat.

And then she stops. Because that's all she can do.

31.

It's funny, she wasn't here long, but sometimes you feel like you see her everywhere. In the bathroom, in the kitchen. A black shape that turns and moves and cascades down the hall. A shadow. This girl. And his dead wife. Where did they go?

That man came to your door today. In the pouring rain. The man Gibson wanted to eat. Why would your dog turn so violent? Maybe this man, maybe he is the abuser, maybe he is the reason she disappeared into the night, the reason she had nightmares? Maybe it isn't the father, like she said. She did, after all, look up and to the left whenever she told you about him. From the research you've done, looking up and to the left is a sure sign of lying. You want so much to know what went on that night, the night she left everyone and turned into a black shadow, days before you saw her in the park, drugged out, lost, afraid of everyone.

What happened to her?

You wonder, often, why you didn't really ask her what happened. In detail. Sure she told you some things – after babysitting she was high and she disappeared into the night, she didn't remember much – but the nights she would wake screaming you knew that more had happened that night than she let on.

Then the man knocked on your door and Gibson went ballistic.

You really think you must do something about your dog. Training? Dog obedience? Can you take a vicious dog and make him sweet again?

Is the babysitter running around Toronto in your wife's skirt right now? In your old shirt?

The US may be going to war with Afghanistan. The Taliban. The library is quiet these days. Everyone is quietly typing away on the internet, searching the news. No one is reading fiction anymore. No one is reading books.

It is midnight and the rain hasn't stopped. If you were real, if you were alive and living in reality, then maybe you would be in the Roof Lounge at the top of the Park Hyatt hotel having drinks with some friends. If you had friends. You would be wearing the suit your wife helped you pick out for your wedding anniversary with the blue-green tie. You would have carried your green umbrella over your forearm and you would have ordered a gin and tonic. If you were real. And if your wife wasn't dead she would be with you. She would hold your arm, the one without the umbrella on it, and she would be wearing her red dress and white pearl necklace and earrings. She would have touched her lips with a tiny bit of pink lipstick and she would have curled her hair. She would smell wonderful. Chanel perfume. Baby powder. Soap and shampoo.

Instead of a drink with your wife you are debating whether or not to take your crazy, wild dog out into the night. He needs a walk. You need a walk. But it is raining hard. You are still standing on the front porch looking out at the rain. Gibson is sitting patiently beside you.

You think of the images on CNN, when all the workers, the

New Yorkers, the people off the street went into the rubble and carried out the bodies on stretchers. Lowered them down the line until everyone had touched the stretcher – an almost holy blessing of the people by the people – and the body was placed in an ambulance and driven off somewhere. Where? Where did they take all the bodies? You think it must have been an overwhelming feeling. All the pieces. Arms, feet, legs, thighs, bones, skin, skulls. There must have been an army of people putting them together. Like jigsaw puzzles.

Suddenly you feel sick.

There are terrorists everywhere. You see them when you are out. Hiding in their big fall jackets. Looking down at their feet. They won't meet your eyes.

If you look up *terrorist* on the internet, will the police come knocking at your door? Will that man come back? Will the babysitter be found?

The subway. The CN Tower. The SkyDome. City hall with its strange half-circle shape. The nuclear power plants. The water reservoirs. Chemical. Biological. Warfare. It's not fair. Life isn't. You are back to worrying. You have nothing to distract you anymore from thinking like this.

You pull on Gibson's leash. Pull him away from studying his pile of pebbles. Try to act lackadaisical about it. The rain. Your loneliness. "Taking the good dog out for a walk," you say aloud, in case anyone is listening. Going to the park.

Gibson's tail is wagging. It makes you slightly happier to see him pleased. "Out for an adventure, Gibson," you say. "Here we go." Gibson barks. Down the street towards the Danforth. Turn right. You are doing just great. Gibson hasn't killed anyone yet. Although no one is really out walking in the rain. You whistle a tune. Gibson growls at the odd passerby. Walk across the Bloor Street Viaduct. It's always longer than you think. A towering bridge. A suicide pact.

Way far down. Then down Bloor towards you don't know where. It's empty out. Everyone is inside and dry. Toronto is vacant.

That's when you see him. The man who knows you. The man who knocked on your door and pretended he was at the wrong house. The man she babysat for. You see him walk up a side street, away from Bloor. On instinct, you turn towards him. You follow him like he followed you. Up the street. Slowly. Gibson panting.

"Don't bark," you whisper to Gibson.

Don't worry.

You watch the man move purposefully up the front walk of a nice brick, detached house. On the porch there is a recycling box, a baby stroller with a cover on it, a wagon. It is cluttered but in an organized way. The lights are off in the house. You stop farther down, on the other side of the street. The man reaches into his pocket for the key to his house and then you watch him go inside. Into the darkness.

"Ah," you say. And you decide to wait a bit. To see what will happen. Maybe the girl is inside that house. Maybe she will appear out of nowhere. Maybe she is in that house right now, watching out the window for you. Wanting to escape. Wanting to run.

The night goes on.

You lean on a post. Gibson falls asleep on the ground. Suddenly the door opens and the man comes out again. He is angry. He slams the door and you see him rush down the street in the direction of Bloor. He does not see you.

You will wait some more. Something will happen. You are sure of it. Something will come out of all of this waiting; something will come out of it that will make you satisfied again. Something will suddenly happen that will make you happy and content. Or if not happy, just content. Satisfied. Able to move on with your life.

"You just wait, Gibson. You just wait and see."

32.

Helen hears him come in. It's late. He'll be sleeping on the couch again. There is no way she's letting that asshole into this room.

But Allan knocks softly on the bedroom door. "Helen, we've got to talk about this. I'm going to the police tomorrow."

"You haven't gone yet? Why haven't you gone yet?"

"Shhh, you'll wake the baby."

"But I thought you were going to the police today."

"I wanted to talk to Paul. I want you with me."

"What did he say?" Helen is lying on the big bed in the middle of the room. She has missed teaching several classes this week but is trying not to think about that. All day, while she lay in bed, the phone was ringing. People leaving messages, wondering where she was. But she didn't answer it. This missing babysitter has caught up with Helen and has swept her into some sort of depressed vortex. And Allan. All about Allan. Everything that has happened. Helen wants to hit someone or something. Break her bed down the middle.

"He didn't say anything. Let me in. I didn't tell him."

"Fuck, Allan."

"I want to talk to you. I want to see you. Can't I come in?"

"No. I don't want to talk to you. I don't want to see you."

"What are you thinking, Helen? Do you think I'm capable of hurting someone? Do you really think that? What do you think?"

Helen sighs. "No, I don't think that. I just –" She doesn't know what she feels. She's angry that Allan lied to her about that night, the night that changed everything. She's angry that he was snooping into their friend's house, that he might have seen the murderer and not done anything about it, that he hasn't been filming commercials like he told her but instead making home movies (and not even home movies, grief movies. Sad, depressing, anxious, horrible movies about people dying), that he let Lindsay walk home by herself crying. She's mad about September 11th and the planes and how that has affected her teaching, her thinking, her life. "God, why did you pass her on the street?" It's so much easier to blame him for all of this.

Helen didn't even like the girl. And now look at her life.

Allan sinks down into the carpet in the hallway. He leans his back on the door of the bedroom.

"Jesus, Helen. We've talked about this. You let her go too. I thought she'd be scared if I came up to her. I was drunk. I don't know. I was covered in compost. I was too lazy to walk her home."

Helen begins to cry. "A teenage girl is missing, Allan. Can you imagine what her parents must be feeling? And it's our fault."

"Yes." Allan groans. He feels defeated.

"What if she's dead?" Helen gasps. "What if she's dead and it's our fault?"

"Listen, Helen. I don't know what happened to Lindsay. I don't. I feel awful about it –"

"Awful? Allan, awful? That's a stupid word to use."

"Shhh, you're too loud."

"I don't care," Helen shouts. "I don't care if I wake the baby."

But the baby doesn't wake. Allan waits for the cry. Helen waits for it. Nothing.

Allan tries the handle on the door. It won't open. He sighs.

There is a noise outside the house. In the back. A thump. Allan stands and walks over to the window that looks out the back of the house. He can't see the porch under the roof. Kids. There are always kids fooling around in the backs of the houses around here. Doing drugs. Getting drunk. In the alleys that back up to the yards.

"Allan? Are you still there?" Helen has stopped crying.

"Yes." Allan moves back to the bedroom door. He hears a dog bark. Ah, he thinks. A dog must have gotten into their recycling bin on the porch.

"I think maybe we should take a break from each other," Helen says.

"What?"

"You heard me."

"But why?"

"Oh, Allan – why? What do you mean 'why'? Where have you been lately? Where has your brain been lately?"

"I was –" What should he tell her? That he has been walking the streets all night looking for Lindsay? That he has been stalking the murderer who really isn't the murderer?

"No, really. Where has your brain been? You lied to me so many times. I don't trust you. I'm sick of you, really. And I want to get my breasts reduced." Helen begins to cry again. She gestures at her breasts even though she is alone in the room. Her voice wavers. "You wanted me to get them big and I want them back to the way they were. I want to be the same person I used to be."

"Me?" Allan pounds on the door. "Me? You're the one who wanted to get them done."

"I did it for you," Helen wails.

"But I didn't ask you," Allan says. "I never asked you to do it. I liked them better before."

"What? What do you mean?"

The baby begins to cry.

"Oh," Helen says. "The baby is crying."

Allan looks up at the ceiling, as if the plaster will tell him something. All he can see in the whiteness is one spiderweb dangling down.

"Are you still there, Allan? Get the baby."

"No," Allan says. "No, I'm not still here." He turns and walks down the staircase. He puts his leather coat back on. His shoes. Allan opens the front door and walks out into the wet night leaving his baby, his wife, his house behind him.

"Where will you go?" Helen calls out. "Where will you go?" she whispers to her reflection in the mirror when she hears the front door close. And she doesn't know if she means to be asking Allan this, or herself.

The baby continues to cry.

33.

Sophie is knocking on Helen's door. First thing in the morning. Seven o'clock. She didn't know where else to turn. Helen, she thought. Helen will be the one who will understand this. After all, Helen was there on the last night with Paul, the night before he met Vivian Middleford. That was the night, Sophie thinks. The calm before the storm. The beginning of the end. She doesn't care. Sophie knocks on Helen's door over and over.

And then she sees the doorbell.

She rings it and can hear the baby cry and this makes her think of Rebecca and her full breasts ache like a charley horse in her chest, and they leak onto her sweater.

After throwing up her spaghetti, Sophie left Paul with Rebecca and went out into the night. She walked around in the rain until, somehow, she doesn't know how, she ended up in front of her parents' house. A long way from her house. She stood there, in the downpour, watching the shapes and shadows move across her parents' front windows as they went about their evening existence. And she thought. Sophie thought about how much she has disappointed her parents, about how all she ever wanted in life was to be a lot less like them and now she's just like them. Except for the divorce, which is, most likely, inevitable. She hasn't pulled it together like her father and mother did or would have or could have. If either of them had had an affair they would have pushed it under the carpet. They would have got through it. They would have ignored it.

"It's not an affair," Paul had said. "I'm in love with Vivian."

As if that will last, Sophie thinks. Nothing lasts. Definitely not love.

Sophie stood in front of her parents' house and then, finally, exhausted and giving up, she walked right in. Caught them watching a sitcom on TV. She stormed into the living room with her wet clothes, her wet boots on, and there they were, sitting in chairs (not on the couch together), watching TV and drinking – Sophie's father with a glass of amber liquid, Sophie's mother with a glass of white wine. There was a TV tray in front of Sophie's mother (they own a TV tray?) and the remains of a meal (could it be microwave dinners?).

"What's going on?" Sophie said.

"My God," Sophie's mother said. She jumped up and immediately took the TV tray and rushed awkwardly into the kitchen.

Sophie's father turned off the TV. Reluctantly, Sophie thought.

Now, this morning, after sleeping in her old bedroom, under the new designer sheets her mother bought to replace her teenage pink ones, her breasts aching, full of milk, her legs stiff from all the walking, Sophie knocks, knocks and finally rings the doorbell at Helen's house in the Annex.

A bleary-eyed Helen answers the door. "Sophie? What are you doing here?"

"Can I come in?" Sophie begins to cry. "Can I talk to you?"

Helen looks around. Sees an older man across the street, just standing there, his dog pissing against a pole. She pokes her head out of the house, holds her bathrobe tight against her (large) chest and says, "Of course, come in."

Behind Sophie comes Grace. Starting her day of work. The nanny shuffles past Helen and Sophie in the front hall, tutting about the water Sophie is dripping on the carpet.

Helen watches Grace carry Katherine up the stairs towards the second-floor playroom. Grace has taken the baby's bottle and she nods and bows to Sophie and Helen and rushes up the stairs as quick as she can. Helen cringes when Grace begins to sing her Tagalog lullaby again. Katherine hushes and stares, in awe, at Grace. Helen knows her child loves the nanny's voice, her eyes, her kindness.

Helen wonders about that quietness in Katherine, that maybe her baby can feel Grace's hunger for her own children. Helen sighs and wishes for the millionth time that her life were different. She wishes she didn't need a nanny to help her raise her child. She wishes Grace didn't need the money. She wishes she could just balance everything at the same time. But can she? Why can't she?

Helen looks from the stairs to Sophie and then at the clock. She rubs her eyes. She often wishes she were kinder to the nanny but she forgets to be and then she feels awkward. Did she even say, "Good morning" to Grace? And why was Grace so early this morning?

"Seven in the morning, Sophie, what's wrong? Is it Paul? Rebecca? Are you okay?"

Helen remembers she asked Grace to come early last week when she thought she would try to go to the gym in the morning.

Sophie takes off her coat and boots and walks into Helen's living room. "Is Allan home?"

"No." Helen looks awkwardly around, as if expecting Allan to jump out at her. "No, he left for work early. I think."

"I need to talk to someone," Sophie says, sitting on the couch. "I didn't know who to talk to. I tried my parents but they don't listen. And then I thought –" Sophie looks up at Helen who is still standing there, clutching her robe "– I thought, I don't have any friends." Sophie begins to cry. "You are my only friend and I don't even know you." Sophie was about to say, "I don't even like you," but caught herself in time. There is no way she would be getting any sympathy if she told Helen she doesn't like her. But really, Sophie thinks, I don't really like her. Look at her there with her nanny doing everything and her beauty and her large breasts that aren't even real and don't ache and leak. Sophie really bawls now. Crying so much that her nose runs down to her lip.

"Kleenex?" Sophie manages.

"Yes, of course." Helen walks into the kitchen and brings back a box of Kleenex. Sophie goes through many Kleenexes before she calms down. Helen sits beside her and waits.

"Paul left me," Sophie says.

"Left you?" That's the last thing Helen expected. "Left you?" Helen expected something else – some little breastfeeding tragedy or that Paul is back in bed, his back, once again, in distress – not marital problems. She didn't expect this.

"For Vivian Middleford."

Helen thinks that name sounds vaguely familiar. A character from one of the books she teaches? "Vivian Middleford?" she echoes.

"Yes." Sophie sobs.

"Who?"

"The woman whose brother was murdered. The woman who –"

"Oh God, I remember that name now," Helen says. "Oh dear, Sophie. Tell me what's happened? Did he move out? Where's Rebecca?"

Sophie begins to tell Helen everything. She starts with the dinner party, the cleanup, the raccoons, then the scream the next morning and Paul missing for hours. Then 9/11, of course. She talks about the towers falling and how she and Rebecca watched them on TV and it didn't seem real. Helen listens. Then there is Paul's absence. From work. From her life. Sophie talks about how she would be in the kitchen and she could hear Paul watching TV upstairs in the bedroom, groaning every time he moved. He lay still at night. Not moving a muscle. At first, he wouldn't talk to her about the murder and then he talked incessantly about it, about the dead man's body, his blood, the wounds. Sophie talked about it with him until, she says, she closed up, couldn't think straight. Two towers fell, killing all those people (planes and people jumping out of the sky).

"It was enough to drive you crazy," Sophie says. "I shut off my brain."

Helen nods. Holds her tongue. What brain?

"And now," Sophie says, "and now, all I can think about is Paul and Vivian Middleford lying naked next to each other, touching each other." Sophie puts her hands up, palms towards the ceiling. She shrugs. "I don't know what to do."

Helen sighs. "I kicked Allan out last night."

"What?" Sophie feels like she's been slapped. Here she is, telling Helen everything about herself, and what does Helen do? She has to equal Sophie's story. Fuck, Sophie thinks. This is why I don't have friends. Friends take your pain and make it theirs. But Sophie puts on a nice face, touches Helen's knee. Fakes it. That's what women do, Sophie thinks. We fake it. "What do you mean?"

So Helen tells Sophie about Allan. She starts with the dinner party too and Sophie is appalled to hear that Allan watched her strip her clothes off through the side window, that he watched her try to seduce her husband (did he see Paul laughing?) and that he was the raccoon outside setting off the motion detector. All Sophie can think to say is "Men." She grunts it. She feels sick. "At least," she says. "At least I wasn't so fat then."

But when Helen tells Sophie about the compost, about Allan coming home and needing a shower quickly, when she tells her about some vague man with a dog and how Allan hasn't been working when he says he is – all the lies – when Helen says, "I don't trust him," Sophie thinks of how Allan drinks his beer out of bottles, how uncouth he is. She thinks about his leather jackets (does he have more than one?) and how he always kisses her on both cheeks and lingers there, his cologne reeking. She thinks about what Vivian Middleford (slut) said about the neighbour seeing someone sneaking through backyards.

"Do you think he murdered that man?" Sophie says, before Helen even proposes the idea.

"Allan? No." Helen closes her eyes. She leans back on the couch. "No. I don't think so. I don't know." Suddenly Helen is angry. "Of course not. No. Why?"

"The babysitter?" Sophie asks. She has suddenly forgotten her problems. This is much more interesting. Allan, she thinks. Who would have guessed? "The police interviewed him. Paul was his lawyer. Oh my God."

"No, Sophie." Helen sits up again. "No. Don't jump to conclusions. I think he just lied about things. He was drunk. Snooping. I don't think he's capable of anything like what you are thinking. It's all coincidence. Honestly. It's just –" Here Helen pauses and thinks. What is it? "It's just that everything changed after that dinner party, didn't it? So much happened on September 11th. Even my students were going crazy with fear. They are usually so self-centred, nothing usually gets in. But then the world expanded suddenly and my students had to stop turning in on themselves. They had to look outside themselves. See what is out there."

"So much worse happens every day, though," Sophie says. "Why should this affect us? Here?"

"I don't know. Maybe it's the way we saw it. The horror of it all coming through the TV live? I don't know." This is what Helen has heard. She has heard that seeing the events live created post-traumatic stress symptoms all over the world. As if the whole world was there when the towers fell.

"The babysitter," Sophie says.

"And the man murdered behind you."

"Isn't it always women?" Sophie says. "Why did a man get murdered? That seems so out of the ordinary."

"It's not always women," Helen says. "What about wars?"

"But don't the men start the wars?" Sophie asks meekly.

Helen and Sophie sit there, on the couch, staring, not at each other, but at the empty fireplace. They have run out of steam, out of things to say that mean anything. Sophie notices the red wine stains on the couch, on the floor by the radiator. Blood? she thinks, but shakes her head. Silence. The women breathe steadily.

"What are we going to do?" Sophie asks, quietly.

"I don't know," Helen says. "I really don't know." We, she thinks, who is we?

Quiet. A car passes on the street. The rain has stopped. Helen hears the nanny tiptoeing behind them, down the stairs, towards the kitchen to get something. The nanny opens the back door and Helen hears her throw a can into the recycling bin on the back porch. Grace is always eating those tins of mandarin oranges with her friends in the alley behind the house. One after another all day long. They live on the stuff. Although Helen shouldn't judge. She'd eat those too if she didn't have to stay slim. And, to be honest, she'd rather Grace have friends in the neighbourhood than be lonely and bored.

What is she thinking? Why is she thinking about her nanny this way? Comparing herself to Grace. Helen cringes, feels entitled and sad and stupid. How did she get this way?

And then the scream. The nanny's scream pierces the air. Sophie's heart almost stops. Helen jumps up, clutching at her throat like a heroine in an old black-and-white movie. And Grace screams and screams and screams, shouting something in Tagalog that Sophie and Helen can't make out. They run to the back door and join Grace on the porch. A slouched shape, a child, a girl, wrapped in a blanket, her clothes filthy, her eyes open, staring, slouched up against the steps. Half fallen, half sitting.

"Oh my God," Sophie says. "What is that? Is that a person?"

The nanny wails. "*Ang* babysitter!" she shouts. "*Ang* babysitter!"

"Lindsay," Helen says, looking down. She shudders once, twice and then begins to cry. "It's the babysitter. It's Lindsay."

Helen and Sophie stand there, in shock, staring down at the girl.

Grace, on the other hand, wraps her arms around Lindsay and pulls her close, hugs her, touches her hair and face, kisses her. "Lindsay," she whispers, her accent strong. "Poor girl. I know."

BEFORE AND AFTER

1.

Lindsay is walking towards Bloor but she doesn't notice Mr. Baxter on the other side of the street. She sees nothing but the math book in her arms. The red fox on the cover. She is crying. It astonishes her that Mrs. Baxter would be that angry with her. For doing nothing. She's done much worse. Tonight she was doing nothing wrong. Only talking (and making out) with Derek at the back door.

What, Lindsay thinks, does a fox have to do with math? Lindsay stops walking and stands there and stares at her book.

Lindsay has smoked a joint. She smoked it with Derek at the back door. Maybe that's why she can't see any connection between math and foxes. Maybe that's what she did that was bad. But Mrs. Baxter wouldn't have known that, would she? Could she smell it on Lindsay?

She called all night. Checking in with Lindsay. Checking up on everything. "Has Katherine had a bowel movement? Did she burp? Is she crying?" Lindsay wanted to throw the phone out the back door. Why bother going out if you are only going to worry about your kid?

Who is crying, Lindsay thinks, and wipes her eyes.

What was in that joint?

Derek and his pot. His drugs. His meth and coke and ecstasy. His Valium. Uppers. Downers.

Lindsay walks again. She feels like she's wearing high-heeled shoes. Tottering down the street. Her legs ache for some reason. Her calves have charley horses.

Fox. Charley. Horse. Nope, no connection. Nothing firing. Her neurons are not firing. She wants to shout this. Laugh.

And cry.

"Knock that joint right outta my head," she sings quietly.

She turns on her achy, high-heeled horsey legs towards Bloor Street, but it's not Bloor Street, it's an alley off Bloor Street with a big dumpster in it. A man asleep on the ground. A bottle beside him.

Hallucination. Lindsay thinks she is hallucinating. The fox on the cover of her math book comes out at her. Jumps out. And knocks her over.

No. Nothing like that happens. But she'd better put the book down. Beside the sleeping guy. Or is he dead? Lindsay doesn't really care. She drops the book beside him and continues down the alley.

Mrs. Baxter screaming at her like that. What gives her the right? Lindsay sure wasn't as stoned there as she is now. A delayed stone. She's heard of that before. She's actually glad Mrs. B came home when she did. What would have happened if she had been later? Like now? If she had walked in on Lindsay hallucinating on the couch? "A fox, a fox," Lindsay would shout.

She giggles.

Continues down the alley.

Where is Derek? He said he'd meet her on Bloor Street.

Where is Bloor Street?

Lindsay shakes her head again. Her school is doing the musical *South Pacific* and she's been hearing the damn songs coming from the auditorium every day after school.

Was that Mr. Baxter who passed her up the street? All of a sudden she remembers seeing him. His leather jacket. Seeing him drunkenly stagger up the street. He's always drunk when they come home. Those two. That's what her mom says, "Do you have to babysit for 'those two' again?" Like they are different somehow. They aren't "us," they are "those." Them. Those two. Not Lindsay and her mother and her mean father and her stupid little brother.

And her cat.

She loves her cat.

If it weren't for her cat (and sometimes her mom – when her mom buys her things), Lindsay would pick up and move out. Move in with Derek maybe. Although then she'd be stoned all the time.

Lindsay's father always yells at her. No matter what she does. If she gets good marks he says, "Why aren't they better?" If she does well in sports he says, "You didn't try hard enough." Nothing is good enough for him.

Muffles. He is six years old and striped all over. He is long-haired and purrs loudly and takes his claws to the underside of her bed and tears at her box spring when he's happy. Muffles sleeps on top of the covers between her legs, and Lindsay can't move once he's there. Her legs cramp. But it's worth it.

Take Muffles and run, she thinks.

Her head spins. The alley is suddenly foggy. Or is it her eyes? There is another man asleep beside another dumpster with another math book beside him and, oh my God, it's the same fox.

Or has she just walked in circles?

Lindsay sits down. She rubs her legs hard. Puts some feeling back into them.

"Derek," she calls out.

"Lindsay," she wants him to call back. But he doesn't. He is nowhere to be seen.

What did he put in that joint? What did she smoke? What could possibly make her legs disappear and her foxy friend come over and lick her nose? A rat. A rat. She thinks she sees a rat beside the dead man. But he moves and it isn't a rat. Just his hand. And he isn't dead. And the fox is gone. And Lindsay collapses in the alley, waiting for Derek to rescue her.

Damn it, she thinks. I didn't even get paid.

2.

He is waiting for her on Bloor Street. He is cold. The bank machine he is standing near is busy. University students taking money out. The occasional woman by herself. He wants to slip in the doors and lie on the floor and wait for Lindsay in there, where it's warm. Derek doesn't know why he is so cold. It's not that cold out, really. It's the joint, it must be the joint. He is shaking like mad.

Where is she?

Derek starts to walk back up the street he ran down. Just to get his blood moving. Roiling. He loves words and *roiling* is one of his favourites lately. He uses it whenever he can. His blood is always roiling. He pictures it bubbling and steaming.

Maybe it wasn't the joint. Maybe it was the pill he popped in Lindsay's Diet Coke. He only had a sip of it, though. She drank the whole damn can. If he's feeling this weird, what is she feeling? Derek can't remember where he got the pill. Someone gave it to him. By the time he popped it in Lindsay's drink he was so stoned he couldn't remember what it was.

Derek walks up the street, doesn't see Lindsay, and then walks back down to Bloor Street. He sells a baggy to the three university students who confront him by the bank machine. He goes into the all-night convenience store and buys a coffee. He wanders around the block a few times and then he gives up. She must have gone home. Derek walks slowly towards his home, towards his basement crap-hole, towards his deadbeat mother (who probably isn't home anyway. She's probably out with some new guy getting wasted). Derek lights a cigarette.

Home. He thought he'd get a bit of action tonight, but instead he's going home to his cold pullout sofa bed. Lindsay's lips are so big and luscious. That's another word. *Luscious*. Derek wonders how you spell it. Her luscious lips make his blood roil.

God, that's good. Sometimes, when he is stoned, Derek thinks he could be a poet.

Feeling warmer after the coffee and the walking, Derek takes the key from the chain attached to his pocket and lets himself into the apartment. It's dark. All the lights are off. Derek feels around for the switch and when he turns it on and surveys the mess of the room he sighs. He lies on his sofa bed, fully clothed, and tries to fall asleep. Derek wonders why nothing is ever different. Why can't he turn the light on and see the apartment clean, his mom baking? He tries not to think of Lindsay's clean house and double bed with pink princess sheets. He tries not to think of the fact that at Lindsay's house there is milk in the fridge and cereal in the cupboard. He tries not to think about how he has to get up for school tomorrow. And he wants to go to school tomorrow because he has English class first thing with Mr. Hamblin and he likes English and has even read the play he was supposed to read. Although right now he can't remember any of it. In fact, he can't remember what play it was. He'll skip school after English. He just has to get to English class.

Derek closes his eyes. He drifts off. His stomach rumbles.

Later he wakes to hear his mother come crashing through the apartment door with some big biker guy. She waves at Derek, lying there in his clothes, and then drags the big man through the living room into the one bedroom. Laughing. Derek listens to the grunting and swearing, the squeak of the bed, until he can't bear it anymore and then he puts the pillow over his ears to drown them out. It is early in the morning.

The pillow doesn't work.

His blood is roiling.

Hamlet, he suddenly thinks. That's it. *Hamlet.* One cool dude that Hamlet guy. One cool dude. Derek smiles and gets out of bed, pulls his coat around his thin shoulders, hikes up his pants just enough and exits the apartment. Out into the wilderness. Out into the cool air.

3.

Lindsay's father doesn't know what to make of it. He's had a few beers. He watched some TV with Joyce and Matt. He's been waiting for Lindsay for a couple hours. She is late. And now he's standing in her room not really thinking about the consequences ("This is my house," he said to Joyce). He is standing in Lindsay's room staring at what he has found there. Joyce is standing behind him. Matt is asleep – or so he assumes. Holding this crap in his hands Don isn't sure he knows what either of his kids is doing at any moment of the day or night.

"What is it?" Joyce asks. "What is that?"

Don shakes his head. "I'll kill her," he says. He growls this. "I'll kill her."

"I don't know what it is," Joyce says, her voice shaking. "Don."

"Well, it isn't baking soda, Joyce. What the hell do you think it is?" Don holds up the baggy again. He isn't quite sure if it is cocaine. He's never seen cocaine except on TV.

"What if it's baby powder?"

"Baby powder? In a baggy?" Don wants to slap some sense into his wife. He often wants to slap her, but he never does. She seems so out of it. Maybe it's her cocaine. Maybe Joyce stores her cocaine in Lindsay's room so Don won't find it. Maybe that's why she's always stupid.

"It can't be cocaine," Joyce says. "It can't be."

Rifling through Lindsay's drawers Don pulls out more things. Thong underwear. Push-up bras. Condoms. Joyce shudders. Another baggy with rolling papers in it. A small mirror and a razor blade.

"What the hell is going on?" Don says. He wants to cry. He sits down on Lindsay's bed, all of this stuff spread around him. The cat jumps up. Don knocks the cat off the bed. The cat hisses.

"Oh dear," Joyce says. "We have to do something."

"What happened to her?"

Joyce picks up the hissing cat and tries to comfort him. "Oooh, Muffles. Ooooh, oooh."

"Shut up, Joyce."

Joyce sits down on the bed beside her husband. They both look around the room. At the posters of boy bands they couldn't even name if someone held a gun to their heads. At the pictures of Lindsay and her friends, and her boyfriends. She has a pink Care Bear on her dresser. And makeup and jewellery all over the place. She sleeps in a T-shirt and boxer shorts and these are thrown on the floor by the bed. There is lip gloss dripping out of a tube on her bedside table. Joyce sighs.

"Why isn't she home?" Don says. "Where are those two?"

"The Baxters? They are always late."

"It's a Monday night. Where are they?"

"I think they went out to a dinner party."

"That professor. On a Monday night. Goddamnit." Don puts his head in his hands. "Sometimes," he says. "I just wish she were dead."

"No. Don't say that, Don. I'm sure there's an explanation. Maybe this is her friends' stuff?"

"I do. I really do." Don picks up the underwear. It's nothing but string. Bright red. He tries to throw it at the wall but it just floats to the floor lightly. The cat sniffs it and then slowly backs out of the room.

"I don't know what to do," Don says. And Joyce begins to cry. "I really don't."

Joyce thinks, This isn't the first time. Two months ago she found marijuana cigarettes in Lindsay's backpack when she was cleaning out the spilled grape juice. And she found a business card from a man who was the owner of a strip club. Three months ago Joyce smelled liquor on Lindsay's breath first thing in the morning before she went to school. Joyce told herself that it was mouthwash. After all, mouthwash has alcohol in it, right? And five months ago Joyce found Derek and Lindsay in Joyce's bed. Naked. Asleep. Joyce tiptoed in – Joyce must have been aware they were there, although she tells herself she had no idea – she tiptoed in and saw them curled together, young limbs so perfect and long and thin. No blemishes or rolls or cellulose. Her daughter and that boy. Lying together, sleeping. On her bed. On Don's bed.

Joyce feels like it's her fault. After all, she said nothing to no one. She kept it all inside. Like she always does. And now Don has found evidence and Lindsay will be punished and the punishment will hurt Joyce as much as it hurts Lindsay. Part of Joyce, a large part of her, doesn't want Lindsay to come home tonight. Not tonight. Not ever.

4.

"And you come with me and you come here." The homeless man in the alley stares at the girl lying on the ground near him. He can't lift his head. She's so pretty. Like a bird. A rare bird. A parrot. Lying by him in the alley in this loud city. The girl doesn't move. The bird doesn't fly away. It is dark. Even with the street lights it is dark. But the man realizes that he just has to open his eyes and it won't be dark anymore. So he does. And she's still there, beside him. And it is still dark, but less so.

"I have things to do and places to go," the man mumbles.

The girl stays still.

Birds don't stay still. They fly away.

The man tries to stand, he falls, he stands, he crouches, he falls.

Teeth ache. Mouth aches. Hungry stomach moving and noising and making moving noises.

"Come with me," he says.

The girl opens one eye. She laughs.

"Ah," the man says. "You're a bird."

"Fox," the girl says. Or he thinks that's what she says but she could have said anything and he wouldn't have known what she said.

Where did he put his aerosol can? Where did he put the cooking sherry?

"Did you take my drink?" the man says.

"Fox."

The girl leans her elbows on the ground. She laughs again. Then she tries to get up and, like the man, she falls and gets up again and ends up in a sitting position leaning on the dumpster.

"Oh my God, my head," the girl says.

Birds fly away, the man thinks. He finds his cooking sherry and he drinks it and then he lies back down and goes back to sleep. Warm stomach. No more noise. The bird goes away. Parrot. Fox.

Lindsay stumbles out of the alley and heads down Bloor Street in the wrong direction. The wrong direction for her home or even for Derek's apartment, but the right direction for everything else. Away from that stinking man. From his horrible teeth and crusty face and bloody hands. Across the Bloor Street Viaduct. She's been walking a long time. She's not really walking, now she's stumbling, now she's lying down, now she's up again and running, now she's half asleep on a park bench. Hours it seems. But it can't be hours. She's still way too stoned.

That man in the alley. He was horrible. Lindsay got away as fast as she could. She's going somewhere now, not quite sure where, but away from where she is used to, away from her part of the city. Up some streets. Leafy streets. An adventure. Nice streets. Big houses smashed together so tight. Lindsay swerves in and out of parked cars. What time is it? She passes a man and his dog coming out of his house, leash in hand, but he doesn't see her. Is she invisible? He doesn't look around, but the dog does. The dog looks right at her. The dog looks like a Muppet. She can't even see his eyes they are so deeply set into his face, into his curly mophead hair. Lindsay wants to laugh. Past the man, past the dog, up another street and down one. Where is she going? What was in that joint? Derek. Where is Derek? Did he just go home? Why didn't he try to find her? Lindsay should have gone to Derek's house. Oh shit, she's going to be in trouble. Her dad is going to kill her. She's so late. She's late and lost in Toronto. She was babysitting. That's all there was to it. Smoke a joint, talk to Derek, drink a Diet Coke, babysit a tiny baby who was fast asleep. And do your math homework. Lindsay stops and looks at her hands. Where is her math book?

"Hey, are you okay?" A woman comes out of a house in an orange housecoat and almost walks into Lindsay. Or Lindsay almost walks into her.

"Yeah," Lindsay mumbles. She can't move her lips. They are numb. Her face is numb. She reaches up and touches her face to make sure it's still there.

"You're not okay. Look, you're bleeding. I could hear you crying out here." The woman points down to Lindsay's pants. Her jeans have black bloodstains on the knees. Her hands are bleeding too. Scraped up. Lindsay runs those bloody hands over her face. War paint. The woman takes her arm and says, "Hey, sweetie, come with me. Come on. I'll fix you up. Did you fall down? Or did someone do this to you?"

Lindsay looks at the woman. She's pretty and nice enough looking. Tall. Thin. Long hair. Trustworthy. Normally Lindsay wouldn't go anywhere with any stranger. Normally. But tonight, this night, isn't normal. There must have been something laced in that joint. Ecstasy? Meth? Fuck Derek. Lindsay hopes Derek is okay. He is okay, right?

The woman leads Lindsay around the side of a house, towards the dark backyard. Why aren't they going in the front door and why is Lindsay going with this woman into her house, behind her house, beside her house? Muffles, Lindsay thinks. Oh where is Muffles? Did Muffles smoke the joint? No, she was babysitting. The baby? Did the baby smoke the joint? Or smell the joint and then die, die, die? Lindsay's head is spinning and her eyes are still foggy.

"My name is Vivian," the woman says. "What's your name?"

The woman leads Lindsay into the house, into the back of the house, into the kitchen. She turns on some lights and sits Lindsay down on a kitchen chair. She rolls up Lindsay's pant legs and checks on her cuts.

This is weird, Lindsay thinks. Why is she touching me?

"What's up?" A man comes out of nowhere. "Who's she?" He stumbles. "Man, I drank too much."

"I don't know," Vivian says. "She won't tell me her name. What's your name, honey?"

"She's strung out."

"Don't you think I know that, Richard?"

"Why'd you bring her in? Where did you find her?"

"On the street. I saw her stumbling up and down the street. I went out and got her. Brought her in. I'm just trying to help," Vivian says. Richard rubs his eyes. Stretches.

"Only in Toronto," Richard says.

"You don't get wandering teens in Florida?"

Lindsay went to Florida once with her father and mother. Before Matt was born. She can't remember much of it. Just that she was too small for some of the rides at Disney World and that pissed her off.

"What will we do with her?" Richard says. "Why did you bring her in? Should we call the police?"

"She's bleeding," Vivian says. "She's wrecked. I'm just helping out. It'll be okay."

Richard puts his arm on Vivian's shoulder. Lindsay watches them. A strange embrace. Something off. Not husband and wife. They are stiff with each other. Back-patting.

Lindsay would rather be sitting in that alley with the man and the fox right now. Really she would. There is a vibration in the air, a wild buzzing vibration moving all around her. She opens her eyes, having closed them when they touched. She opens her eyes in time to see Vivian coming towards her.

"I need to go home," Lindsay says. "Or to school. What time is it?"

"Isn't she sweet?" Richard says. "On drugs. Still thinking about school."

Vivian sighs.

Lindsay closes her eyes again and slumps over on the kitchen table.

5.

The homeless man in the alley wakes up again. He wakes up and he gets up and he wipes the drool from his chin and he crashes down the alley swearing. He crashes down the alley and ends up on Bloor Street slumped in front of a bank building. He keeps thinking of foxes for some reason. And small birds. Parrots. He pisses himself and the warmth spreads around his pants until it becomes cold and he shivers. He remembers the woman he passed on the street earlier – a foxy woman, come to think of it. In her high heels. And then, later, a man who smelled like shit.

"Got any money?" the man says to no one. It is empty on the street. Everyone home in bed.

Home, the man thinks. In bed. Safe and sound. He sometimes remembers what that feels like. And he sometimes doesn't.

6.

Vivian is getting angry that she doesn't know what to do with the girl who is now asleep with her head on the kitchen table, and Richard is absolutely no help. Richard is popping pills for a headache coming on and is reminded of some of the reasons he doesn't like his sister. She does not have the ability to stop. Ever. With anything. Sex or drugs or anger. Her anger is well known in the family. At their cousin Bruce's wedding in Sarasota Vivian took the cake-cutting knife (silver with a crystal handle) and tried to stab their father for making her walk the half-block to the reception instead of riding in the limo. Richard sighs. What is it with the women in his life? His wife, Jennifer, and Vivian. Even his mother was always angry and screaming.

Richard had knocked on the door this afternoon with his suitcase and Vivian had to take him in. There was no turning him away. He'd finally left Jennifer once and for all.

Vivian was a crazy teen with black-lined eyes and jet-black hair. Everything dyed – hair, nails. Tattoos. Lip rings. Vivian looks normal now, which makes Richard think that she must be hiding her deviant behaviour inside. Before it was outside, for all to see. Before she was a girl with a ring coming out of her lower lip, a girl you expected to go off the deep end. But now Vivian is dressing like a housewife in her orange robe. Her hair is highlighted and long, her lips coloured pink.

And now there's this girl who looks pretty normal asleep at her kitchen table.

"I think we should call the police to pick her up," Richard says.

"I don't know," Vivian says. "What if they charge us for taking her in."

"Us?" Richard says. "I didn't take her in. I just came into the kitchen and she was here."

"What do you think she's on?"

"Can't tell really," Richard says. "But she brings back memories of you, doesn't she? Kitchen table at home. Mom cursing you out."

Vivian sighs. She's sick of being reminded of her teenage years. She was sixteen, for fuck's sake. Teenagers do stupid things. Before Richard knocked on the door, asking her to take him in, save him from his screwed-up marriage, Vivian was finally starting to feel normal. She's been alone for almost a year now, without Ted, and she was finally feeling like she could go it alone, that she didn't need anyone to survive. She didn't need a man in her life. Vivian, in fact, just before Richard came in, was in the process of cutting Ted out of her photo album, getting rid of his face and body in some pictures, or just throwing the whole picture out if she didn't look good in it. Four years with that man and he suddenly tells her he's gay. It makes no sense to Vivian.

The last thing she needs in her life right now is her brother to come charging in with memories of her past, of the stupid things she's done.

But now Vivian, in her orange housecoat, looks at Richard. Richard, who is all grown up, who has been married twice and is now running from a woman; Richard, who smiles and the kitchen lights up. Her baby brother.

"We should be on what she's on," Vivian says, nodding at the girl.

Why, Richard thinks, do they have this girl in the house?

Vivian saw her outside, drunkenly wandering, shuffling, falling down on the front sidewalk, heard her crying, and her instinct was to protect the girl from the outside. To pull the girl into her house and sit her at her kitchen table and then what? Why? How old is this girl?

Vivian's semi-normal life was finally under control. Now Vivian has a drugged-out teen (is she still alive?) at her kitchen table. Vivian both hates Richard and loves him. He has a tendency to always mess up her life. Bring back the past.

Vivian both hates being alone and loves it.

She seems to always be alone. Even as a kid she was alone. Even when she was with someone she was alone.

Vivian takes a headache pill from Richard and pops it in her mouth. She moves it down her throat with a rye and ginger. She can't believe that she's drinking again.

"So what are we going to do tomorrow?" Richard says. "What's there to do in this city?"

Vivian nods at the girl. The magic feeling of being helpful is over. She wants the girl gone. Out of the house. But the girl looks so peaceful, sleeping there.

Richard stands up, wobbling. Vivian can see a tattoo on Richard's arm – "Jennifer," it says. Christ, you'd think he could have thought of something more original. Obviously Richard felt strongly about his wife at one time.

"See if she has any identification," Vivian says. "We can't leave her outside without any ID."

"Why would we leave her outside?" Richard looks comically

confused. Like a cartoon character. His brow furrowed, her mouth open. He's quite drunk. Vivian can tell.

"We can't take her to her home," Vivian says. "Her family might think we drugged her. We can't take her to the police station. They might think we were up to something."

Richard sits down on the floor, suddenly. "I feel weird."

"Maybe," Vivian says. "Maybe you should have thought of this before you started drinking so much earlier and then popping those pills."

"I wanted to sleep tonight. I wanted a deep sleep," Richard says. "One I won't wake up from." He laughs.

"Those are sleeping pills? I thought they were Tylenol. Shit."

"Are we fighting?" Richard lies on the linoleum. "I've only been here a couple of hours and we're already fighting, Viv. Why is that?" Richard rolls onto his side.

Vivian takes a deep breath.

"We could go up the CN Tower tomorrow," Vivian says. "Or go to the art gallery?"

"You know why I left her, don't you? Did Mom tell you?"

"No, Richard." Vivian sighs. The girl sighs at the table, deep in sleep. She is drooling slightly. "I don't know why you came here. I just opened my door and there you were."

I just opened my door, Vivian thinks, and suddenly I wasn't alone anymore. Suddenly I was drinking again. Almost nine months without a drink and then Richard appears. A bottle in hand.

"Look." Richard sits up. The Jennifer tattoo visible on his arm. Vivian breathes deeply. And around her name, the tattoo, is an open wound surrounded by a bruise. There are more over Richard's body. There are small burn marks too, as if someone put out a package of cigarettes on Richard's skin. "Can you see them? Can you see what she does to me? For no reason. And I'm so goddamned nice to her. I am." He laughs.

"Don't laugh," Vivian says. She stands but the sleeping pill has made her feel wobbly. "Did she do that to you?"

"Yep," Richard says. "Good ol' Jennifer. I'm a fucking man, Viv. I'm a man."

"Why? Why would she do that?"

"I was a bad husband, I guess," Richard says. "I don't know why. There is no why. Just because."

Richard sits there, revealing all, his shirt pulled up, his body scarred and burned. Vivian crouches down near her brother and takes Richard's hand in hers.

"I didn't know."

"Neither did I," Richard says. "Just out of the blue one day. She used to be so nice. And then this. This. I couldn't take it anymore and so I left. She doesn't know. I'm scared about what will happen when she finds out I'm gone. And no one will believe me. Will they? A man? His wife?" Vivian takes Richard in her arms and rocks him. Vivian kisses her brother's forehead.

Richard's voice is faint. "I feel like I'm going to pass out. I've had way too much to drink tonight and those pills."

Vivian stands and pulls Richard up to his feet, they both wobble slightly, right themselves and then Vivian pulls Richard into the guest room off the kitchen.

"Let the girl sleep it off at the table," Vivian whispers. "I'll make her pancakes in the morning and send her off."

Richard lies down on the bed and curls up in a fetal position. Vivian's little brother. Vivian looks at him. And then she rushes to the washroom and retches up her rye and ginger ales and the sleeping pill. Then she moves back to Richard on the bed. And she tucks him in. He is sleeping now and Vivian is sure everything will be better in the morning.

7.

Don and Joyce begin to phone the Baxters. But the phone rings and rings and rings, with no answer. And then it breaks into an answering machine and Helen Baxter's voice comes on all sickly sweet and Don wants to throw the phone against the wall.

One in the morning.

Two.

Three.

They keep phoning.

No answer.

"Where is she?" Joyce cries.

"I'm going over there. I'm going to find my daughter."

Joyce wants to try Derek first. She thinks that maybe Lindsay went to Derek's and spent the night there. Maybe the Baxters don't know this and just assume Lindsay is home in her own bed. Maybe Don's incessant phoning has woken up their baby. Maybe they have unplugged the phone.

"Does a phone ring when it's unplugged?" Joyce asks. "I mean, if the Baxters have unplugged the phone do you think it would still ring on our end?"

"What are you talking about?" Don is putting on his coat and shoes.

Joyce wants to tell Don all about Derek. About the smells on Lindsay's breath, about the sex on their bed. But she's terrified Don will go off the deep end. Perhaps have a heart attack. His doctor recently said he has to watch himself. His doctor said his cholesterol is high. And Don has packed on the pounds recently. Joyce has substituted skim milk for 2 percent and so far no one has noticed. Although Matt did ask if the milk had gone bad and Joyce had just said, no, it was a different brand.

Matt. Her son. He's the only one who cares about her sometimes. He's the only one who still snuggles up to her, as if he's not ashamed of the way she looks, the way she feels. Because Joyce feels rotten inside. She feels old and heavy and ugly all the time. As if her insides are rotting. It's the way Don makes her feel. And the way Lindsay makes her feel.

"Are you coming?" Don is standing by the door, holding it open into the crisp night air. The street is silent. Empty.

"Yes, yes, of course." Joyce bundles her coat over her sweatpants and T-shirt. It's a good thing neither of them were ready for bed when they discovered everything in Lindsay's room.

Don watches his wife bend to tie her running shoes. He watches her butt spread. He thinks of his lovely daughter, so beautiful. She's a princess. But she's also horrible. Don thinks about the way she treats her friends, the way she treats her boyfriends, the way she treats this whole family. She's always smacking Matt when she passes him in the halls (although Matt often deserves it), and she hasn't said anything that is not condescending to her mother in years. Often she'll sit up with him and they'll watch TV late into the night. Even with that forced coziness, Lindsay will scowl at anything he says. She'll scowl at him until he feels like shit.

What is it with girls? Look at his wife. Her huge ass. Her stained track pants.

"Hurry up."

"I'm coming, I'm coming." Joyce pauses at the door. Half in, half out. "Do you think we should tell Matt we're going out?"

"He's asleep."

"Should we leave him a note?"

Don starts walking down the front steps. Joyce runs inside and scrawls a note on the grocery list on the kitchen counter. Then she rushes back out and locks the front door. Follows Don down the front steps at a quick pace. They round the corner together, heading towards the Baxters' house, looking for their daughter.

The note on the kitchen table reads: *Ketchup, applesauce – Matt, we're looking for your sister. She's disappeared. Dad is mad. xo, Mom.*

8.

It isn't until Derek is in English class, studying *Hamlet*, listening intently to his teacher, Mr. Hamblin, as he reads from the play, that he hears the two things that change his life: first, two airplanes have crashed into the World Trade Center in New York City, and second, Lindsay is missing.

Gone. Disappeared. No one can find her.

The airplane thing doesn't affect him that much. At least not immediately. Not until he starts to hear the whispers around the school, the kids all talking about it. There is a low rumbling noise throughout the hallways. And this bothers him. It feels like an imminent disaster. Derek then passes the cafeteria where someone has set up a TV and he sees the planes crash over and over. He hears the reporters shouting. His classmates are silent. That's what is the eeriest. All these kids, these assholes, usually so loud, and they are silent. Watching. Mesmerized.

"Jesus," the girl beside him says. "Is that people? Is that people falling out of the buildings?"

Derek looks closely and it is people. People jumping, not falling. People coming down. It's a rainstorm of people. Derek closes his eyes.

The principal finds him in the hall.

"Derek, can I speak to you?"

Derek follows him into his office. Even before the principal says it, Derek knows what is going to happen next. Planes are flying into buildings in New York City and Lindsay is missing. The principal wants to know where Lindsay is. This man is going to accuse him of doing something. Lindsay probably took off, stoned, maybe stayed the night at her friend's house, and Derek is going to get shit for giving her a joint, for slipping that pill into her Diet Coke. Derek shakes his head. He answers all the questions as honestly as he can. Everything legal, of course. Derek isn't dumb enough to convict himself before he hears from Lindsay. Perhaps she's said nothing. Perhaps she's at home, tucked under her quilts. He's not about to say the wrong thing. Not yet.

Out in the halls again, Derek looks around for someone with a cellphone he can use. But the cellphones are down; the lines are down in Toronto. "Too many people calling about the World Trade Center," some kid Derek doesn't know says.

Derek nods and moves off down the hall and out of the school. He went to English class. Now he can leave. Maybe he should go look for Lindsay. But Derek is exhausted. He waited for Lindsay a lot of the night. He knows his mother will be asleep this morning, sleeping in, her arms wrapped around that biker dude, but it will be silent in the apartment for a couple of hours. Derek decides to go home and get some rest. Then he'll go look for Lindsay.

As he walks home he notices that most people's faces are looking shocked. He sees the Chinese grocery store owner staring intently at his little TV above the counter, he sees a woman with a baby in a carriage rushing past looking horrified.

Derek stops outside of Honest Ed's department store and, with all the people standing there, watches as the first building goes down. It collapses upon itself. Disappears in a huge cloud of dust. Almost slow motion. Everyone on the street is silent. Everyone stares at the TV. Derek shudders. He tries to imagine being in a building that is collapsing. He can't imagine it. It's beyond anything he can think about. It's beyond everything. A building crashing down. Desks. Chairs. Computers. Those little divider walls. Windows. The coffee machines and water coolers. Derek closes his eyes. His bloodshot eyes. When he opens them he sees a guy standing there beside him, staring at him. He actually smells the guy before he sees him.

"Fuck off," Derek says, under his breath. The guy starts moving off. "Hey, come back." Derek moves up quickly to him. "What's that? Where'd you get this?" The guy has a book under his arm. "That's Lindsay's math textbook. Where'd you get it?" The man shrugs, happily hands the book over to Derek and shuffles on down the street. Derek stares after him. He opens the cover of the book and sees Lindsay's name scrawled on an empty page. He also sees "D + L" written in several places. And Xs and Os scattered about. A drawing of a cartoony looking cat. Derek touches the book, runs his hands over it. He begins to walk home carrying it. Thinking about the World Trade Center. Thinking about all those dead people. Ripped up bodies. And all those people, they have kids and mothers and fathers and families. Girlfriends and boyfriends.

Where is Lindsay? Surely she's not missing. But Derek looks again at the book in his arms. What the hell was that guy doing with it?

It then occurs to Derek – if something did happen to Lindsay then her math book is evidence. And if her math book is evidence then Derek shouldn't be touching it. He shouldn't have it.

"Shit." Derek drops it like it's a hot coal. Then he picks it up again and walks back down Bloor Street, away from his apartment, away from Honest Ed's, and towards an alley he knows of. He wipes his handprints off the book with his shirt and then drops the book in a dumpster. He hides behind the dumpster and smokes a joint. Then he heads back towards home. It's later now, mid-morning, his mother might be up. She'll be up and she won't know anything about New York yet. She'll be smoking and drinking her coffee and listening to her music and she won't know that all those people were crushed and mashed at work. Derek's mother won't know that Lindsay took off last night and no one has heard from her since. She won't know, either, that the world feels like it has changed. She won't know about the looks on people's faces in the streets.

Derek shakes the fuzz out of his head and continues home. To sleep. To watch TV. To figure out what is happening. Or, better yet, what is going to happen.

9.

When Vivian goes into the kitchen in the morning to get a cup of coffee to take back up to her bedroom while she does her makeup, the girl is gone. Vivian stands in the kitchen in her bra and underpants, scratching under her armpits, stretching and yawning. She looks around. The girl has dirtied the handle on the sliding glass door, but other than that it's like she wasn't even there. Funny, Vivian thinks, I didn't hear her leave last night. After Richard fell asleep Vivian left them – the girl at the table, Richard in the back room – and went up and had a bath. She soaked and then collapsed into her bed. It was very late. Very early. Vivian isn't sure what you call that time of night or morning. After all that booze last night she did have to pee once, but other than that she slept like she was dead. Vivian makes a cup of coffee. She rubs her eyes. And then – coffee coursing through her body, eyes clear of morning guck – Vivian looks down at the floor and sees all the mess. The black mess. Smeared mud? And what is that smell? What did the girl do to her house?

"What the hell?" Vivian groans. She bends down to look closer at the stuff. She sniffs it. The smell is definitely coming from whatever it is.

Vivian didn't want to clean today. This is ridiculous, she thinks.

Vivian peeks around the door into the room Richard is in. Just a quick peek. Maybe Richard rolled around in the garden last night after Vivian left? Totally drunk? Maybe he was the one who tracked dirt in? Or the girl did and they didn't notice when they were talking in the kitchen? It's reddish dirt. Strange. Vivian looks in quickly. Sees the lump of her brother sleeping. Goes back into the kitchen.

It then hits her.

What she just saw.

Her brain processes it. Works hard. She can almost feel the cogs and wheels turning.

At first she thinks she may be hallucinating from getting back on the booze last night.

But then she looks back into the room. She looks back into the room. She looks back into the room.

Richard? Not Richard? What is it?

Richard. Vivian begins to run. To scream. In her underwear. Her bra. She begins to scream and run and rushes out the front door and into the street. Screaming until she's almost hoarse. And then she is covered by a warm bathrobe that smells of Old Spice and she is rushing behind a man into her house, down the hall, into the kitchen and back to Richard. Or whatever that is. That horrific mound of flesh and blood and bones. Vivian flicks the light on and the man collapses in front of her. Vivian watches him go down in slow motion. He is standing there one minute and then the next minute he is down. He fainted in the blood. Vivian bends to touch him. Slightly balding, tall man. Attractive. She touches him and it feels like electricity.

Call 911. She jumps up quickly and rushes to her phone. Call 911.

The man came out of nowhere and covered her with his warm bathrobe and took care of her. And now he's fainted and Richard is brutally dead and Vivian is, once again, all alone. The way she was before Richard came knocking at her door, knocking back into her life. Vivian opened her front door yesterday and her brother stood there, smiling, his suitcase in his hand.

"I'm here," Richard had said. As if he was expected. As if he had called before he came.

And Vivian had put down her scissors and tidied up the pieces of her old boyfriend, of Ted, on the dining room floor and the brother and sister had opened the rye he brought and got to work on it.

Alone. Now Vivian is all alone. Again.

10.

Derek and Lindsay are at Cherry Beach. They are hidden by the bushes, smoking a joint. Lindsay tells him over and over what she saw that night, she tells him about the man with the dog and his house and how he didn't touch her and, in fact, helped her, and she hangs onto Derek for dear life. She tells him not to say anything, not to tell anyone where she is, because she needs some time to figure everything out.

"Did I do it?" Lindsay asks. "Did I kill that man? Did I just imagine a person coming into the kitchen?"

Derek shrugs. "I doubt it. Why would you kill someone? And you didn't have any blood on you. Did you?" He looks down at the old lady clothes she's wearing now from the man with the dog. "Plus it was a man, right? How could you overpower a man? And where would you get the duct tape and stuff? And why?"

"I know," Lindsay says. "I know you are right."

She looks up into the sky.

Derek shudders, thinking of September 11th and how Lindsay

didn't see it happen. If you don't see it happen, he thinks, then you aren't affected the same way. Kind of like the murder that happened with her eyes closed. You can process it, sure, and know it was bad, but it's not like seeing it happen live on TV. Or being there as it happened. Like the people in New York and Washington and Shanksville and on those planes. Derek imagines over and over all the people who were engulfed by the dust running up the street. He sees over and over the man who dove down from the top of the one building. His graceful swan song. His dive. His last effort to be something different. To be somebody.

Lindsay snuggles into Derek's arms. "I'm going to disappear," she says. "Just until I can't take it anymore. I'll sleep down here."

"Will you be okay?"

"Yeah. I might need some stuff, though. Do you have more?"

Derek looks at her. His drug-addicted girlfriend. He made her that way. He sighs. "Yeah." Derek puts his hands in his backpack and takes out a bunch of baggies. He gives Lindsay all of them. "Take them. I don't want them anymore. I was going to sell them. But I don't want to now."

Lindsay laughs. "Right."

Derek wonders how he is going to pay the guys who sold him that stuff. He'll figure it out, though, he knows he will. Somehow.

"What are you going to eat?"

Lindsay begins to cry. "I just don't want to go home right now. What if they think it's me?"

"The newspapers say they are looking for the man's wife from Florida. They don't even have your fingerprints and it looks like the woman there, the other woman, the sister, didn't even tell the police about you."

"Why wouldn't she say anything?"

Derek shrugs. "She really shouldn't have taken you into her house, right? Maybe she thinks the police will think she stole you or something?"

Lindsay feels her legs stiffening from sitting wrapped up in Derek's arms. Her back is hunched over. But she doesn't want to move. She looks out at the water. If you look far enough, she thinks, you don't see the pollution and garbage floating near the shore.

"Do you think you can hide out for much longer? People are looking for you, Lindsay. Lots of people. Where will you go now?"

Lindsay shrugs. "I can try. For a while, anyway. I don't want to go home. I can't go home now."

Derek kisses her. He lights another joint. They smoke it together.

"I don't know why I went into the room to see it, to see him," Lindsay says. "I wish I hadn't."

Derek thinks, Once you see it, you don't ever *not* see it. It's always there. Like the dead man in Lindsay's mind. She says she closes her eyes and sees nothing but blood. She says it's black blood. Soaking through rooms, dripping slowly. Derek thinks Lindsay will never be the same again. He wonders if her family is ready for this. He wonders if her cat can take it. Her pink room. Her teenage life.

Derek stands and stretches. "I'd better go," he says. "I should go back to school. I've got to keep the cops off me. They think I have something to do with your disappearance."

Lindsay nods sleepily. She has snuck a few pills from the baggies Derek gave her and her body is numb. Her mind is foggy.

"Bye, sweet prince." She giggles as she lies back in the grass.

Derek walks through the streets of Toronto. It is a bright sunny day. A good day to be a teenager, skipping school with no drugs in his backpack. He loves Lindsay, but something in his head, some switch that clicked on just when those planes hit the buildings, something is telling him that she won't be his girlfriend for very long. Derek thinks he may just make it in the world.

He may go somewhere.

Not down.

He won't go straight down, diving out of a collapsing building. Even if he wants to make something out of himself and that's the only way to go. He'll go up. Straight up.

11.

Sophie is running up the street, towards Helen's house. She is holding her breasts in her hands. Her shirt is soaked through.

Paul has parked the car down the street. He is walking towards Helen and Allan's. Suddenly Sophie is behind him.

"Oh God, Paul," Sophie pants. Paul can see her breasts are leaking. Milk. "What are you doing here?"

"I've been looking for you," Paul says. "The baby needs feeding. And they caught Richard's killer. At the border. His wife."

"Rebecca," Sophie says. And then she begins to cry. "Richard?"

"What happened, Sophie? What's going on? Why are you crying? Richard. The man I saw murdered."

"Paul." Sophie catches her breath. "Wait. Slow down."

"Me? You slow down."

She leans on his car. "I went to Helen's in the morning to talk to her."

"You told her?" Paul says, meekly. "Why would you tell her?"

Sophie ignores him. "And we were talking and then suddenly the nanny screamed."

"What nanny? What did she say about me?" Paul asks. "Was Allan there?"

Sophie glares at him. "On the back porch there was a body. Wearing a skirt, a sweater. We thought . . ."

"Whose back porch?"

"Helen's back porch. That's why the nanny screamed."

"Helen's nanny?"

"Paul. Let me finish."

Paul is scuffing his feet on the ground. "I can't believe you talked to them before we even had a chance to talk. We don't even know what we are going to do yet."

"Jesus, Paul, listen. We found the babysitter."

"What babysitter?" Paul is having trouble following this conversation.

"Okay," Sophie says. She has caught her breath. "Would you please shut up and listen?"

Paul is silent. People are passing at intervals. Sophie and Paul watch a young woman in high heels click up the street.

"The babysitter who went missing the night we had our dinner party, Paul, was lying on Helen and Allan's back porch this morning."

"Oh." Paul looks confused still. And then "Oh," he says again. Suddenly realizing. "Was she dead?"

"That's what we thought. We thought she was dead. She was lying there, looking really bad in weird clothes." Sophie smiles. "But she's not dead. She's okay. We called 911 and an ambulance came. She was drugged out. Dirty. But okay." Sophie stops smiling. "Wait? They caught the person who killed Vivian's brother? It was his wife?"

"Wife. Although I guess he just left her, so maybe they were exes? I'm not sure about that. She came up from Florida – broke in.

Murdered him. Can you believe it? He was really drunk so he didn't struggle too much, supposedly. Had some sleeping pills too. Still hard to believe."

Sophie looks at Paul. Studies him. He's shaking slightly. But it is chilly outside.

"So what happened? Why are you here? Outside the house? Where are you coming from?" Paul asks.

"I just told you, Paul. We called 911. The ambulance came and they took her to the hospital. That's where I was just now. We went together. Me and Helen and the nanny and even little Katherine. They're still there. The babysitter's parents are there. Everyone is talking at once." There is a sparkle in Sophie's eyes.

"No, I mean what happened to the babysitter that night? Where has she been?"

"They aren't sure yet. That's the weird thing. She isn't talking. She isn't saying anything. Just crying a lot. The doctors say she's in some sort of shock. They don't know whose clothes she is wearing."

"Where is Allan? Was he with you?" Paul asks. "I want to tell him about Richard."

"No. Well, not in the morning. He took off last night supposedly. They fought. He left. But he came to the hospital later. God, you should have seen how excited he was to see the babysitter alive. He was so relieved. He cried a lot. Helen hugged him a lot. I think Helen thought he'd murdered the poor girl." Sophie pauses. "You know, you should have seen the babysitter's parents when they came into the hospital. It was like –" Sophie stops to think. "It was like they went from being old, shrivelled up angry people to, I don't know, to attractive people. To people who had a reason to live again. And her brother, her little brother. He was crying the whole time."

Paul says, "Allan and Helen are having trouble?"

Sophie shrugs. "They may be having trouble," she whispers,

"but at least there is no other woman involved. Not anymore, at least. They found the babysitter. It's a little less complicated, I'd guess, Paul. A little less."

"I don't know," Paul says. "It's always complicated, Soph. Always. No matter how it happens."

Everyone is breaking up, Sophie thinks. At least she may have company. Her parents' generation tended to stick it out. Even if it wasn't nice. Or healthy. But Sophie can go out with her other divorced friends and, perhaps, meet someone new. She can move on with life. She can live.

"Where's Rebecca?" Sophie suddenly looks around frantically. "Oh God, Paul? You didn't leave her with my mom, did you? Did you?" Sophie smacks her hand on Paul's car.

"I –"

"Let's go," she says. "Hurry. We have to go save Rebecca."

"Save her? From what?"

"From my mother. I have to get my purse." Sophie runs up to Helen's house, opens the front door with a key and enters. Paul stands there, watching his wife disappear, out of his life, and then appear again carrying a purse. It's over, he thinks. But he knows it's over with Vivian too, before it even began. Suddenly he knows that it's all over.

"Okay, let's go." Sophie gets in the front seat of his car. Paul hesitates. Sophie says, "Come."

12.

You see it happen. And you hear the news later. The girl is safe. She left your house and ended up on the back porch of the people she was babysitting for. You don't know how. You were standing out front of that house with Gibson and suddenly they all come running out front and an ambulance pulls up and there she goes, the girl, with your wife's clothes on. This is a relief. For you. For Gibson. Although you are waiting for the police to knock on the door, ask you what you were doing with the girl in your house, arrest you. You are waiting for prison, for the title of pedophile, even though you never touched her. It wasn't about that. It was about grief. About loneliness. You needed a friend.

They have mentioned your wife's clothes on the girl on TV and how she hasn't told them who gave the clothes to her.

You still need a friend.

But things are getting better. The relief you felt when she left. The relief when you saw she was okay. That's all you needed. Each day passes and you feel slightly more secure.

Now you walk the streets with Gibson. Leisurely. You might take him to obedience training – for his aggressive behaviour. You hold his leash tight, just in case, and you cross the street when anyone else is walking by. Gibson's especially not fond of other dogs. In sweaters. If any dog wearing a sweater approaches Gibson, he attacks.

You're getting older. You will retire soon. You might move. Out of Toronto and into the country. Somewhere far from airplanes and buildings. Gibson would love that. Nothing can happen in the country, you think, but then you realize, you know, you are sure, that something, anything can happen anywhere, at any time. After all, your wife died. After all, it was just a Tuesday morning in September. The sky was bright blue and cloudless. Everyone was turned away for a minute, a second.

A Tuesday morning. That's all it was.

ACKNOWLEDGEMENTS

I originally wrote this book (then titled "The Night Before the Day After") in 2006. My agent at the time, Hilary McMahon, should be acknowledged for making a lot of effort to sell it. Even though I got great feedback, most publishers weren't interested in fiction that referenced 9/11 in 2006 – a few amazing books were being published, but not that many. Especially fiction. It was, and still is, such a raw period in history. People were still trying to make sense of it. I put this book in a box for a while, but thought about it often. I pulled out a bit of it ten years later, the starting chapter at the time, about Sophie and Paul and the Wedgewood butter dish and cleaning up the dinner party, and sent it in for publication with Sam Hiyate's *Don't Talk to Me About Love* magazine in May 2016. I realized then that I was still intrigued by the characters and story. I fiddled with it a bit more. But it wasn't until I sent it to Paul Vermeersch at Buckrider Books that it found a home. Paul read it in one weekend and immediately, and enthusiastically, accepted it. Noelle Allen, my publisher, was also excited and, as usual, keenly supportive. And although Paul was my brilliant editor for my last novel, *The Prisoner and the Chaplain*, he thought I'd benefit from another editor this time and passed this book on to the talented Jen Sookfong Lee, who took this novel and played with it and shaped it and helped me see through it and over it and behind it better than anyone. Jen is a novelist and poet herself and knows instinctively how to explain what she sees is and isn't working. She knows when to step back and when to push forward. She also propelled me along with her unwavering enthusiasm. Thank you, Jen and Paul and Ashley Hisson, who came in at the end to tidy it up and fix all the mistakes. And thank you to Ingrid Paulson for the striking cover.

I have so many people I could thank for this book but there are a special few who stand out in my mind. My friends Peter and Janet Harris, Karen Kretchman, Jen Wales and Kevin Oickle. During a rough five years they have had my back constantly, giving me mental, physical and emotional help anytime I needed it. Thank you all. My appreciation to Heather Hudson and Dr. Neil Hudson, for never giving up. Erin Twohey, Sarah Cullingham and Jessica Bosnell, my amazing staff at Hunter Street Books. A special thanks to Erin for reading this book ahead of time and boosting my confidence. My daughters, Abby and Zoe, for always being encouraging and even a little bit proud of their mom. My husband, Stu, for pushing me to work harder and always do better – because he knows I can. My parents, Margaret and Edward, for editing, reading, supporting, clapping and being plain proud parents (and for always turning my book covers out at all the bookstores they enter). My Barbados family, Dave, Nicola, Alec, Josh and Rachel. Because of visiting you, I thought up this title standing in the ocean at the beach near Port St. Charles. Lastly, the pets can not be forgotten: Sebastian, Max, Buddy and Maybe. There is so much laughter in my life because of these four-legged family members.

For five years now I have owned a bookstore in downtown Peterborough. During the pandemic it became solely an online bookstore. I have learned a lot about the book industry, about why people buy books and about the choices people make about what books to buy. I've also learned that I can't predict anything – buying practices or personal taste in particular. I can only hope *Everything Turns Away* makes it on some customers' lists and becomes a favourite.

Michelle Berry, June 2021

NOTES

The title of this novel, *Everything Turns Away*, comes from the poem "Musée des Beaux Art" by W. H. Auden, written in 1938 while Auden was staying in Brussels. In the poem Auden discusses the impact suffering has on humans. In the musée he contemplates the painting *Landscape with the Fall of Icarus* – a painting he thought was by Pieter Brueghel the Elder. (It is now believed to be an early copy of Brueghel's lost original, painted by an unknown artist.) The painting depicts the goings-on of ordinary life, but in the lower right-hand corner the artist has depicted Icarus's legs sticking out of the ocean, the aftermath of his wings melting from flying too close to the sun. Auden notes, "How everything turns away / quite leisurely from the disaster."

This poem feels personal. You can imagine Auden sitting on a bench staring at this painting. He plays with the vernacular in an almost lighthearted way and notices how the world, even with this mythical boy falling into the water, continues on. For me, this poem and this painting sum up what is happening in my novel. The world continues on and everyone interprets the news of the world in different ways depending on where they are and what they are doing. The characters (and even the dog) go on with their lives.

You can view *Landscape with the Fall of Icarus* on the British Library's website at www.bl.uk/collection-items/landscape-with -the-fall-of-icarus. You can read "Musée des Beaux Arts" on *The Poetry Daily* at https://poems.com/poem/musee-des-beaux-arts/.

Michelle Berry is the author of three books of short stories and five previous novels. Her short story collection *I Still Don't Even Know You* won the 2011 Mary Scorer Award for Best Book Published by a Manitoba Publisher and was shortlisted for a 2011 ReLit Award. Her novel *This Book Will Not Save Your Life* won the 2010 Colophon Award and was longlisted for the 2011 ReLit Award. Her writing has been optioned for film and published in the UK.

Berry was a reviewer for the *Globe and Mail* for many years, and taught online for the University of Toronto. She was also a mentor at Humber College. Berry now lives in Peterborough, ON, where she owns an independent online bookstore, Hunter Street Books. Please visit www.hunterstreetbooks.com/.